CHRONOS: REVOLUTION

CHRONOS: REVOLUTION

Dean Palmer

XULON PRESS

Xulon Press
2301 Lucien Way #415
Maitland, FL 32751
407.339.4217
www.xulonpress.com

© 2020 by Dean Palmer

All rights reserved solely by the author. The author guarantees all contents are original and do not infringe upon the legal rights of any other person or work. No part of this book may be reproduced in any form without the permission of the author. The views expressed in this book are not necessarily those of the publisher.

Unless otherwise indicated, Scripture quotations taken from the Holman Christian Standard Bible (HCSB). Copyright © 1999, 2000, 2002, 2003, 2009 by Holman Bible Publishers, Nashville Tennessee. All rights reserved.

Paperback ISBN-13: 978-1-6322-1040-1

Ebook ISBN-13: 978-1-6322-1041-8

Prologue

His feet were heavy with fatigue, his nose raw with dust. His face burned hot with anger. He looked out over the desolate valley, and his anger burned hotter still. *This place was once so beautiful, so lush.* He paused and took a deep breath of rich air. Strengthened anew, he glared at the summit above. *They will pay for their wickedness.*

He placed his hands on the rock in front of him and began the laborious climb up its face. Another twenty feet, and the trail would level. Remembering the instructions from his father, Jared, when they climbed together in his youth, he took care to keep three points of contact secured on the rock, moving only one hand or foot at a time. Halfway up the rock face, he saw a bright light streak by above. He jerked his gaze to the sky, and one foot slipped off its precarious perch. He scraped his leg against the unforgiving rock and clutched his handholds with all his might. *Surely one day we'll have something better than sandals for this job.*

Minutes later, he thrust one leg over the top and pushed himself to his feet. He swept dust off his tunic, bent over, studied the throbbing abrasion on his leg, and sighed. *It'll heal.*

He glared at the summit once more and resumed his hike between craggy rocks. As he neared the top of Mount Hermon, he saw the intended recipients of the sober message he carried. They

Chronos: Revolution

shone with glory from the Most High, glory they had misused in their wickedness. He missed the days when their glow inspired awe. Now it stirred nothing but indignation.

The man emerged on the bald summit to a splendid array of glowing winged *authorities*, angelic warriors clad in golden helmets and armor bearing fearsome swords. They surrounded twenty glorious winged *rulers,* angelic beings of higher rank, wearing white robes and wielding golden scepters with white orbs at the end.

Fury shook every muscle in his body. Among the countless tens of thousands who composed the rebellious one-third of the angelic realm, these two hundred *rulers* and *authorities* were by far the most audacious and murderous, with the sole exception of the one who had started the war in the first place.

His foot shuffled against a high spot on the ground, and a warrior turned to look. The angel narrowed his eyes and placed a hand on the shoulder of his nearest comrade. Within seconds, the warriors parted, forming a clear path to their center and staring with cold malevolence as the man walked through.

He met their glares courageously, knowing full well they could murder him painfully and with no effort. He walked straight up to their leader and stared into his eyes.

The warrior next to him—by all appearances his deputy—turned to his leader. "Shall I destroy him, Semyaza?"

Semyaza shook his head and spoke with his characteristically quiet arrogance. "No, dear Azazel, of course not. If a son of Adam dares come into our midst, he must have a good reason." He stared down at the human with his eyebrows raised. "Welcome, Enoch,

Prologue

esteemed Scribe of Righteousness. To what do we owe the honor of your visit?"

Enoch prayed silently and humbled his heart, careful not to let even his righteous indignation lead him to transgress his own ordained boundaries. He was, after all, a member of a lower order than any of the angels present.

Despite his best efforts, his voice shook with anger. "You may dispense with the pleasantries, Semyaza. I have come with a message from the Most High, from Him who sits on the throne in Heaven."

Semyaza turned his head a few degrees, his eyes still fixed on Enoch.

"You have wrought great destruction on the earth. You have left Heaven and *defiled* yourselves with the daughters of men." Enoch gestured below the mountain. "Your half-human sons, the great Titans, are testimony to your wickedness. They foolishly believe themselves to be immortal and beyond God's judgment. They afflict, oppress, attack, and wreak destruction all over the face of the earth."

Semyaza's gaze drifted into the distance. His lips curled slightly.

Enoch turned slowly to address the entire assembly. "Therefore, you shall watch your sons destroy themselves."

Semyaza's smile melted.

"Their years will be five hundred and no more. Being the brute beasts without souls that they are, after they die, they shall wander the earth as evil spirits—as unclean ghosts—and they shall haunt and torment the children of humanity."

Semyaza's eyebrows slanted. "Our sons?"

Enoch faced the impudent ruler again. "As demonic spirits, they shall hunger and thirst with no food, water, or rest, always striving to possess bodies of the unredeemed and defenseless, and even those of wild beasts."

The warriors began to murmur among themselves.

"There is more."

The assembly fell silent.

"Because of your master's rebellion, he who audaciously accuses God's children before the throne day and night, God's beloved image-bearers on earth are born under a curse of sin and death. And yet the Father offers them grace. They may choose to call on His Name for redemption. But you..." Enoch's anger got the best of him, and for the first time, he pointed indignantly at the angelic leader. "You were born under grace and yet rejected it and chose the curse. Therefore," he looked around for emphasis, "you shall have no peace, nor shall you *ever* find forgiveness."

One warrior shouted, "No forgiveness? What does that mean?"

Another shouted from the opposite side, "Then what is to become of us?"

Enoch turned toward the voice. "You will be imprisoned in the Abyss, the deepest part of Hades, for seventy generations, and when you are released, you will be cursed creatures, like locusts with scorpions' tails, to torment rebellious mankind for five months. You will resemble horses with armor. You will have the face of a man, the hair of a woman, and the teeth of a lion, and your final destination will be the lake of fire—" he swept his hand, "—for all eternity."

Warriors cried out as some fell to their knees. "This is too much! This is too much for us to bear."

One of them fell before Enoch, his hands clasped in supplication. "Please, please...you must plead our case before the Most High."

Prologue

Semyaza's shout shook the mountain. "Stop groveling, you fools! You bound yourselves with oaths. We all bound ourselves." He grew a foot taller and stared down at Enoch. "And just who is going to imprison us in the Abyss, Human? Would that be you?"

A deep, booming voice made him shudder. "That would be my job."

The assembly turned as one to the speaker. A mighty archangel landed firmly on the mountaintop. The crowd around him spread to make way.

Semyaza's eyes widened. "Raphael... It is a great honor—"

Raphael walked through the crowd. "Your *honor* was to serve the Most High, Semyaza, but you have chosen to serve yourselves, corrupting and murdering His beloved image-bearers." He stood a head taller than Semyaza, shook his head, and practically whispered. "Semyaza, Semyaza. You should have known better." He stepped next to Enoch and placed a sinewed arm around the man's shoulder. "The Scribe of Righteousness speaks the truth. You are hereby consigned to the earth, never again to see Heaven, and your days here will be numbered."

Even the white-robed rulers gasped.

Semyaza pointed a finger in the air. "Our master will never permit this."

Raphael's stare melted the ruler's indignation. "You think Lucifer cares about you?" He shook his head. "I assure you. You will find no help from him. To him, you are completely expendable—tools to be used and discarded in his master plan to raise up his false messiah." He panned his gaze across a long series of shocked expressions. "Yes, the Most High knows all about your master's plan.

Chronos: Revolution

He is eternal, after all. The One who created time is more than able to stand outside it." He turned to one of the rulers. "Is it not so?"

The ruler bowed and lowered his scepter to his side. "It is so, Archangel."

Another *ruler* turned his head to the side, his tense eyes trained on Michael. "Will our judgment, our imprisonment, begin now?"

Raphael squared his shoulders toward Semyaza but turned his head to speak. "No. First you will witness your sons' destruction. Your imprisonment will come later—when the earth is cleansed of your filth."

"Then we may...go?"

A moment of tense silence followed. "All but one." Raphael stepped away from Semyaza, walked in front of the white-robed ruler he had addressed earlier, and stared, inches from his face. "All but you, Yomiel."

Yomiel jerked his head back and forth. "Me?"

"Yes you, Yomiel, guardian of time. Since you have chosen to leave your station and rebel against your Creator, your power will be too great for you to remain free. In your arrogance, you have already threatened to undo the very fabric of creation." Raphael's nose practically touched Yomiel's. "That was a grave mistake. And so, you shall be restrained." He glanced over his shoulder. "The rest of you may leave now."

The angels scattered like a startled flock of birds. Their desperate, scurrying flights more resembled those of bats than eagles. Within moments, only Raphael, Semyaza, the trembling Yomiel, and Enoch remained.

Prologue

Yomiel fell to his knees before Raphael. He looked up at Semyaza and implored, "Help me, Master...please."

Semyaza spread open his hands. "Raphael, I am his—"

Raphael's gaze remained fixed on Yomiel. "Leave him or join him."

Semyaza scoffed, "Fine."

Yomiel watched his master abandon him and fly away.

Still staring down at the trembling angel, Raphael took a few steps back. Yomiel dropped his scepter and clasped his hands in front. "Please, please, I won't...I mean, I'm sorry for what I said. I *promise* I won't..."

On the ground, the orb of Yomiel's scepter began to brighten. He stood and stared at it. Raphael placed an arm across Enoch to prevent him from walking forward. Yomiel's scepter lifted off the ground and hovered in front of him. Its glory became blinding. He raised both arms across his face. "Please! Please don't do this!"

Enoch shielded his eyes with a raised arm. Even Raphael turned his head and squinted. The glowing scepter grew into a large, bright, blinding sphere of energy. It subsumed the screaming Yomiel, who disappeared into the blinding glare. Seconds later, his screams silenced. The sphere shrank and settled to the ground. Its glare diminished and disappeared. A blue and white orb remained.

Raphael extended his right hand. The orb lifted off the ground. A gold cylinder with pointed ends and two rows of stones set near each end appeared around the orb, encasing it inside.

Raphael placed a hand on Enoch's back and gently pushed him forward. "Take it, my friend."

Chronos: Revolution

Enoch stepped forward, carefully grasped the gold-encased orb, and plucked it from the air. He turned, stepped in front of Raphael, and held it out.

Raphael raised a hand and shook his head. "No, my friend. No angel may touch it. You must guard it. When the Two Hundred are imprisoned, we will imprison Yomiel with them." He lowered his hand. "You will need help, Scribe of Righteousness. You cannot do this alone."

Enoch stared at the gold cylinder. "I will raise up a team of Guardians. We will keep it safe. I cannot even imagine the consequences were this to fall into the wrong hands." He furrowed his brow and looked up. "Are you certain Yomiel is the only angel who must be restrained like this?"

wwwwwwwwww

May 7, 1946

Dockhands below and crewmembers above secured the gangway against the ocean liner. It sloped gently from the ship's deck to the crowded dock below.

Carrying a single, small bag, leaning on a new cane, and sporting a new, brown fedora, Karl Aufseher looked down from the ship's deck at the crowd gathering below. The hair on the back of his neck stood. He glanced discreetly over his shoulder. A man in a dark overcoat and a dark, wide-brimmed hat walked past, looking at him.

Karl saw two shadows in the corner of his eye. He looked at the deck above. Two ghostly spirits of *sheddim*—the middle caste of the *Nephilim*—stared down.

xiv

Prologue

Karl took a deep breath and prayed silently. *I'm glad I don't have it, Father.*

He made his way to the gangway, pressing the end of his cane onto the deck with every other leaning step. He inserted himself into the queue, grabbed the rail that ran down the long ramp, and carefully descended. Halfway down, he spotted a dark-blue hat with a black band waving up and down. He looked at its owner, smiled, and nodded.

Wearing a blue suit for the occasion, Joseph Michaels—the trusted friend Karl first met on the *Graf Zeppelin*—grinned from ear to ear and placed the hat back on his head. Karl reached the ground and half-walked, half-hopped with surprising speed toward his old friend. Joseph hurried toward him with open arms, and they practically collided.

Joseph lifted Karl off the ground in a bear hug. "Welcome to New York, my friend! It's so good to see you."

Karl's voice was a little wearier. "It's good to see you too, Joseph. How's Elsa?"

Joseph grabbed Karl's bag, placed an arm around his shoulder, and led him away. "She's just fine, and so is our son. We named him Karl."

Karl smiled sheepishly and looked away. "I'm happy for you, Joseph. Truly happy." He looked at Joseph. "And Anna?"

"She's well. She's been staying in our Georgetown apartment. She misses you." Joseph looked more serious. "You look good."

Karl looked down. He was finally beginning to *feel* good.

"It took me a long time to track you down." Joseph shook his head. "I mean...*Dachau*...a concentration camp, of all things. No

Chronos: Revolution

one should have to endure such evil." He looked at Karl. "I'm sorry you had to go through that. How did you survive?"

"In Jesus's Presence, Joseph, His wonderful Presence. I learned to sleep with my head on His chest and walk with His arms around me." His eyes watered. "After everything I went through…all my anger…I finally learned how to stay in the Father's sweet, sweet embrace." He smiled as his eyes glistened. "In my spirit, anyway."

Joseph was silent for a moment. He looked down and nodded. "Then as you resume your ministry and calling here, I will be your first disciple." He wiped his eyes. "Abiding in His Presence like that is exactly where I need to grow." A moment later, he took a quick breath and checked his watch before gesturing with his head and leading them through the crowd. "I wish I could have come to you, Karl. How long did it take you to recover?"

"Oh, months, but the journey to recovery was easy by comparison. I was in good hands."

Joseph stopped. "Is that why you didn't want Anna to know you were coming today?" He pulled an envelope out of his overcoat pocket. "I got your letter."

"No, no. I just wanted to preserve our date. We're meeting tomorrow at Martin's Tavern. I want it to be perfect."

"On the first anniversary of the Allied victory in Europe."

"Yes."

"Sounds like you might have had some foreknowledge on the subject?"

Karl allowed his eye to twinkle just a bit. "I might have. Can I make it to DC before then?" he asked, looking at his watch.

xvi

Prologue

"You're on the two o'clock out of Grand Central Station—after we have lunch together."

Karl smiled. He reached out and rubbed some material from Joseph's sleeve between his thumb and forefinger. "You seem to be doing well for yourself."

"Very well, actually. I had family connections here, so we've been able to establish ourselves pretty quickly."

Karl nodded. "That's wonderful, Joseph."

Joseph turned and kept walking. Karl stayed put. "Would you help me with something else?"

Joseph turned back. "Of course. Anything."

"I need you to help me—help us—take a trip. A long trip. An expedition, really."

"I'm happy to. Where do you need to go?"

Karl cleared his throat. "Antarctica."

wwwwwwwwww

Modern Day

Kat sat in an old, green, vinyl chair and leaned toward the hospital bed, her hand on the man's chest. She felt it rise and fall as he drew slow, labored breaths.

He lay with the bed at an incline, tubes coming out of his nose, his right arm plugged into an IV that dripped from a bottle suspended on a rolling stand beside him. His eyes were closed. His eyebrows squeezed together from time to time. Kat couldn't tell if that was an indication of pain or simply the effort of breathing. She hated seeing him like this—a shadow of his former self.

Chronos: Revolution

He drew a deeper breath, opened his eyes, and pulled them into a faint smile. His voice was scarcely more than a whisper. "Hello, Kit Kat."

"Hi, Daddy."

"How long have you been here?"

"A couple of hours, I think."

"You don't need to be here." He seemed to enjoy the gentle rebuke. "You have a family to take care of, now."

"You *are* family."

His eyes smiled again. He looked toward the foot of the bed for a moment. "You know, I know you're a career woman and all that, and I'm *very* proud of all you've accomplished..."

Kat longed for her father's approval. She leaned in.

"...but I always imagined having a big family. Lots of grand-kids over for Christmas." He looked into her eyes. "Does that surprise you?"

Kat's heart sank. "A little." She remembered the seventeen years she spent in the ancient, pre-Flood past, and something tugged at her. Deathbeds, after all, were a place for confession. "Actually, you almost got your wish."

He pulled his eyebrows together. "How?"

"Joel wasn't our only child. We had three more."

His face froze in an expression of deep concern. He slowly turned his hand a few degrees. "What happened?"

She saw his hand move and took it in her own. She sniffed and wiped an eye with her other hand. "Oh, you know. They didn't make it."

"Why didn't you tell me?"

xviii

Prologue

Kat felt like someone was watching. She looked over her shoulder. Joel stood at the door with a sober look on his face. Kat bit her lip. Joel was the last person she wanted to hear her talk about her other children. She didn't want him to see how much she missed them, how painful the memories were each and every day. She pulled her lips into a faint smile and gestured with her head.

"Come in, Joel." She turned back to her father and tried to change the subject. "You know, I really hoped that our mission would—I don't know—give me a chance to find a miracle cure or something."

He sounded pained. "Oh, but you did, Kat. You did. You cured me completely."

Kat was puzzled. Her father wasn't given to this kind of humor. "What?"

"Your story was just what I needed to convince me."

"Of what?"

"Of him."

Kat turned to Joel, who watched from the foot of the bed. "Of Joel?"

"No, Kat. Of Him." He raised a trembling finger and pointed up. "You convinced me to call on Jesus—for the first time in my silly, wasted life."

Kat had been so awash in her own regrets, she had forgotten the obvious. "Your life wasn't a waste, Daddy. When Mom left, you were all I had." She was terrified she was about to lose him, too.

He squeezed her hand. "And you gave me the strength to keep going, too." His smiling eyes grew serious. "Now, our lives have come full circle, haven't they? And," he wheezed a breath, "we are right where we're supposed to be."

Chronos: Revolution

Kat didn't expect him to say that. "And where is that?"

"In His hands." He wheezed hard and struggled to draw his next breath. "Now, we know we have our happy ending coming—our happily ever after." His eyes smiled again.

A wave of tears pushed up from Kat's throat. She was surprised to feel joy mixed with the grief. "You're right, Daddy."

He pulled his chest up and wheezed another breath. "I love you..." His last words were barely audible. "...Kit Kat." His chest fell, and his final breath escaped. His eyes froze in their sweet smile.

Kat was overwhelmed. The hope that he could still hear her gave her the strength to push her words out. "I love you too, Daddy." She rose from her seat and kissed his forehead.

Joel gasped, "Grandpa!"

Kat turned and looked.

Joel stared above the opposite side of the bed, his eyes wide. Then his eyes rose as if watching something disappear into the ceiling.

Chapter 1

Under the front row of a sea of black umbrellas, Joel shivered between Grace and his mother, Kat, his cold hands clenched in tight fists in his overcoat pockets. This was his second funeral in as many days. He stared at the mahogany casket, remembered the moment he saw his mentor die, and wallowed in regret.

Next to the casket, the minister finished a prayer. "And it is with profound respect for members of all faiths represented here that I offer this prayer in the Name of my Lord and Savior, Jesus Christ. Amen."

With his silence, the raindrops tapping on the canvas umbrellas seemed to get louder. A man in his nineties wearing a dark blue suit with a traditional yarmulke on his head shuffled next to the minister, placed a black ribbon around his neck, grasped it with bony hands, and tore it lengthwise. He chanted a weary, melodic psalm in Hebrew before addressing the crowd. His aged voice rang with a subtle German accent. "I was a young boy when I first saw Karl Aufseher," he gestured with a trembling hand to the headstone of the adjacent grave, "and his lovely, sorely-missed wife, Anna."

He kissed his fingers and placed them on Anna's headstone. "Anna helped hundreds of Jews emigrate from Germany right up to the day it became illegal to do so. Soon afterwards, she found herself working in the office of Reichsmarschall Goering, and like Queen Esther, she chose to recognize that she had been raised up" —his weary voice broke— "for such a time as this."

He turned his head, blinked several times, and sniffed. He slowly drew himself as straight as his hunched back permitted. "Karl and Anna Aufseher rescued over two hundred of us," he slowly raised two fingers, "twice over. They smuggled us from Germany through Occupied France to the relative safety of Morocco—saving our physical lives. But with their friends, Joseph and Elsa Michaels" — he gestured toward a nearby pair of headstones— "they also introduced us to our beloved *Mashiach Yeshua,* saving our very souls."

He placed a hand on the casket and gazed into the sky. "Dearest Karl Aufseher, you deserve the title of Righteous Among the Nations, and yet, we have honored your request and remained silent. Now that you have passed on to your well-deserved reward, though, I will remain silent no more. I will honor your memory."

He shuffled slowly to a woman farther down the front row to Joel's right and took her gloved hand in his own. He bent down, kissed it, and clasped it with both hands. "Your father was a great man, Joanna."

Joel studied the woman carefully. "That must be her."

Grace whispered. "That must be who?"

"Dr. Joanna Michaels, Aufseher's daughter who married Joseph Michaels' son. We hid in her office right before..." Joel didn't want to finish the sentence.

His father, Will, reached around Kat and squeezed his shoulder.

The old man shuffled one step to his left and reached out to the next woman. She extended her own gloved hand.

Chapter 1

After kissing it, he looked up. "I thank God for your grandparents' bravery and sacrifice."

Joel watched with interest. "That must be Joanna's daughter."

The owner of the gloved hand leaned forward and kissed his forehead. It was Jamie.

Kat slapped a hand over her mouth. Joel's mouth fell open. His mind raced as he connected dots in his memories.

As the old man shuffled away, Jamie glanced over at Joel and his parents and gave them a subtle nod. Joel watched his father nod back.

As the ceremony drew to a close, Will turned behind to Kemuel, the stowaway aboard *Chronos* who had become their priceless ally, and whispered, "I'm guessing we know how Aufseher got close enough to *Snowm—*" he glanced both ways, "—got close enough to *Snowman* to smuggle you on board."

Kemuel stared into the distance. Will reached out and placed a hand on Kemuel's arm. The touch seemed to snap him out of his daze. "Hmm?...Oh." He tightened his lips and nodded subtly. He leaned in. "We, uh, need to meet you briefly before returning."

Kat stepped closer to tighten their circle. "We?"

Kemuel gestured over his shoulder with his head. "Every member of the councils who was available is here to pay respects to the Seer."

Will kept looking at Kemuel. He looked concerned for his friend. Joel watched them both. Kemuel *did* seem out of sorts. Gemaliel, wearing an uncharacteristically modern, dark-gray suit, stepped forward with his wife, Zemirah, who was wearing an equally modern, dark-gray skirt with a matching jacket. He held a large black umbrella for both of them. She reached out and shook each of their hands in turn.

Will spoke for them. "Your presence is a great honor for the professor."

She spoke with warmth and authority. "It is the least we can do." She glanced at the casket. "We are puzzled that the Lord would take the Seer home before—"

Gemaliel stepped closer and wrapped an arm around her. She glanced at him with a warm smile before looking back. "We can discuss this later."

Kadmiel and his wife, Keturah, joined them. He held an umbrella above them while she held his arm. He pulled a card out of his inside jacket pocket and extended it to Will. "We need to talk more, but not here. The *Timekeeper* is docked at National Harbor."

Will accepted the card, glanced at it, and placed it in his own jacket pocket. "You brought the *Timekeeper*? Is that safe? I would have thought the Coast Guard would still—"

Kadmiel glanced toward Jamie. "Dr. Michaels was able to wipe that slate clean for us. We needed a secure venue, and besides," Kadmiel looked discreetly in both directions, "we can portal to and from the station from on board without fear of discovery."

Kat smirked, "Good idea."

"We thought so." Keturah gently tugged at his arm and smiled. He nodded. "We must go pay our respects. We look forward to seeing all of you."

Beneath a line of umbrellas, the elders streamed toward the casket, nodding respectfully on the way.

Joel leaned to Kemuel. "Is Uruk here?"

4

Chapter 1

Kemuel shook his head. "He volunteered to help guard the orb. He's pretty passionate about it, now. We can't pry him away."

Jamie and her mother approached with Chris, the engineer from the *Chronos* mission, right behind.

Joel, who was closest, extended a hand to the elder of the two. "It's a pleasure to meet you, Professor Michaels. I'm sorry for your loss."

She gave Joel's hand a firm shake. "Thank you, young man. So, those must have been your textbooks all over my office floor?"

From her subtle accent Joel guessed she had spent a fair amount of time in one of New York's outer boroughs. She extended an arm toward Grace and pulled them both into a hug.

"The two of you were my father's pride and joy. He took great pleasure in sponsoring your studies."

Joel hung his head. "I kind of feel like we squandered it, not having any degree to show for it."

She drew her head back. "Oh, pish posh. That isn't why he sponsored you, and you know it full well." She turned to Jamie and raised her eyebrows in an apparent question.

Jamie nodded. "Yes, Mom. Grandpa passed his...ministry on to Joel, here."

Joanna Michaels nodded, looked at Joel, and placed her hands on his cheeks. "Then I will pray for you, young man. I promise to be your greatest prayer warrior, alright?"

Jamie nodded. "I promise, too."

Joel was surprised how much the gesture touched him. He tightened his lips and nodded.

Joanna turned to her daughter and kissed her cheek. "Well, I'm guessing these nice people are going to have some questions for you. If you want to find me, I'll be rummaging through my father's office." She glanced at each of them and squeezed her eyes in a tight smile, betraying her tears for the first time. She dabbed them with a tissue and walked away.

Jamie stood with her feet only a few inches apart, clasping a black clutch bag with both hands. She threw a pained glance at Joel before turning to his parents.

Will spoke first. "So, it was you who enabled your grandfather to smuggle Kemuel on board?"

Her expression was open, but she said nothing.

"Why did you do it?"

She looked down. "Because I had to."

Kat furrowed her brow. "That isn't really an answer."

Jamie looked apologetic. "I don't mean to be evasive." She looked toward the casket. "I trusted my grandfather," she glanced at Joel, "even as I'm sure you trust your son."

"Because Joel inherited your grandfather's..." Kat seemed to be searching for the word.

"Anointing. I can't think of a better way to say it." Jamie looked at Joel. "It's a great burden, I'm afraid." Her eyes watered.

There was a moment of silence. Kat stepped closer. "I'm sorry, Jamie."

Jamie blinked and wiped a tear with one finger. "Why?"

"Well, I'm sorry for your loss, for one." Kat looked down. "And I'm sorry for how I treated you at the base. I was kind of...awful." She looked at Jamie. "I had no idea what kind of burdens you were

Chapter 1

carrying. I'm proud of you for—I don't know, for bucking up under the pressure so well."

Tears streamed down Jamie's cheeks. She dabbed her eyes with a tissue and pressed it against her nose. "It means a lot to hear you say that...Kat."

"Well...we Barbies gotta stick together, right?"

Jamie burst out with bright laughter. "And don't you forget it." She sighed. "Thank you. I needed that." Her expression grew more serious. "I don't know what happened to you during the mission, but you changed."

"How?"

"Well, when you took off, you were..." Jamie shrugged, "...kind of a tomboy, but you came back..."

Will smiled, "All woman."

Jamie nodded. "But still strong, as only a woman can be."

Kat placed a hand on Will's shoulder and smiled. "I had good reason."

Joel was awash with sweet memories from his childhood. Then his siblings' deaths swept across his mind's eye. Deflated, he stared at the ground.

Will leaned over. "What is it, Son?"

He shook his head. "Nothing, Dad. Thanks." He could feel Grace's knowing look from the side.

Kat looked at Joel with concern for a moment, then turned back to Jamie. "So, what will you do now that you're the program's director?"

Jamie shook her head. "The program's canceled."

"Canceled?"

Jamie nodded. "And I've resigned." She glanced at the casket. "Grandpa saw to it I'd be well taken care of—and very busy." She smiled. "He and my grandmother had a ranch in Montana, which is why you didn't see him much on campus." She took a deep breath. "And they adopted enough children that they had to bring in help." She looked at Joel. "He was always ready to take more children in when needed."

Joel drew his lips in a tight smile but furrowed his brow. He wasn't sure why she directed that comment to him.

She looked intently at Will and Kat. "As soon as you can, you *must* come visit. Please. I'd like you to meet my...extended family."

There was a moment of silence, painful for Joel. He knew his parents were thinking of the children they had lost in the far distant past, children who wouldn't have died had Joel been more responsible. Their names played over and over in his mind, piercing his heart like arrows: *Joshua, Christina, Joy...Joshua, Christina, Joy.* The last thing his parents would want to see is other people's children.

Will broke the silence. He stepped over to Chris and squeezed the top of his arm. "What about you, Chris? I never thought of you as a *ranch* sort of man."

Chris smirked. "It actually suits me well. It gives me a nice home base to work from."

Jamie reached over and took his hand. "Chris is working with a ministry to refugees from ISIS. He travels a lot."

"And thanks to Jamie's grandfather, I can do it full-time, now."

Jamie looked up at him. "Just be sure not to be gone too much."

He smiled and kissed her cheek. "I promise."

Chapter 1

Kat threw an inquiring look at Will before turning back to Jamie. "We'll see you as soon as possible, okay?"

Jamie nodded and smiled. She and Chris exchanged a long series of hugs and handshakes with the others before leaving. Will placed his arm around Kat, and they waved as Jamie and Chris walked away.

Grace stepped next to Joel and looked toward the casket. She looked concerned. Joel followed her cue and looked. Kemuel stood in front of the headstones, staring.

The hair on Joel's neck stood up. He scanned the thinning crowd. His eyes landed on the one man staring at him some distance away, his tidy, brown hair and tan skin shadowed under his umbrella. Joel was certain he recognized the man. He couldn't help but stare. He racked his brain but couldn't place him.

He turned his head and stared into space. *Maybe it's the suit.* Then an image from Nimrod's tower struck him. He jerked his head back in the man's direction, but he was gone.

Grace took his hand. "Are you alright?" Will took a step closer to listen.

Joel gestured with his eyes where he had been looking and spoke under his breath. "I could swear I just saw Turiel."

Grace looked down to one side.

"You don't believe me?"

She opened her eyes wide. "Oh yes, I believe you. It's just not like...his type...to be seen like that."

Joel looked at his father. "We should get to the *Timekeeper*."

Chapter 2

Following his parents, Joel and Grace climbed down the ladder from the *Timekeeper's* upper deck. Seth greeted them with an enthusiastic smile. "Welcome aboard, all of you." He gestured for them to follow and led them through a handful of bulkheads and corridors to the compartment just off the *Timekeeper's* bridge.

Joel couldn't shake the image of Turiel in the cemetery. A portal opened against the wall opposite the room's entrance and revealed the control room of the Guardians' station on the far side of the sun. A pair of waiting crewmembers stepped through from the Timekeeper to the station. Joel saw a shadow in the corner of his eye, and a brief flash of the old, hauntingly familiar pain poked the inside of his skull. He squeezed his eyes closed for a moment.

Seth's expression grew serious. "Are you alright, Joel?"

Joel suspected Joachim could be nearby. He looked around and saw nothing to explain the shadow or the pain, which disappeared as quickly as it appeared. He shook his head. "Sorry. I'm just jumpy, I guess." He peered through the portal and spotted Uruk speaking with another elder and a guard. The sight of the friendly elder brought a wave of relief.

Uruk spotted Joel and nodded with a hint of a smile. Joel returned the silent greeting before the elder next to Uruk

Chapter 2

extended his hand and squeezed it into a fist. The portal disappeared with a pop.

Joel's head hurt for another brief instant. He took a deep breath, then looked at his umbrella, which was dripping onto the dry deck. A crewman took it from him, tagged it, and placed it in a cylinder next to the door, already full of umbrellas. Joel scanned the now-empty compartment. "Is this room just for portals?"

Seth nodded and grinned. "We like to call it the transporter room."

Joel couldn't restrain a chuckle. "I didn't know you were movie buffs." Seth smiled and led them into the passageway to the conference room.

When they entered, they found Kadmiel, Keturah, Gemaliel, and Zemirah already seated along the opposite side of the conference table. The long row of windows behind them provided a sweeping view of the hotel and shops at National Harbor, as well as the tall white Ferris wheel that served as its showpiece, all backlit by a cloudy glare.

The four elders stood. Kadmiel gestured to the row of chairs facing him. "Please, have a seat."

Joel pulled out a seat for Grace, then took his own. A crewman surprised him from the side. "Excuse me, sir." He held out Joel's old bookbag. "You left this here before."

Joel accepted it. "Thank you." He placed it on the floor next to him and took his seat.

Kemuel sat at the head of the table. Kadmiel folded his hands on the table and addressed Will and Kat. "Colonel Stark, Major

Chronos: Revolution

Stark—" he looked at Joel, "—and young Seer—welcome. Thank you all for coming."

Keturah's rich, mellow voice was warming. "First, we want to thank you from the bottom of our hearts for what you did for us." She took care to look at each of them in turn. "We owe you our lives."

Will spoke for them. "You're more than welcome." He looked at Kadmiel. "But I'm guessing that isn't why you invited us here."

Kadmiel nodded. "You're right. Thanks to you, we have overcome the final incursion. Our mission is nearly complete."

Kat rested her forearm across the table. "Nearly?"

Kadmiel looked like he was searching for words. "We're not even certain what to make of everything. You all surprised us so much when you arrived five thousand years ago with the second orb." He took a deep breath. "As you know, Joachim betrayed us and stole the first orb."

Joel glanced at Kemuel, who was boring a hole through the table with his eyes.

"Because of your heroism and sacrifice both during and after the final incursion in Kansas City, we were able to recover the orb you had used to return from the pre-Flood past. Even now that orb is powering our station." Kadmiel parted his hands and opened them before folding them again. "We have to assume the orb you returned with is the same one Joachim stole, but...well...nothing is certain."

Will rested his forearms on the sides of his chair and laced his fingers together. "Then to complete your mission, you must recover the orb that's still missing."

"Yes, with one added detail. Enoch's instructions to us were to hand the orb to a Seer, a man whose arm would have Enoch's mark."

Chapter 2

Zemirah spoke for the first time. "Karl Aufseher had such a mark, though it had been defaced during his time at *Dachau*—and yet he asserted that he was not the one we were seeking. He told us we must look for another."

Gemaliel leaned forward. "To be honest, we were hoping you, Joel, would be that man."

Joel remembered the last time he was in that conference room. He looked at Kadmiel. "That's why you looked at my forearm?"

Kadmiel nodded.

"I see." Joel was puzzled. "Why would Enoch want you to hand the orb to anyone?"

"We don't know." Kadmiel took a deep breath. "But we have a more pressing matter at hand. Based on your own testimony, and that of the Seer—the old Seer, that is—we know the missing orb's housing was damaged."

Joel nodded. "The orb was removed from its housing and then hidden."

"Yes." Kadmiel turned his head a few degrees, his eyes still trained on Joel. "We were also rather hoping you would know where. Did the Seer tell you?"

"He told me where he hid it, but he also told me it isn't there anymore." The elders lowered their heads. Their disappointment was obvious. Joel wished he had better news. "But he told me that with help I would figure it out when the time comes."

Kadmiel glanced at Keturah. She closed her eyes and nodded. He turned to Joel. "You have certainly earned our trust. We will leave the *Timekeeper* here as long as possible. When you ...*figure it*

13

out, as the Seer said, please let us know." He turned to Kemuel. "You will return to the station with us for a much-needed rest, Kemuel."

Kemuel straightened. "Sir, I would much rather—"

"I understand, Kemuel. Seth can handle things here for a while."

"Very well, sir."

A short time later, Joel slung his bookbag over his shoulder, placed a hand above his eyes to shield them from the glare, and watched the tall white Ferris wheel as its cars revolved slowly around its axis. He panned down, and his eyes landed on the restaurant where he planned to get a table for Grace and his parents. He warmed his hands in his overcoat pockets and strode away from the pier past the Ferris wheel.

As he approached the open plaza overlooking the harbor, laughter caught his attention. He gazed down at children playing in a sandy beach area and climbing on five separate aluminum sculptures that protruded from the sand, together depicting a seventy-two-foot giant struggling to free himself from the ground. He knew this sculpture well. It was called *The Awakening*, and it had been moved some years before from Hains Point, the southern tip of East Potomac Park's island golf course between the Washington Channel and the Potomac River, a few miles north of National Harbor.

Joel stared at the distressed-looking giant and lost himself in dark memories. In his mind he heard cackling *se'irim* and the bellowing laughter of *sheddim* and giant *overlords*—the *Nephilim* castes from his pre-Flood childhood—and his body shook. Then right on cue, the last images and sounds from the fateful day the *Nephilim* took his brother and sisters returned to torment him.

Chapter 2

Their names haunted him over and over in a demonic singsong to remind him of his unworthiness: *Joshua, Christina, and Joy... Joshua, Christina, and Joy.*

Someone grabbed his shoulder and spun him around. The startling gesture nearly made him cry out. He found himself staring at a man in a dark suit. The memory of the tall, murderous *men in black*—or MIBs, as Grace referred to them—caused him to jump back.

The man was only about Joel's height with dark, close-cropped hair—clearly not an MIB. His suit looked official but not necessarily wealthy. Joel tried to slow his heartbeat.

The man pulled a wallet from his inside jacket pocket and flashed a badge. "Are you Joel Stark?"

Joel was wary. He nodded slowly.

"We need you to come with us, sir." The man grabbed Joel's arm and started walking. Two other dark-suited men walked just behind them on either side. He pocketed his badge before Joel could get a look at it. "We need you to help us with a matter of national security, Mr. Stark." He whipped out a picture and flashed it in front of Joel's face.

Joel blinked and studied the picture. It was an old photo of Aufseher.

"We understand you knew this man—Dr. Karl Aufseher." He pocketed the picture. "Aufseher stole something that is very important to us." He stopped and looked at Joel. His expression was all seriousness and concern. "We want you to tell us where he hid it."

The other two men took positions on each side, looking out.

Chronos: Revolution

Joel suddenly felt like he had tumbled into the middle of a film noir. He thought quickly. It occurred to him that the man hadn't said what the hidden *something* was. He furrowed his brow. "May I see your ID again?"

"Mr. Stark, you have no idea how much danger you're in. We want to help you, but you have to tell us where it is."

Joel shrugged. "It?"

The man huffed and shook his head. "You know what I'm talking about." He gestured over Joel's shoulders with his eyes and spoke under his breath. "Look, if you want your loved ones to be safe, you need to tell us where to find it."

The familiar, welcome voice in Joel's spirit reminded him he wasn't alone. *Pay attention, Joel.*

Joel tilted his head a few degrees and tried to take a deeper look. Something was wrong with the man, but it wasn't like the tall MIBs he had encountered. It was something else. "Have we met?"

The man's expression grew stern. "Tell me where, Joel."

Joel's adrenalin spiked. He looked around for help.

Suddenly the man looked concerned again. Too concerned. "Joel, these people can't help you, but *we* can. Help us."

Joel racked his brain. He couldn't figure out what was wrong. He heard a distant, echoing tap. He stared at the man's face. The man's impatience was apparent. "Help us, Joel...*now*. Tell us when and where he hid it."

Joel's gut surged again. The man had said *when*. He knew.

The man grabbed the lapels of Joel's overcoat and pulled him to his face. "Give me a time and place, Joel, or..." He tightened his lips

Chapter 2

and stared into Joel's eyes, giving him a long look. Then he let go of Joel's overcoat, grabbed his arm, and pulled him away.

Joel struggled against the man's grip, but the other two men pushed from behind, practically lifting him off the ground. Joel realized they weren't taking him to a car. They were heading toward the water. "Where are you taking me?"

Chapter 3

The strange man in the dark suit threw an urgent glance at Joel. "You need to help us, Joel."

Joel could still hear the strange tapping. He got another good look at the man's eyes. Then the tapping triggered a memory: the old man's walking stick in Nimrod's tower chamber. He played out the scene in his head.

It suddenly hit him. "Your eyes! It's your eyes!"

The man stopped and stared.

Joel pointed into the man's face. "You're Turiel." He suddenly felt indignant. "And you've been *warned*."

The man's hair faded to a lighter brown and grew in length as his face morphed into the tan one Joel had seen at the top of Nimrod's tower. He squeezed his nose into a vicious snarl and leaned inches from Joel's face. "Give me a time and place, Joel—*now*."

Tell him.

Joel blinked and prayed silently. *You want me to tell him?*

Tell him.

Turiel grew a few inches, pulled Joel off the ground, and snarled again. "Time and place, Joel."

Joel half-smiled. "Tunisia...1855." Turiel let go of his lapels and let him fall.

Chapter 3

Grace shouted a short distance away. "Joel, are you alright?" She looked puzzled. Joel turned back to point an indignant finger in Turiel's face. Turiel and the men were gone.

Grace walked up to him. "What's wrong?"

Tense from the encounter, Joel looked into her eyes and immediately felt calm. He wanted her so much. As Kemuel's daughter, she was perfect for him, but the singsong kept playing in his head. *Joshua, Christina, Joy...Joshua, Christina, Joy.* Then he realized why Grace had come into his life. She was his punishment, a reminder of what he could never have, because God couldn't trust him with anything so wonderful.

Grace looked concerned. "You know you can talk to me, right?" Joel wanted to say so much, but he was stuck in his own personal torment. Grace nodded slightly and gestured behind her. "Your parents are waiting for us."

Even in his selfish anger, Joel wanted to be a gentleman. He helped Grace remove her coat and pulled her chair out before moving to his own seat at his parents' table. It was a weekday mid-afternoon between tourist seasons, so the restaurant was nearly empty.

He draped his overcoat over the back of his chair and sat. He felt something pressing against his back and remembered he had been wearing his bookbag under his overcoat. He pulled it off and set it down.

Grace still looked concerned. "Joel, I didn't say anything outside, but I could swear you were floating a few inches off the ground."

Will and Kat furrowed their brows and looked at him.

"What happened out there?"

Joel licked his parched lips and glanced to the side before speaking. "I just saw Turiel and two of his...angelic goons."

Kat leaned in and spoke under her breath. "The same Turiel you mentioned before?"

Joel nodded. "From Nimrod's tower, yes."

"What did he want?"

Joel opened his eyes wide. "He wanted to know where," he made quotation marks with his fingers, "*it*...was hidden." He looked to his left and shook his head. "They came disguised as government agents. I'm beginning to think I'll never know who to trust again."

Grace placed a hand on his shoulder. "You're a seer, Joel. You can always know."

He met her gaze and stayed there for a moment. He liked it there.

A server placed their drinks on the table. Joel pulled his eyes away from Grace and found his mother staring with a faint grin. He looked down and ran his fingers through his hair.

Will leaned in. "It looks like we need to figure out where *it* is. What did Aufseher tell you?"

"He told me what I just told Turiel."

Kat blinked. "You told Turiel?"

"As strange as it may seem, the Holy Spirit told me to."

Kat blinked again. "Okay. Just *what* did you tell him?"

"Tunisia, 1855."

"Then we need to...what...fly to North Africa?"

Joel shook his head. "No. The professor told me it isn't there anymore."

Chapter 3

Will huffed a brief laugh. "Then I guess we know where Turiel is right about now." He looked around the table with a wry grin. "Just how long would it take him to get there, do you think?"

Joel shrugged. "Not long enough."

Kat rested her forehead against the ends of her fingers. "Then where is it?"

Grace leaned in. "The professor told Joel he'd figure it out when the time comes." She looked intently at Joel. "Can you remember anything else he might have said? Anything else he might have given you?"

Joel replayed his time in Professor Michaels' office. He shook his head. "He seemed lost in his own memories most of the time."

"What was the last thing he said to you?"

Joel scrunched his face. Then he suddenly remembered. He reached over, yanked his bookbag off the floor, unzipped it, and reached in. He pulled out a book sealed in a clear, watertight bag and held it where the others could see. "He put this in my bag before he helped me escape."

Everyone stared with wide eyes as Joel retrieved the small, leather-bound book from the bag, flipped through the pages with one thumb, and lay it open on the table. It was blank, save for a single hand-written page. He leaned forward and read it aloud in a low voice:

Supply delivered what was found
After 96 years without light or sound.

Observed by one who brought liberation

Chronos: Revolution

Celebrating the birth of his great nation

Beneath Alaska and Idaho is its place.
Above Hawaii and North Dakota it shows its face.

A palm tree is guarded by a horse.
Concealing a most destructive force.

DAVID MORPH TREE, P.P.

Joel suddenly felt like he was in an entirely different movie. He stared at the page. "Who is David Morph Tree? It sounds like a name from Harry Potter."

Kat scoffed. "Harry Potter?"

He looked around the table. "No one else thinks that?" He shrugged it off. "Anyway, does this mean anything to any of you?"

Kat leaned over to see better. "Could 'Beneath Alaska and Idaho' mean south of them?"

Grace shook her head. "I don't think so, because that would mean 'above' means north. You can't be south of Idaho and north of North Dakota."

"Then maybe 'beneath' means buried?"

Will placed his elbows on the table and shook his head. "It can't be buried in two different states."

"Well, it would have to be Hawaii, right? That's the only one of the states listed where you would expect palm trees."

Grace folded her arms on the table. "I think we're going about this the wrong way." She pointed at the page. "Look at the third

Chapter 3

stanza. 'Observed by one who brought liberation.'" She looked up. "Who would the professor think of who brought liberation?"

Kat gestured with an open hand. "Jesus."

Grace tilted her head. "Well, if that's the case, then the birth of His nation could refer to Israel."

"And 'supply' could refer to him supplying all our needs."

"I don't think that helps us, though. What about the references to American states?"

Joel lowered his head and swept his hands over his hair. "You know, Professor Aufseher and his wife had a significant role in World War II, and the World War II Memorial has pillars from each state."

An hour later, Joel stared across an elliptical pool with a long series of arched fountains surrounding taller fountains near each end. A large elliptical plaza surrounded the fountain, set off with a semicircle of granite pillars and a stone pavilion at each end. The capital mall stretched in either direction from the ellipse's sides.

Grace stood next to him. "I've always liked this memorial. The whole nation came together and sacrificed like never before—or since."

Joel nodded. "It was a pivotal time in history in many ways. It represented a change of international orders, from colonialism to a new wave of nationalism the whole world over, from the *Pax Britannica* to the *Pax Americana*." He looked at Grace. "Professor Aufseher had me take graduate-level international relations."

She chuckled and shook her head. "He had us taking the weirdest hodgepodge of classes."

Chronos: Revolution

"And language studies."

"No kidding. I can order dinner almost anywhere in the world." They shared a brief laugh.

Joel furrowed his brow. "Why do you think he had us do all that?"

She shrugged. "I have a feeling we'll figure it out soon enough."

They listened to the fountain. He sighed. "I only met him a few times, but I miss him."

"So do I. I was surprised what a sense of loss I felt when he died. He was such a sweet old man."

"But he seemed so...burdened."

"Yes, but also gracious. He figured out how to carry his burden well." She faced Joel. "You know it took him nearly a year to recover from the war and make it to the States." Her gaze drifted to one side. "He told me he had a date to keep at some restaurant, but he never told me what it was about. I couldn't be sure, but the memory seemed to make him sad. I guess the war was hard on him."

Joel couldn't help himself. He reached out and held her hand. He thought she might have blushed.

Will and Kat approached from one side, having walked around the pool. Kat spoke first. "We've checked the pillars for each of the states in your poem," she shook her head, "and we can't make sense of it."

Joel gave Grace's hand a squeeze before letting go. "I don't...*feel* it here, anyway."

Will placed his arm around Kat's waist. "You know, I wonder why Turiel would need your help to find it in the first place. As an angel, I would think—"

Chapter 3

"Contrary to popular belief,"—the familiar, weary voice surprised them all. Wearing a brown overcoat and matching sport cap, the old man leaned on his cane with a warm smile— "angels do *not* know everything."

Joel knew the man at once.

Will spoke before he did. He sounded incredulous, one finger pointing at the man's chest. "You were at Lamech's house. You spoke English."

Joel glanced at his father. "And he saved me from Turiel on Nimrod's tower." He smiled and looked into the man's eyes. "You're pretty tough for an old man, you know."

"Looks can be deceiving."

Kat looked at Joel, then at the old man. "Thank you, sir, for saving my son."

"He's a special young man."

"Yes, he is." Kat's lips disappeared.

"But you resent his calling."

Kat glanced to the side. "I suppose I do. I've lost enough children to this war. If the professor had been successful, none of this would be necessary. I'm sorry if that sounds bitter."

The man's tone was soothing. "Don't apologize. You're being a mother—and a good one." He straightened a little. "It's hard to measure success in endeavors like those of Karl Aufseher. It's rather like trying to measure what *didn't* happen." He leaned forward slightly. "But trust me, he was *very* successful." He looked at Joel. "As your son will be."

Joel looked down and shuffled a foot. He wasn't so sure.

Chronos: Revolution

Will leaned in. "My experience with...your kind...has led me to believe you *do* know everything."

The old man took a deep breath. "Intelligence—even great intelligence—is still not omniscience. That's reserved for the Almighty." He nodded slightly. "We know exactly what the Holy Spirit tells us."

"So, do you know where it is?"

He shook his head. "I'm afraid not, but I do have the impression you're getting warmer." He leaned in and nearly whispered, "Just the same, be mindful of who might be listening."

Joel and the others exchanged glances and nodded. When they looked back, the old man was gone.

Joel huffed, slapped his arms at his sides, and faced the afternoon sun, high above the Lincoln Memorial. "It's getting late. If we don't get out of town quick, traffic's gonna be a nightmare."

Grace cupped her hand over her eyes and looked with him. "I agree. I hate rush-hour in this town."

Kat watched the fountain in the center of the pool. "We're no closer to finding it than when we started. Coming here seems to have been kind of a waste."

Still facing west, Joel had a new thought. "You know, maybe it wasn't." He pointed. "Maybe the poem refers to the birth of *this* nation. If that's the case, then who would be the one who brought liberation?"

Grace followed his cue and looked west toward the Lincoln Memorial. Her eyes went wide. "Of course. President Lincoln issued the Emancipation Proclamation, bringing liberation to slaves...and if it's 'observed by one who brought liberation'..." She turned and looked the other way down the capital mall. "Then it could be

Chapter 3

hidden anywhere here." She pointed east. "Maybe in the Capitol Building."

Joel stroked his mouth with his hand. "The states have provided statues that are displayed in the Capitol. Maybe it's—"

"Joel, that's it! Gifts from the states." She held out her hand. "May I see the poem again?" Joel pulled the book out of his overcoat pocket and handed it to her. She opened it, read it with wide eyes, and faced east again. She smirked. "I can't believe I didn't see it before." She looked at Joel. "We need to get to the *Timekeeper*—fast."

Chapter 4

For the second time that day, they climbed down the ladder into the *Timekeeper*. Kadmiel emerged from the corridor, his eyes wide with hope. "So, did you figure it out?"

Joel gestured to Grace. "*She* did."

Kadmiel led them into the passageway. They followed him into the conference room and found a handful of elders and crewmen standing around the table. Kadmiel gestured to their seats and walked around the table. After Kadmiel and Seth took places at opposite ends of the table, Kadmiel extended a hand, palm-up, toward Grace. "The floor is yours, young lady."

Grace cleared her throat. "Aufseher told Joel he hid the orb in Tunisia in 1855, but he also said it isn't there anymore." She held the book up. "Joel found a poem from the professor that tells us where it's hidden, a poem auspiciously written by one David Morph Tree."

Seth leaned on the table. "Sounds like a name from Harry Potter."

Joel widened his eyes and nodded. "Thank you." He smirked at his mother. Kat rolled her eyes with a slight grin.

Grace opened the book. "*Supply delivered what was found; After 96 years without light or sound.*" She looked up. "The USS Supply was a nineteenth-century stores ship. In 1855 it delivered a memorial stone from Tunis to the States. It's called the Carthage Stone,

Chapter 4

a gift from the son of the American consul." She turned the book around and pointed at the page. "The name at the bottom—David Morph Tree, P.P.—is an anagram. The inscription of the real name on the memorial stone reads 'vid Porter Heap, M.D.' His name was David Porter Heap, so I'm guessing the strange mark before 'vid' was meant to abbreviate the name...or the first two letters wore off."

She lowered the book. "After it arrived in the US, it was displayed briefly and then lost for decades. It turned up under a dark stairwell in 1951, ninety-six years after it was sent." She raised the book and continued to read. "*Observed by one who brought liberation; Celebrating the birth of his great nation.*" She looked up. "The date on the stone commemorates Independence Day, 1855, and it's hidden in plain view of the Lincoln Memorial." She pointed at the page. "The last stanza reads, '*A palm tree is guarded by a horse; Concealing a most destructive force.*'" She looked around the table. "The stone has an image of a horse standing in front of a palm tree." She closed the book. "The orb must be hidden inside the stone."

There was a moment of silence. Kat interjected, "Didn't you skip a stanza?"

Grace blinked. "Oh, yes." She opened the book and pointed on the page. "*Beneath Alaska and Idaho is its place; Above Hawaii and North Dakota it shows its face.*'" She looked around the table and smiled. "Each of the states, along with quite a few nations and masonic lodges, sent memorial stones for display. They're all in the same place. Alaska's is the highest. Idaho is next, followed by the Carthage Stone, Hawaii, and North Dakota."

Kat blinked and nodded. "Where?"

Chronos: Revolution

Grace smiled. "The Washington Monument. The stones are mounted on the inside wall all the way up the tower, but if you take the elevator, you'll miss most of them. This one is only visible as you descend the stairs."

Kadmiel gazed into the distance and shook his head. "What a brilliant hiding place." He focused on a black set of speakers mounted on the center of the table. "Did you get all that?"

Uruk's enthusiastic voice squawked from the speakers. "Indeed, we did. It has been hidden in the Washington Monument all these years. Incredible. You must bring them here so they can retrieve it."

A few minutes later, they stood in the compartment adjacent to the bridge. Seth made sure they remained away from where a portal could appear. The deck vibrated and listed to port as the *Timekeeper* backed out of her berth and turned north.

Kadmiel's tone was urgent. "The station will open a portal here shortly. When they do, we'll have them send you into the Washington Monument." He checked his watch. "It will be closed for tours, so it should be empty."

Seth leaned through the doorway to the bridge, his hands on each side of the frame. "Take us as far up the Potomac as you can."

The helmsman responded with a crisp, "Aye, sir."

Seth turned back to Joel and the others. "We'll get as close to you as possible—in case you need help."

The portal popped open with a sustained hum. The station's control room was visible on the other side. Uruk stepped out and extended an arm to usher them back through. Joel's head throbbed,

Chapter 4

and he felt a chill. A shadow flashed by. Kat placed her hand on the back of her neck, and even Uruk winced a bit.

Joel saw the worry in his mother's eyes. "You felt that, too?"

She dropped her hand and nodded.

Joel turned to Uruk. "And you?"

Uruk looked sober. He placed an arm around Joel's shoulder, walked with him toward the portal, and spoke in a near whisper. "Many of the elders have been complaining of discomfort when we use the orb to portal. I fear it could mean Joachim is near."

A crewman emerged behind them on the bridge and spoke urgently. "Sir, someone has stowed away on deck."

Joel stopped and exchanged a worried glance with Uruk. "It might be Dr. Aelter...I mean, Joachim."

Seth headed aft and spoke over his shoulder. "I'll take care of him."

Uruk was trembling. His face was completely ashen. "If Joachim is here, then we must keep the station's orb safe at all costs. We mustn't...He mustn't be allowed..."

Kadmiel raised two hands in a gesture for calm. "Not to worry, my friend. Let's continue with our mission while the crew take care of our stowaway." He gestured for them to follow and stepped through the portal. Will, Kat, and Grace stepped through after him.

Uruk kept a hand on Joel's shoulder. He glanced nervously in all directions: up, around the bridge, and into the passageway.

Kadmiel's distorted voice sounded from the other side of the portal. "Come, Uruk."

Uruk looked down, and his eyes darted back and forth.

"Uruk, let us not delay."

Chronos: Revolution

Uruk placed his arm around Joel's shoulder again and walked with him through the portal. Joel winced from another brief flash of pain. Uruk looked sympathetic. "I don't know about you, but I find that truly vexing."

In the station's control room, two more elders and a handful of guards looked on. Gemaliel and Kadmiel exchanged nods. Gemaliel extended an open hand and closed his fingers into a fist. The portal shut with a pop.

Kadmiel looked at each of them in turn. "After we send you into the Washington Monument, we won't be able to help you. If we were to open another portal from here, it's possible he could..." He furrowed his brow, and his lips disappeared.

Will nodded. "We understand."

Kadmiel turned to Will, Kat, Joel, and Grace. "I assume all four of you will want to go."

After their experience in the underground lab in Kansas City, Joel knew his father needed to go. He didn't want to be responsible for his mother or Grace. Will looked at Kat, who took his hand. He nodded to Kadmiel. Joel found himself nodding with his father, then immediately wished he hadn't.

Kadmiel looked intently at each of them. "Very well. After you retrieve the hidden orb, you will need to use it to get yourselves back. Understand?"

Will spoke for them all. "Yes."

Kadmiel nodded. He turned to Uruk, who was shifting around nervously, "Would you care to do the honors, my friend?" Uruk opened his mouth but said nothing.

Chapter 4

Gemaliel stepped forward and spoke in a low voice. "One of us should do it, Kadmiel. Uruk has been rather...gun-shy ever since his return. He seems to prefer letting others open portals right now."

Kadmiel nodded. He extended his fist and opened his hand. The portal reopened. A tight space was visible on the other side of the field. To the left was a steel-framed white glass wall. Joel guessed the monument's elevator mechanism was behind it. On the right, clear, steel-framed glass covered the stone interior of the monument's observation deck and formed a partition for one of the windows. Ahead, the short passage turned left ninety degrees around the white-glass wall. In the corner ahead and just to the right, a stairwell led down.

Will and Kat stepped through. Joel took a deep breath. He reached out for Grace's hand. She took it and nodded.

Joel led Grace through. As soon as he emerged onto the other side, a deep sense of foreboding gripped his heart. He knew at once they weren't alone. Still reaching back through the portal, he squeezed Grace's hand and held it back. He hoped with all his heart she would recognize his cue and stop.

She did.

He turned back to face her. She lowered her head slightly, her eyes fixed on his, and let go of his hand. He opened his hand in a gesture to stay. She nodded.

He pulled his hand out of the portal and stared into her eyes until it closed with a pop. He was glad she was safe, but part of his heart seemed to rip off when the portal closed.

Kat looked back. "Where's Grace?"

33

Chronos: Revolution

Joel flashed an urgent look at her and shook his head quickly. She seemed to recognize his cue for silence. She nodded.

Will made way for Joel and gestured down the stairway. Joel nodded and led the way down. The short flights wound down a few levels until they began to wrap around the black, iron-framed elevator shaft. The stone-and-mortar outer wall had a crude, unfinished look, and the lights were dim. Each step on the metal walkway echoed in the tall, hollow chamber. The stairway opened to a flat landing along one side of the memorial. In the center of the wall to his left, a rectangular stone was mounted with an image of Alaska and the words *THE GREAT LAND* carved in bold, capital letters. Joel gestured with his head as he walked by.

They descended several more flights and passed the second stone. It was a smaller, gray rectangle framing the word *IDAHO* carved in bold letters in beige granite. Roman numerals were carved below the state's name. Joel took a deep breath. The Carthage stone was only twenty feet below, and he could feel the orb's power. He felt a rush of anticipation as he rounded the next couple of corners.

He saw the stone. It was nearly square, made of variegated red and white marble. In the center was a black inlay with a deep yellow image of a horse standing in front of a small palm tree. Joel stopped in front of it and ran his fingers over the surface. *Professor Aufseher once looked on this same stone.* He suddenly felt a strong connection with his mentor, as if a circle were somehow becoming complete.

Will and Kat stood on each side of him. Will placed his hand on the surface and closed his eyes for a moment. He looked at Joel and nodded. Clearly, he felt it too. Will and Kat moved back a step and watched.

Chapter 4

Joel looked at the stone, placed his hand over the black inlay, and closed his eyes. He felt the orb's power surge. He had never opened such a precise portal. He concentrated hard and drew his hand back a few inches. A small portal popped open between his hand and the stone.

He opened his eyes and studied it. The portal led to the center of the stone. His hand trembling slightly, he reached in. It was a strange sensation, feeling particles of marble displaced by time. Unable to see what was inside, he closed his eyes again and felt around carefully. He moved his hand back and forth until he felt the solid, round orb, the one thing unaffected by the time-displacement field. He carefully wrapped his fingers around it and drew it out. The tiny portal popped closed. The memorial stone looked completely unchanged.

Joel felt a rush of success. He held the blue and white orb in front of him and stared. Will and Kat placed an arm around each other's backs and smiled. Joel took a deep breath. Now he only needed to open a portal to the station, and it would all be over. He carefully moved the orb from his right hand to his left, then extended his right hand and concentrated.

A blue spark fizzled in front of him.

He tried again. Nothing happened. He looked at his parents. "I don't get it. I can't seem to open another portal." He spotted movement over his parents' shoulders.

The angel's voice surprised them from the corner. "I may not be able to operate your device, but I *can* prevent you from using it."

Will and Kat spun around. Joel's abdomen squeezed tight. "Turiel. How did you know to come here?"

Chronos: Revolution

Concealed in a shadow, the angelic *ruler's* tone was mocking. "Don't you know? Angels know everything."

Joel knew better. "Why don't you show yourself?" Turiel emerged from the corner. The dim glare of a light bulb illuminated his tidy brown hair and dark overcoat. "What, no robe and scepter?"

Turiel narrowed his eyes into an intense glare and extended his right hand. A golden scepter with a white orb at the end materialized in his grasp with a crack that echoed up and down the tower's interior. He pointed the orbed end toward Joel. "I just got back from a very long trip to North Africa." He shook his head. "Tsk, tsk, tsk. Angels don't like being sent on wild goose chases." He extended his left hand. "Now give me the orb."

"We both know you're not allowed to hurt us."

"Under normal circumstances, yes," he jutted his head. "But this isn't exactly a normal circumstance, is it? With the orb, I can go anywhere I want, to any time." He rolled his eyes in a circle. "I can undo the very fabric of creation—the dimension of *time* that holds it all together." He shouted, "Now hand it over!"

The white orb at the end of Turiel's scepter began to glow.

Chapter 5

Joel stared at Turiel's glowing scepter and prayed silently. *What do I do, Father? What do I do?*

Ask your dad.

Joel turned his head back towards his father, his eyes still locked on Turiel. "Dad, I think this one is on you."

Turiel snarled and raised his scepter. Its light became blinding.

Will jumped in front of Joel, knelt on one knee, and raised his right forearm across himself. The orb grew hot under Joel's arm.

Turiel swung his scepter down with a fierce yell. His scepter struck an invisible force just above Will's arm, blasted from his grasp with a fierce clap of thunder, and struck the wall behind. The memorial tower leaned a few feet with a deep roar and wobbled back and forth. Dust fell from the walls. Joel and Kat grasped the railings on each side.

Turiel spun around and extended his hand. The scepter flew back into his grasp. He faced them again and glared.

Joel wasn't sure they could keep doing this. "Father God, what now?"

Distract him.

Joel leaned down to his father. "Dad, we need to break his concentration...just for a moment." Will nodded.

37

Chronos: Revolution

Joel stared at Turiel. He held a fist in front of himself and concentrated on the orb. He would only have an instant.

Turiel shook his head and scoffed. He pulled his scepter close and ran toward them.

The orb again grew hot under Joel's arm. Will extended his hand and pushed it toward Turiel. A blast of energy struck the angel like a locomotive. Turiel hit the wall behind him. The tower rumbled and wobbled again.

Joel opened his fist, palm-down. A portal opened under their feet, and they dropped through.

They landed on grass in the capital mall as the portal slammed shut. The evening sun silhouetted the Washington Monument. Kat looked around. "Couldn't you have gotten us to the station?"

Joel slipped the orb into his overcoat pocket. "Sorry, I only had a fraction of a second." He gasped and stared where the portal had been. "Wait a minute, the, uh, Nemesis should have been pulled through with us." He looked down to one side. "I wonder why he wasn't."

Will stepped closer. "Maybe it has to do with the other device, Son." He gestured toward Joel's pocket. "Try again. Let's get the orb to the station."

Joel slipped his left hand into his pocket and grasped the orb. He extended his right hand and concentrated.

Nothing happened.

Joel shook his head. "Maybe Turiel can prevent it from some distance."

"Do you think he knows where we are?"

Chapter 5

"Let's not take any chances. We need to get to the *Timekeeper*."

Kat pursed her lips. "That's a long run."

Joel thought for a moment. "We can take the Metro." He scanned around and pointed south. "L'Enfant Plaza station. The Yellow Line crosses a bridge over the Potomac."

Will took Kat's hand. "I don't have any better ideas."

Kat slowed Will down. "We should walk. If he's anywhere nearby, he'll be looking for people running."

Will nodded.

Joel walked ahead toward a cylindrical building suspended on buttresses with an open plaza beneath. They hurried underneath, past the tall fountain in its open center and toward Independence Avenue on the other side. After making their way to the opposite corner of the intersection, Joel spotted movement in the air above.

He turned up and to the side. Now in full glory and accompanied by two armed *authorities*, Turiel hovered over the capital mall and scanned the ground below. Joel gestured with his head. "There's Turiel."

Will and Kat turned to look. Kat scanned the sky. "Where? I don't see him."

Will looked at Joel. "The Metro station, Son."

Joel nodded and led them south. "It's two blocks from here." As they reached the next intersection, he glanced back. The three angels were sailing in their direction. His body tensed. "They're coming this way."

He ran ahead and led them down the last block and across the next intersection to a crowded corner plaza area with a metal-framed

Chronos: Revolution

glass canopy shielding a set of escalators that led underground. Further south, a commuter train slowly chugged across a bridge.

Kat yelped. Joel turned back. With Will's help, Kat pulled herself off the ground and hobbled a few steps. Will pulled her close, wrapped her arm over his shoulder and helped her along. She grimaced. "I twisted my ankle."

Will nodded to Joel. "Lead the way, Son."

Joel hurried through the crowd to the top of the escalator and looked back. His parents were right on his heels, his mother leaping along with her husband's help, her injured foot barely touching the ground.

Joel hurried down the left side of the descending escalator, excusing himself as he pushed past the few people who weren't following the commuter protocol and standing to the right.

At the bottom, an arched concrete tunnel curved left to a row of turnstiles. Joel stopped in front of them and felt his pockets. He turned back to his parents. "I don't have my Metro card."

Will placed his hand on the console next to one of the turnstiles. "No worries. I've got it."

Joel could feel the orb grow warmer. Will nodded for Kat to go through, then Joel. The turnstile obediently swung around for each. Will followed and wrapped Kat's arm around his shoulder again.

Joel led them down another short escalator to the platform. Flush floor-mounted lights along the track were already flashing to warn of an approaching train. From the dark tunnel at the opposite end of the stop, a light shone, and a diesel horn tooted twice. Joel hoped against hope it would be the right train. He looked at

Chapter 5

his parents. "It has to be the Yellow Line—not Green. The track splits ahead."

A boxy stainless-steel train rumbled toward them. The signs near its doors read *YELLOW*.

Joel heaved a sigh.

The train rushed by, swirled the air around them, slowed to a stop, and opened its doors with a hydraulic hiss. Joel hurried in with his parents and grabbed a pole near the door on the opposite side of the car. Within seconds, the doors hissed closed, and the train pulled away. A voice squawked on the speakers, "Next stop, Pentagon."

The train rumbled through the station and into the dark tunnel. A series of fluorescent lights flashed by. Joel scanned the crowded car. He looked at his parents. "Do you think we lost them?"

Will shrugged. "I hope so. Just where does this train go, Son?"

Joel reviewed the map in his head. "It crosses the Potomac, stops at the Pentagon and Reagan National Airport, and runs south through Alexandria." Joel thought for a moment. "Alexandria Station will be the closest stop to National Harbor."

Kat shook her head. "The *Timekeeper* won't be there anymore."

Joel's heart sank. He had forgotten that. The track angled up gently, and the train emerged into the evening light and began its course across a bridge over the Potomac.

Joel felt a chill. Something was wrong. He looked at his parents, who stared back. In the middle of the bridge, the train squealed and lurched to a sudden stop. Passengers shouted. Two people tumbled to the floor. The lights went out.

Chronos: Revolution

Joel looked out over the Potomac. The *Timekeeper* was just south of the bridge, turning hard in an arc past their position. He pointed. "Look."

His parents ducked and looked out the window. Joel scanned the bridge outside. It would take a big jump to get to the water. A loud impact shook the train. Passengers shouted again, steadied themselves, and looked around.

Kat reached out, turned Will's head to face hers, and looked into his eyes. "I can't run. I'll just slow you down. Take Joel. Help him get the orb to the *Timekeeper*."

Will paused a moment before nodding. He placed his hand on the back of her head and kissed her. "Get off at the airport and call Jamie."

Kat nodded and kissed him again. "I love you." She turned to Joel and pulled him into a hug. "Be safe, Son. Promise me you'll be safe."

Joel didn't think he could promise that. "Just keep praying for me, Mom."

Another loud impact rocked the train. Muffled screams came from the next car. Will placed his hands in the seam in the middle of the door next to them and pulled the doors apart with a loud grunt. Joel reached into the seam and pulled with him. It didn't budge. Kat hopped one step on her good leg, reached above the door, shattered a plastic cover with her fist, and pulled an emergency lever. The door hissed open. The door at the end of the car opened. Three men in dark overcoats pushed their way through shouting passengers.

Will turned his back to the open door, pulled Joel's back against his chest, and wrapped his arms around him. "Ready, Son?"

Joel nodded.

Chapter 5

Turiel and his goons were only yards away. The orb grew hot. Joel and his father launched backwards out of the car, sailed in an arc over the side of the bridge, and plunged into the cold water.

The loud splash became a muffled gurgle. Every muscle in Joel's body seized with the intense cold. He reached his arms out, spread his legs, and thrust himself to the surface. He sputtered and gasped. "Dad!"

"I'm here, Son."

About twenty feet away, the *Timekeeper's* stern was angling toward them as the yacht faced south away from the bridge. Joel thrust himself toward the yacht as quickly as he could. Seth ran across the *Timekeeper's* deck toward them. Next to him, a white-haired man held a gun.

Joel stopped swimming and shouted in frustration. He pointed. "It's Joachim." He looked at the bridge above and behind them. "Now what? We can't let Turiel get the orb, but we can't let Joachim have it, either."

"They're probably working together, Son."

Joel's body began seizing up from the cold. He was losing his ability to stay above the surface. He couldn't imagine how things could get worse.

They did.

Joel's father shouted and plunged beneath the surface. His arms, thrown up from the force, disappeared last.

Chapter 6

Joel gasped. "Dad! Dad!" He turned himself in the water, looking each way.

Something clutched his ankle. Joel gasped for air. He was yanked underwater and pulled along with a mighty force. His head rushed. He needed to get to the surface to breathe, but he couldn't even see what was pulling him. In fact, he could barely see anything. Within seconds, he was under what he thought was a metal surface. Desperate for air, he reached up to try to push himself around the object. A round opening appeared a short distance from him, and light shone out. The invisible force pushed him under the opening and let him go. The water in the opening shimmered as if there were air above. He swung his arms down and thrust himself through.

He emerged into a hollow, round metal chamber and gasped in a deep breath. His father grabbed his arm and pulled him out of the water and to the side. Instead of closing, the opening simply disappeared, replaced by a solid metal surface with no hint of a seam. Joel ran his hand over the surface.

His father pulled him to his feet. A few feet away, two seven-foot-tall, pasty-skinned men in dark suits stared at them before turning away and busying themselves with something Joel couldn't see. Between them, a handsome, strong, dark-haired man wearing

Chapter 6

jeans and a black leather jacket angled his hands and seemed to be causing the vessel around them to move. He turned away and ignored his new passengers.

Joel shivered as his drenched clothes dripped on the metal floor. He folded his arms tight and stared at their host. To his surprise, he immediately understood where they were. He thought to himself, *I guess being a seer brings some knowledge with it—unwelcome knowledge,* The more he put together, the more he wished he *didn't* know what he did.

His father didn't look so certain. "Where are we?"

Joel turned his eyes toward his father, still facing the dark trio. "I think the colloquial term would be a UFO."

Will lowered his head and blinked. "A UFO?" He looked around and seemed to resign himself to the possibility. "I suspected for some time that, well...*if* they existed, they were probably demonic."

The black-jacketed man spun around and practically struck his own chest with his thumbs. "Do I look like a demon to you?" He scoffed, shook his head, and turned around again.

Joel narrowed his eyes at their host. "Think of it this way, Dad. If it's ghostly, a mere shadow that must possess someone else's body, then it's an unclean spirit—a demon, a *Nephilim* ghost." He gestured toward their abductor. "But if it can take physical form," he looked around with his eyes, "and if it can manipulate matter, then it's a rebel angel—one of the *rulers* and *authorities* the Apostle Paul warned us about."

"So why all the stories of...you know..." Will spoke the last word quietly. "...abductions?"

Joel wasn't sure whether to speak under his breath. The hollow vessel's acoustics made every word reverberate. "They've been doing what they did before the Flood—tinkering with bloodlines—in this case, searching for residual *Nephilim* genes."

Will furrowed his brow. "Why?"

"To breed hosts—or really, to breed *the* host." Joel gestured to the tall, dark-suited men. "These goons won't cut the mustard for the spirit they have in mind."

The men stared for a moment.

Now Joel's father *was* whispering. "Who?"

"The same Titan who inhabited..." Joel didn't think that word was adequate, "who *possessed*—Nimrod, and maybe some others throughout history." Joel felt a deep sense of foreboding. "I think they already succeeded, at breeding *the* host, that is, and he's out there somewhere."

The man in the black leather jacket huffed.

Joel stared at his back. "You don't like your normal uniform?"

He turned around and ran a hand down the jacket's lapel. "I like leather. It means something was killed so I could wear its skin. Linen is for wimps."

Joel gestured to the man's jeans. "But *cotton* is somehow...tougher?"

The angel jutted his head a bit and shook it mockingly. Joel was surprised. He had never seen an angel act so petty. He looked around the small chamber they were in, pursed his lips a moment, and lowered himself to the floor. He leaned against the angled wall.

Will looked puzzled for a moment, then sat next to his son. "Do you have any ideas?"

Chapter 6

Joel looked at his father. He wasn't sure what to say. There wasn't much they *could* do against an angel, not alone. "Sit, I suppose. The way I see it, if *they* can hit *us* when we're in a cargo plane, something else can hit them. I figure sitting is safer."

Still looking at them, the black-jacketed angel jutted his head. "Whatever." He pointed to himself with his thumb. "Now the Master will remember that the orb's custodian was captured by—"

Joel raised his hand in a cue for silence. "With all due respect, I don't care about your name. I've learned that lesson. The only name I care about is—"

"What, are you going to *rebuke* me in His Name?"

Joel shook his head. "No. I know my rank. May the Lord rebuke you, Himself."

The dark angel shuddered, seemed to regather himself, and scoffed. He extended his fist, and a golden scepter with an orb at the end materialized in his grasp. He aimed it at Joel. The two tall, dark-suited men stepped back to give him space. Joel remembered the raw power he saw in Nimrod's palace when Turiel struck with his own scepter. The orb at the end of the scepter began to glow. Will slowly reached his arm across Joel.

Something struck the vessel and rocked them hard. The dark-suited men fell over. The angel staggered and dropped his scepter. Joel and his father placed their hands against the surface to steady themselves. Something hit them again, and the vessel was yanked straight up. Joel's head swam. They stopped abruptly, and a force pushed them hard to one side. Joel slid across the floor with his father. Then, without warning, they plummeted for a full second and struck the ground hard, listing to one side.

The side of the vessel ripped open like tinfoil. The weary looking aged man who had visited them at the memorial ambled into the opening and leaned on his cane. He stared at the man in the leather jacket. "Get out, Aphiel."

Aphiel picked up his scepter, pointed it toward the old man, and glared. The old man extended his left hand. The scepter ripped out of Aphiel's grasp and flew into the old man's hand.

"You have forgotten your place, Aphiel." He lifted his cane and swept it in a circle. Starting at the top, the vessel around them dissipated, leaving them on the cold, damp ground in the dimming twilight. A cold breeze swept across the ground. Joel shivered in his wet clothes. He and his father climbed to their feet, folded their arms tight, and stood behind the old man.

Joel looked around. Steam puffed from his mouth with each shivering breath. They were on Hains Point between the Potomac and the Washington Channel. He looked at the ground beneath them. The aluminum statue of the giant struggling to pull himself out of the ground used to be right there.

He knew what the enemy was doing—their grand plan to bring their false messiah—and the knowledge weighed on him. He wondered what kind of dark ceremony was involved in transferring a Titan's spirit into a newly bred host. The thought made him shudder.

Just north of them, on the road that curved from one side of the narrow island to the other, a few bikers and runners watched them curiously. Joel spotted movement west of the island on the Potomac. The *Timekeeper* was following the riverbank from their previous position to the north. Joel could see Joachim brandishing his gun on the deck.

Chapter 6

Beyond the *Timekeeper*, Turiel soared across the water toward them, his wings stretched wide. He slowed, allowed his feet to settle under him, landed smoothly next to Aphiel with a series of flaps, and folded his wings behind. Both armed *authorities* Joel had seen at the summit of Nimrod's tower followed. They landed behind Turiel on each side, folded their wings, and drew their swords.

Joel turned to the people watching from the street. They didn't seem fazed. A police car with flashing lights stopped next to them. The door opened. A police officer emerged and spoke with the gathered people, and within moments, the runners and bikers continued on their way. The police officer stood near his car, folded his arms, and watched.

Joel's heart began to thump. The situation was worse than he thought.

The two dark-suited men grabbed him and his father by the arm. Aphiel walked up to the old man and stared down at him. "You have overstepped your bounds, old man." He reached down, yanked his scepter out of the old man's hands, returned to Turiel's side, and transformed into his glorious, white robe. His wings appeared and folded behind him.

Joel couldn't help himself. "Nice linen."

Aphiel sneered.

The old man pointed a bony finger at the quartet of angels. "The Lord rebuke you, Aphiel—and you as well, Turiel. You know better."

Two more *authorities* streaked to the ground behind the angelic *rulers* with claps of thunder. They drew their swords. Two more appeared. Soon, with a series of thunderous booms, dozens of rebel angels in golden armor stood in a perfect line with their swords

Chronos: Revolution

raised. Energy sparked along their weapons' blades as if they were enveloped in lightning. Two white-robed rulers struck the ground on each side of Turiel and Aphiel. They extended their white-orbed scepters and glared.

Joel exchanged a worried glance with his father. He wondered how the old man could help them this time.

Turiel's angry voice echoed. "You're on the wrong side of history, old man. Stop taking this pitiful form and join us."

The old man shook his head. "I take this *pitiful form*, as you put it, for good reason, Turiel. I will not tempt God's image-bearers to worship me."

"Why not?" Turiel looked at the angels on his right and left. "Do we not deserve to be worshiped?" He gestured to the people jogging away. "The only reasonable purpose for these humans is to worship and serve us."

"Many of them *have* worshiped you, Turiel, and look at what has become of them."

Turiel waved that off. "Why should I care whether they live or die? Why should I care whether they suffer eternal damnation?" His tone was mocking. "They're here to serve *me*—not the other way around. They're not my problem." He extended the orbed end of his scepter. It began to glow. "Now join us."

Joel glanced back toward the street. People jogged and rode their bicycles in both directions, completely oblivious.

The old man looked over each shoulder at the dark-suited men, his questioning eyes wide. "Are you sure you two want to be here?" The tall men looked at each other for an instant. They released Will and Joel and ran behind the line of angels.

Chapter 6

The old man faced his opponent. "Mark my words, Turiel. One day there will no longer be a place for you in Heaven—or for your Master, the accuser."

"That all depends, now, doesn't it?" Turiel directed his scepter toward Joel. "With the orb in our hands, we will be *unstoppable*. And don't forget, old man: there are legions of us. Countless tens of thousands." He shook his head. "You cannot stop me this time."

The glowing orb at the end of his scepter became a blinding light. Joel's forehead began to hurt, and the pain grew quickly. He lowered his head and grimaced as it grew even more intense. Soon he thought his head might split in two. He doubled over, clenched his fists against his temples, and cried out. The orb in the pocket of his drenched overcoat became hot. It pulled him toward the rebellious *ruler*.

Will cried out, "Joel!" He put his arms around his son and pulled back with all his might.

Joel drew the orb against himself with his left arm, his right fist still pressed against his head. He leaned away from Turiel, but the force dragged him and his father along the ground. He was powerless to keep the orb from the angels, and he knew it. The pain was excruciating.

The old man placed his arm in front of Joel and held him in place. "And don't *you* forget, Turiel," he tossed his cane and grasped it in the middle, "there will always be twice as many of us as there are of you." His cane transformed into an orbed scepter and glowed bright. The pain in Joel's head disappeared.

The old man's weary voice became a deep shout. "And we serve the Most High God, *Yahweh Elohim*." He stood up straight and transformed into a fierce, white-robed warrior with a golden breast-plate. "And we fight in the Name of His Son, *Yeshua HaMashiach*, whose Kingdom will one day fill this earth!"

Two *authorities* struck the ground on each side of him with claps of thunder. Then two more. A series of lightning bolts struck the ground in a line with explosive blasts, and an opposing line of angels faced off with the rebels, their swords raised in flexed arms, their fierce expressions hard as flint.

Joel and his father found themselves behind a line of righteous angels. He pursed his lips and looked back and forth. "It's a war."

The angel whose protective arm was still extended across Joel looked over his shoulder. "No, young Seer, this is merely a skirmish. The war is coming."

Will let go of his son. "Some skirmish."

Turiel shouted, "Get the orb!"

The white-robed *rulers'* scepters blasted energy toward Joel. The two *authorities* on each side of Joel and his father jumped in front and raised their forearms. The scepters' energy struck them hard, illuminating invisible shields on the angels' arms. The *authorities* grunted and slid across the ground a few inches with the impact. The energy deflected away with an explosive clap.

Turiel raised his scepter above his head, yelled, and charged toward Joel. His line of *authorities* uttered a fierce shout, raised their swords above their heads, and charged forward with him. Joel watched them approach.

The righteous line shouted back, raised their own swords, and ran ahead of Joel to meet their attackers. The energy on their blades glowed bright orange with crackles of red.

Chapter 6

An attacking angel swung down. Baring his teeth, his opponent met the blade with his own. The energy combined with a deafening clang and a blast of lightning that flashed into the sky. All along the line, swords collided with flashes of lightning, blasts of thunder, and fierce shouts. Within seconds, one of the rebels took to the air to attack from above. The defenders rose to meet them, and the battle raged with a flurry of wings, clangs, flashes, and explosions.

Joel and Will stayed behind their white-robed defender. Two *authorities* remained on each side to shield them. From above, two attackers broke through the line and streaked toward them with swords outstretched. Two others ran across the ground from each side. The righteous *authorities* on the ground drew their swords and flexed their free arms over their heads.

The attackers above struck their invisible shields and pushed hard against the resisting force. The defending *authorities* on the ground grimaced, fell to their knees, and swung their swords against the attackers on the ground, their forearms still flexed above them. The white-robed defender extended his scepter and blasted the attackers away with a series of bright pulses.

Joel looked at him and shouted over the din, "Look, I promise not to worship you. May I *please* know your name?"

He drew his square jaw into a grin. His booming voice resonated. "Very well, young Seer. My name is Phanuel." The *authorities* with him shouted and fended off two more pairs of attackers. Phanuel looked up, held his scepter with both arms, and blasted the attackers away with a rapid series of bursts. He looked at the *authorities* next to him. "We must get them to safety. Bring them and stay close."

53

The golden-armored *authorities* sheathed their swords, stepped behind Joel and his father, and placed one arm around them. Phanuel stretched his wings up, pulled them down with a rush, and leapt into the air. The *authorities* held their charges tight, swept their wings down, and rose alongside Phanuel, their free arms raised as shields. Joel found himself lifted into the darkening night sky. Phanuel's shout to his squadron echoed. "Cover us!"

Half a dozen *authorities* swept in next to him and soared ahead in echelon formation. They raised their shields, collided with the line of attackers, and swept out, making a broad path through the middle. Phanuel aimed his scepter and blasted any would-be attackers away while his accompanying *authorities* carried Joel and his father over the river.

A trio of *authorities* attacked from below on Joel's side. Phanuel fired down and warded them off. He led them higher. Joel heard shouts from his right. He jerked his head to look. Another trio attacked from above on his father's side. Phanuel blasted two away, but one got through and struck the angel carrying Will. The three of them plummeted in a flurry of struggling arms, legs, and wings.

Joel cried out, "Dad!" He watched them tumble toward the *Timekeeper.*

On the yacht, Joachim leapt to the side as the trio landed hard on the deck. Will rolled across the surface and slid to a stop. The wrestling angels tumbled over the side and splashed into the water.

Joel watched his father stare at the gun-wielding Joachim and raise his hands in submission. Joel hollered ahead to Phanuel, "We have to go back and—"

Chapter 6

Something struck the angel carrying him. The angel lost his grip, and Joel plunged toward the water. His body tensed with the rush of weightlessness. A strong arm reached around him from behind, held him fast, and pulled him back into the air. Phanuel shouted, "I've got you." His wings waved up and down with mighty force, carrying them through the air at a tremendous speed.

Joel watched the river speed by, then the ground. He looked behind. Aphiel and two *authorities* were right behind, gaining on them. They weren't carrying a full-grown man.

Phanuel shouted "You must open a portal. I'll toss you through. They won't be able to follow."

Joel shouted back, "But Joachim will be pulled through with me, and besides—" A blast of energy struck Phanuel. He grimaced and kept flying. Joel continued. "Turiel has been preventing me from opening—"

"I'll see to it you *can,* and your Nemesis won't follow either. Trust me, and *hurry.*"

Joel felt a wave of relief. "I'll take it to the station."

"No! You mustn't take it there. Trust me, Joel. Take it forward in time." Another blast struck Phanuel. He gritted his teeth and pressed on. The strain appeared to be slowing him down.

Joel shook his head. "I've never been further forward than this time. I won't know—"

"Just go as far forward as you can, Joel. The Father will guide you. Hurry."

Joel extended his hand and concentrated. A blue field began to grow ahead. A third blast struck Phanuel and made the mighty angel cry out. They plunged toward the ground and missed the portal,

Chronos: Revolution

which disappeared with a pop. Phanuel swept his wings down hard and thrust them forward again, baring his teeth and struggling to maintain speed. He began to sound winded. "Hurry, Joel."

Joel concentrated again. A blue field appeared ahead and below. Phanuel tossed him forward just as another blast struck him. Joel soared in an arc toward the field and glanced behind. Phanuel curled up and spun to the ground. Joel looked forward and concentrated to keep the blue field open.

Chapter 7

Joel held his breath and sailed through the portal. The rush of wind and shouts of battle silenced.

This portal felt different. Instead of the normal, instant gateway, Joel sailed through a wild display of colors and sounds. An invisible force stopped him, yanked him back, and pushed him forward again. A loud sucking sound grew in his ears. A moment later he popped out of the portal into silent, warm, and dry nighttime air. He sailed through the air for a moment, struck ground, curled into a ball, and rolled head over heels for what felt like an eternity. He straightened his body just in time to collide with a wall.

The impact knocked the wind out of him. He slid down the wall, crumpled to the ground, and struggled to draw breath with his tense muscles. His head swam, and his vision tunneled. He tried with all his might to remain conscious, but his narrowing spot of vision disappeared.

wwwwwwwwwww

Will climbed down the ladder into the *Timekeeper*. He saw Seth and hurried toward him while Joachim climbed down after him.

He pointed at Joachim. "Seth! You need to arrest him or something. Whatever you Guardians do to criminals."

Chronos: Revolution

Joachim pocketed his pistol. Seth shook his head apologetically. "I'm sorry, Will, but I can't." He gestured toward Joachim. "He's an elder, and I've sworn to obey him."

Will was incredulous. "You've *got* to be kidding me, Seth. He stole the orb." He jutted a finger against Seth's chest and pointed it at Joachim. "*You* need to relieve *him* of his command."

Joachim tilted his head up and stared down at Will.

Seth drew his lips into thin lines. "I'm sorry, Will, but it doesn't work that way."

Will stared at Joachim. "You can't let this *coward* win."

Joachim clenched his fists and took a step toward Will. Then a cool, dispassionate look swept across his face. "Seth, I want you to get me to the station. Tell them to open a portal for us."

"I'm sorry, sir, but you're kind of...*persona non grata* right now. They decided not to open any portals from the station until the Seer returns with the hidden orb."

There was a moment of tense silence. "How are our battery stores?"

"Ninety-five percent, sir."

Joachim swept his hand over his mouth. "Then take us out into the Atlantic. We'll take off from there and get to the station the old-fashioned way."

Seth raised his eyebrows. "You call arcing around the sun, accelerating and decelerating at one-G old-fashioned?"

Joachim looked impatient. "How long will it take?"

"Four days, eight hours."

"What if we double the acceleration?"

"Two Gs? A little over three days."

Chapter 7

"And three Gs?"

Seth shook his head. "Just over two-and-a-half days, sir, but the rest of the crew just learned the hard way that the human body doesn't take three Gs well for that long. Trust me, sir, as an older man, you won't want to experience that."

"Very well. Three days it is. Make our acceleration two Gs." Joachim stared at Will and huffed a deep breath. "Go lock our guest in the galley."

"The galley?"

Joachim raised his eyebrows. "I'm not a bad host. He might be hungry."

Seth looked conflicted. "Sir, we could just drop him on shore before taking off."

"No...We may yet have need of him."

〰〰〰〰〰〰〰〰

The *Timekeeper* jetted water from her stern, lifted her bow, and carved a path through the water in search of open ocean.

Hovering above the river's surface, Turiel watched.

〰〰〰〰〰〰〰〰

Joel felt someone shake his shoulder. He heard a muffled voice. His head hurt, and his back was killing him.

He opened his eyes. It was broad daylight, but everything was blurry. He took a slow, deep breath.

He was leaning sideways against a brick wall. He could just make out two figures standing over him. *Father, where am I?*

Chronos: Revolution

One of them spoke to the other, but it was too muffled for Joel to understand.

The second one appeared to shrug. He got down on one knee, looked in Joel's eyes, and said something else. This time Joel heard it clearly, but he still didn't understand a word. The man looked at his comrade for a moment, turned back, gave Joel's shoulder a gentle shake, and spoke again. He sounded sympathetic.

Joel slowly shifted around until he was sitting. He placed a hand on his forehead and spoke slowly. "I'm sorry, but I don't understand you."

"Ha!" The man turned to his comrade. "I told you he was American." He looked back. "Are you alright, sir? We need to get you out of here."

His friend sounded less sympathetic. "We should arrest him for being drunk."

Joel shook his head slowly and allowed the closer man to help him to his feet. "I'm not drunk." He blinked several times, and his vision became clearer. The two young men wore gray uniforms with black patrol caps. They had automatic rifles slung around their shoulders.

Joel tried to read the closest man's nametag. It was written in Hebrew characters. He took another deep breath. "Am I in Israel?"

The man blinked and stared. "You don't know where you are?" He turned to his friend. "Maybe he *is* drunk."

"It's a long story." Joel placed his hands in his overcoat pockets. The orb was still secured in one of them. Finally feeling clearer, he looked into the young man's eyes. "I know this will sound strange, but what year is this?"

Chapter 7

The young man stared. Joel wished he hadn't asked. He began to worry he was about to get arrested. An old man with a cane ambled up. Joel felt a rush of recognition, followed by the heaviness of disappointment. It wasn't Phanuel's face.

The old man stopped near them and looked straight at Joel. "Looks like you've been through a lot, young fellow."

The young police officer looked at the old man, then back at Joel. "What's your name?"

Joel dusted himself off. "Joel Stark." It occurred to him he didn't have a passport with him.

The old man pointed at Joel. "Are you by any chance related to the famous Will Stark, the American astronaut?" Joel was surprised to hear the question. He nodded. The old man smacked his gums and clapped his hands. "I thought you had his face." Still looking at Joel, he gestured to the young policeman. "You should have a lot to discuss with Officer Thomas Michaels, here."

Officer Michaels turned to him. "How do you know my name?"

The old man winked at Joel and ambled away. All three of them watched him leave. The name finally struck Joel. "Wait, Thomas *Michaels*?"

The young man looked at him. "*Tom* Michaels."

"Are you related to Dr. Jamie Michaels in America?"

Tom turned his head to one side, still looking at Joel. He furrowed his brow. "Yes...she and my father are cousins."

Joel felt a wave of relief. Certainly, *she* could help. "Would you please help me contact her? She can vouch for me."

Chronos: Revolution

The officer scratched his head. He suddenly seemed apologetic. "I can try...but we might have trouble getting through." He seemed to expect that to be a sufficient explanation. Joel waited for more.

Tom shifted his feet. "Look...a lot of America's infrastructure has been...pretty much wiped out."

Joel's adrenalin spiked. "Wiped out? How?"

Tom blinked and shook his head. "Wow. It looks like we *do* have a lot to talk about."

The rattle of a large diesel motor and the squeaks of burdened axles announced a large, slow vehicle's approach. Tom's comrade grabbed his shoulder and shouted something in Hebrew. Tom gestured in the direction the old man had gone. "Come with us, quick."

A sleek, modern-looking green tank with a red and white star emblazoned over a set of black and orange stripes appeared at an intersection down the street.

Joel laid the fork on his now-empty plate. A young boy looked up from the chair next to him. "You must have been hungry, mister."

Joel wiped his mouth, nodded, and chugged the glass of water in front of him. He looked at the man on the opposite side of the table with round, wire-framed glasses and salt-and-pepper hair on the sides of his head. "Thank you, sir, for the meal. I'm truly grateful."

By the man's accent, Joel guessed he had grown up in or around New York. "You're family, Joel. You're welcome." He looked serious. "My son tells me he found you unconscious a few blocks from here. Do you remember how you got there?"

Tom walked in from the kitchen, now wearing civilian clothes, and sat next to his father.

Chapter 7

Joel wasn't sure how much to share. "I do remember. It's a long story. I'm not exactly sure how to explain."

The man pointed over Joel's shoulder to his overcoat draped over the back of his chair. "Does it have anything to do with whatever's in that pocket...whatever it is you don't seem to want anyone to see?"

Joel tightened his lips. The man was more observant than he realized.

"I trust you didn't bring anything dangerous into my house."

Joel put on his best poker face. *He has no idea.*

"May I see it?"

Joel was grateful to his hosts. He wanted to be careful, but he didn't want to insult them, either. He reached around, pulled the orb from the jacket pocket, and held it out.

The man's eyes went wide. He pointed at the orb. "My grandfather told me of such a thing. He told me about his escape from Germany. He said a man and a woman helped them by using a blue and white..." he swept his fingers toward Joel. "What do you call it?"

"Orb."

"*That's* the word...orb...to stop time. I didn't believe him for years, but one year they had a reunion, and the other people who escaped with them *swore* it was true."

The last hint of the man's smile disappeared. He seemed to be studying Joel. "Is that why you asked Thomas what year it is?"

Joel was tormented. He wanted to trust these people. He nodded slowly.

The man pointed at Joel. "Are you the man who helped my grandparents escape from Germany?"

Joel shook his head. "No, but I knew him. I'm afraid he's...dead."

Chronos: Revolution

"Well of course he's dead. That was more than eighty years ago." His expression softened. "Sorry, my boy. For all I know, it was just yesterday for you." He leaned on the table. "So, what are you doing with it?"

Joel stared at the table. "Protecting it. Trying to get it to safety."

"And where would that be?"

Joel sighed and shook his head. He wished he knew. "I guess back to America. I have friends there who should be able to help."

The man nodded slowly without smiling, pushed his chair away, and stood. "Come with me, young man." He leaned down, put his hand on Tom's shoulder, and spoke in a low voice. "Have your mother bring our guest a drink. He might need it."

"Coffee?"

His father shook his head.

"Oh?...oooh...okay, Poppi."

The man led Joel into the living room, invited him to sit on a rich, floral-patterned sofa behind a coffee table, and sat on a matching seat that faced the end of the table. Tom followed with a small narrow glass of clear liquid, handed it to Joel, and sat in the chair opposite his father.

Joel took a whiff of the drink. It smelled something like licorice. He didn't really want to drink it. The man gestured to the coffee table. "Save it...in case you need it."

Joel furrowed his brow and set it down. "Thank you, Mr. Michaels."

"Call me Jacob."

"Thank you, Jacob." Joel leaned toward his host. He dreaded what he was about to hear, but he was eager for information, just the same.

64

Chapter 7

Jacob grasped the arms of his chair and took a deep breath. "What do you know about New Rome, Joel?"

Chapter 8

New Rome? Joel had never heard of such a thing. He raised his eyebrows and shook his head.

Jacob placed a hand on his forehead. "Oy...where do I start?" He looked at Joel. "What do you know about IR?"

Joel figured with the name New Rome, he should guess something related to his political science experience. He blinked. "International relations?"

Jacob's expression brightened.

"My mentor had me study it, along with a *lot* of other fields." He counted on his fingers. "World History, European History, American History, Political Theory, Theology...German, French, Arabic..."

"But not Hebrew?"

Joel shrugged apologetically. "I'm afraid not."

Tom leaned forward. "Poppi used to teach IR and Political Theory at Tel Aviv University."

Jacob cleared his throat. "Which will make this easier." He took his glasses off. "How would you describe the international order, Joel?"

Joel leaned back. "Sounds like one of my comprehensive exams." He thought for a moment and began what sounded like a cool, classroom report. "The Cold War bipolar order dominated by America

Chapter 8

and the Soviet Union gave way to a brief, unipolar period where the US. was the only superpower. A lot of political scientists believed that was giving way to a new, multipolar regime dominated by the BRICS countries." He counted again on his fingers. "Brazil, Russia, India, China, and South Africa, with the US still dominating North America." He looked around. "Which has been pretty good for Israel, since the US has always..." he shook his head to the side a few times, "...*usually*...been a staunch ally of Israel."

Jacob nodded approvingly. "I'd give you an A, and that gives me an idea where your memory ends." He leaned his head and wiped his brow. "Well, the US split down the middle. A new wave of internationalism took over, and you could say they gave away their position of global leadership." He squinted and squeezed the top of his nose between two fingers. "NATO became useless. The UN was immobilized by disagreements between the US, Russia, and China, so people called for a new regime." He spread his hands in a sarcastic gesture. "*Voila*—New Rome."

Joel leaned forward.

"New Rome is—or perhaps *was*—a federation of ten regional rulers. A *foolish* federation. They threw away two centuries of experience with democracy—with constitutional, limited power, with checks and balances—and replaced it all with an ineffective bureaucracy designed to be ruled from the top. Their New World Order rose from the ashes of the Post-World War II regime established by the US." He shook his head and scoffed, "Peace and safety."

"Even peace in the Middle East?"

He scoffed again. "Peace...some peace. The Palestinians swallowed it, because it got us out of the West Bank...and it got them *lots* of aid." He poked his chest with his thumb. "*We* swallowed it, because they claimed it was provisional...a seven-year roadmap to meet our demands...and because that roadmap allowed us to rebuild the Temple." He widened his eyes and nodded. "Even the Americans swallowed it because they auspiciously retained control over North America. But like everyone else, they lost much more than they gained." He stared into the distance.

"What happened?"

Jacob blinked. "What always happens to fragile regimes—*war*. It started with a coup in Moscow." He stared at the floor. "A bloody coup...by a bloodthirsty man."

"Who?"

"Nobody knows. He stays behind the scenes." He looked up. "China was next. He wiped out Beijing and took over the warm-water ports along the Pacific Rim. Then, with his fleet positioned to defend against the US, he turned the other way." He gestured out the window. "He invaded the Middle East."

"Here?"

Jacob shook his head. "Not exactly." He carved a path with his hand. "He rolled straight through Jordan and captured Riyadh in a day. He had control over—" his next words were a high, descending sequence of tones, "*all* the oil he needed. He made his people rich for the first time in more than a century, so they were willing to follow him to hell and back."

"And then?"

"He left."

Joel blinked.

Chapter 8

"He made a pact with the Saudis, took his toys, and went home, *but*"—he pointed a finger in the air— "now he controlled manufacturing on the Pacific Rim *and* the oil that fueled it. He took it all for his people, and the rest of the global economy went into a tailspin." He twirled a finger toward the ground.

A woman with white hair pulled into a bun stepped in and placed her hand on Jacob's shoulder.

Joel guessed she was his wife. He was trying to digest the implications of what he had heard. "So, a global depression?"

"Not just depression—*famine*. Without the oil, the ships couldn't sail, the trains couldn't run. Countries like Japan, who depend on trade for their very subsistence, were no longer able to import enough food. Starvation and pandemic disease have been rampant for two years, now." Jacob stared into space again. "More people have died than ever before...in all history."

"Since the Flood, maybe." Joel shook his head. He began to connect the dots and realized what was going on around him. "How many people have died?" He had a good idea what was coming.

"At least *two billion*."

Joel leaned back in the sofa. "One-fourth of the world." He covered his eyes with a hand. "Then it *has* begun. It's no wonder the persecution will be so severe. They'll need a scapegoat."

"What persecution?"

Joel wasn't quite ready to advance the subject. "I don't get why America just sat on their thumbs and let this happen."

Jacob looked straight into Joel's eyes. His expression looked pained. "America won't be able to help us for long...not now." He was silent for a moment. "They tried...at least some of them. They

Chronos: Revolution

threatened Russian control over Saudi oil and tried to stabilize the global economy. They argued and debated on the world stage...until *he* ended the debate for them."

A heavy sense of dread hung on Joel's chest. He was afraid to ask the next question. "How?"

Jacob's eyes watered. He picked up a framed picture from the coffee table and wiped his eyes with his hand. "New York was one of the first cities to go." He shook his head and let the tears stream down his face. "He didn't strike for strategy...he struck for vengeance. New York, DC, LA, London..."

A lump formed in Joel's throat.

"He has mounted a second invasion south to secure his oil interests, but this campaign isn't going so well for him. The Americans are furious. They staged their naval forces in Cyprus, and from there, they *just* attacked his forces rolling through Syria."

Jacob's wife knelt beside him. She plucked a tissue from a box on an end table and handed it to him.

Joel tried to swallow the lump down. *Father, what has become of Grace...and my parents?* Something told him his parents *might* be okay, but he had a terrible feeling Grace was gone. He looked to the side.

Tom broke the silence. "I'm sorry to have such news for you, Joel."

Joel felt a spark of anger beneath the tears that were trying to force their way out. He clenched his jaw and forgot to keep his thoughts silent. "Why here, Father? Why now? And how could You..." He forced the next words down. He wasn't supposed to think such things.

Chapter 8

Jacob's wife reached to the coffee table, picked up a TV remote, and pressed the power button with her thumb. "I know this is unwelcome, but you need to see this."

The TV came to life with images of tanks rolling down a street. On the sidewalks on each side, civilians watched, pointed, and scratched their heads. The commentary was in Hebrew.

Jacob wiped his eyes with the tissue. "Please find something in English for our guest, Hannah."

She changed the channel. A helicopter view of an aircraft carrier, listing and on fire, appeared on the screen. Crew members climbed out on deck, slid into the water, and helped the wounded into inflatable rafts. An F-35 slid off the carrier's deck and plunged into the sea with a mighty splash, bobbed for a moment, and sank beneath the waves. An Arleigh Burke destroyer moved into view, its crew members struggling to pull men and women out of the water.

Joel's vision blurred. He wiped his eyes and listened to the commentary. The woman's voice had a British accent. "*All that's left of America's Fifth Fleet in the Mediterranean. The Eisenhower Strike Group was already crippled and limping west when this latest attack came.*"

An anchorwoman pictured in the corner of the screen placed a set of papers on the desk in front of her. "*And can you confirm initial reports that the attack was, in fact, from the Russian Federation?*"

"*That's right, Kelly. They fired from miles away, but there is no doubt, now, the attacking fighters were Russian Su-57s.*" An image of a fighter jet appeared on the screen. "*This is clearly retaliation for the American attack on their forces pushing south through Syria.*"

Chronos: Revolution

The anchorwoman nodded. "*Thank you, Laura.*" She turned to face the camera as her image filled the screen. "*Let's turn now to Tel Aviv for the latest developments.*"

A man appeared on the screen with a mike in one hand and his other hand over his ear. Behind him, a long line of tanks rolled down a main street. "*Yes, Kelly...Russian forces have completely occupied Tel Aviv. They have established checkpoints in and out of the city, and there are unconfirmed reports of summary executions. We have been unable to contact anyone with the Israeli government since forces rolled in yesterday.*"

"*Is it true they are headed for Jerusalem?*"

"*There are indications that some Russian forces have already entered Jerusalem.*" He gestured behind himself. "*We have seen a steady stream of forces heading east out of Tel Aviv, which suggests they intend to seize control over Jerusalem, as well.*"

Jacob looked at his wife and ran his hand across his neck in a gesture to turn it off. She muted the TV.

Joel turned to his host. "You said Israel signed the treaty on a provisional basis, right?"

Jacob nodded. "Seven years. Signed on the first of January."

"Am I right guessing that about three-and-a-half years have passed?"

"Almost."

"Has anyone been counting the days?"

Jacob nodded. "Well...yes. There's a propaganda channel proudly counting off the days of New Rome."

Joel felt his gut squeezing together. "And what day is this?"

Chapter 8

Jacob looked at his son. Tom leaned forward, plucked the remote off the coffee table, aimed it for the TV, and pushed a button. Another news channel appeared. In the corner of the screen, a text box read, *Days of New Rome: 1259.*

Joel stared at the screen. *Tomorrow, all hell breaks loose.*

"Phanuel!" Joel stood in the small, hedged-in yard behind Jacob's house. His frustration was growing. At least before, his father was with him. Now Phanuel seemed to be his only hope. "Phanuel, I need to speak with you." He turned around and cupped his hands around his mouth. "Phanuel!"

The weary, old voice surprised him from behind. "Now that's *exactly* why I didn't want to give you my name, young Seer."

Joel spun around.

He wore the same clothes as the old man Joel had seen that morning, but his face was the familiar one from Nimrod's tower and DC. He rested his bony hands on the arch of his cane. "There you go calling on *my* name instead of the Name you *should* be calling."

Joel had so many questions. "I'm sorry, Phanuel, but I have to speak with you."

"No, you don't. You need to pray—and you need to listen."

Joel's frustration dissipated for the moment. "You're right." He placed a hand on his head. "But so long as you're here..." He looked around. "Why here? Why now?"

"I already told you I don't know everything, didn't I?" His tone softened. "By now you know what's happening, right?"

Joel nodded. "Tomorrow's the day, isn't it? Tomorrow, he... reveals himself."

Chronos: Revolution

Phanuel nodded slowly.

"Then what am I supposed to do?"

Phanuel opened his mouth to speak.

"You're gonna tell me to pray again, aren't you?"

Phanuel stared.

Joel thought of the battle he had seen over Hains Point. "Do any of the rebel angels know I'm here?"

Phanuel looked around. "Well, I should say not, since they aren't here...but if you keep shouting my name at the top of your lungs, that could change."

"I see your point." Even in the angel's presence, Joel's deep sense of dread was growing. "Phanuel...please help me. I don't want to be alone here."

"You are never alone, Joel. The end of the age may be fast approaching, but Jesus promised to be with you through all of it."

That wasn't the answer Joel wanted. He wanted the protection he had enjoyed at Hains Point. He fell to his knees. "Please, Phanuel."

Phanuel swatted Joel's shoulder. "Get up!" He swatted it again. "Get up, young Seer." He pointed a bony finger at Joel's face. "Don't you do *anything* that even *vaguely resembles* worshiping me, do you understand?"

Joel nodded. The lump in his throat returned with a vengeance. He squeezed his eyes shut. "I'm scared, Phanuel. I'm scared."

A firm hand grasped his arm near his shoulder and pulled him to his feet. Joel found himself looking into the fierce eyes of the warrior angel who had fought for him before.

Phanuel now wore khakis and a loose, white pullover. He held Joel by the shoulders, looked into his eyes, and spoke with a resonant

Chapter 8

bass voice. "Joel, it has been my pleasure and honor to follow you and your father all these years—and to fight with you, but I must leave, now."

Joel shook his head. "No, you can't leave, Phanuel. Not now."

"Joel...as God's image-bearer, *you*...you and the rest of the redeemed, are destined to reign on earth, not me."

"But I need your strength. I know who we'll be facing tomorrow."

Phanuel pointed a finger into his own chest with raised eyebrows. "You think *I'm* strong?"

Joel furrowed his brow and nodded. "Of course, I do."

"With Him, young Seer—" Phanuel jutted a finger in Joel's chest twice. "—*you're stronger*. The One who is in you, Joel, is greater than the one who is in the world." He took one step back. "What did Paul tell the Ephesian Church? How does any soldier prepare for battle?"

Joel wiped his face with his sleeve and took a deep breath. "By putting on his armor, I suppose."

"And what can you tell me about that armor?"

Joel didn't really want a theology lesson. He started with his head and worked down. "Helmet of salvation, breastplate of righteousness, shield of faith, belt of truth, feet sandaled with readiness for the gospel of peace, and the sword of the Spirit, God's Word."

"And what's the next verse?"

Joel looked down and to one side. "Pray at all times in the Spirit."

Phanuel smiled. "And don't you forget it. One more thing—" Joel looked at him. "Do you notice anything in common with all of the armor?"

Joel thought about it. *Salvation, righteousness, faith, truth, peace.* He huffed a breath and drew his lips into a faint grin. "Wow, I never picked up on that before." He looked at Phanuel again. "They're all gifts from Jesus."

Phanuel nodded. "Which is why in his epistle to the Romans, Paul simply said, 'Put on the Lord Jesus Christ.'" Phanuel pointed into the sky. "He is your King." He pointed at Joel's chest again. "He is your Captain. Follow Him, Joel. Even in the thick of battle, the safest place for you is *right...behind...Him*." A sad smile crept over his face. He stepped forward and gave Joel a firm hug. "Farewell, fellow servant of the Messiah...my dear friend. I look forward to seeing what He is going to do through you." He drew back and grinned. "I've already seen Him do a *lot* through you...more than you know." He turned to the side and looked to the sky.

"Phanuel?"

Phanuel looked at Joel.

"Thank you for remaining faithful to Him."

He grinned and nodded. "Remember what I told you, Seer, and be sure to pay attention. You're in for quite a show, tonight. Now—" with a burst of light, he transformed into his full glory, "— before tomorrow, I must deliver two witnesses to the Temple." He stretched his wings high, swung them down with a mighty rush, and soared straight up. Within seconds, he was gone.

Joel swept his hand over his hair and watched his friend leave. Bitterness crept up his throat. He struggled to push it down. Despite Phanuel's encouragement, he had never felt so alone.

Someone spoke.

Joel whipped around. No one was there. He was puzzled. Now that he thought of it, he hadn't *heard* anyone. He *felt* the voice. It

Chapter 8

spoke again. The voice felt familiar, but now Joel was doubting his very sanity.

Pay attention, Joel.

He closed his eyes and waited. A breeze washed over his face.

Now...are you ready to listen to Me?

Joel felt a wave of relief. Phanuel was right. He wasn't alone, after all. He took a deep breath, sighed through pursed lips, and nodded. "Yes, Father." He fell to his knees, and the tears returned. "Yes, Father. I'm so sorry." His crying sounded almost like laughter. "I'm so sorry, Father."

Well then, brave young warrior. Let's get to work.

This time Joel *did* laugh through his tears. "Yes, Father."

A light streaked up into the sky in the distance. Joel stood, cupped a hand over his eyes, gazed toward the horizon, and followed the light up. It was an angel. Seconds later, another shot skyward, then another. Joel panned across the horizon and saw dozens, then hundreds, of angels soaring up with more and more joining them. They streamed together into formations, and the formations streamed together into larger ones. Joel stared as tens of thousands of angels left their earthly posts and flew heavenward.

"Why are they leaving, Father?"

Chapter 9

The last of the setting sun was dipping over the horizon, casting a blanket of purplish gray across the sky. Joel stepped into Jacob's house and found him sitting with his wife, Tom, and the young boy Tom had introduced as his nephew. They all stared at the television. Joel was determined. He had to give them a head start. He pointed outside. "Can you all see this?"

Tom leapt to his feet and followed Joel's pointing finger. "See what?"

"You don't see all those lights heading into the sky?"

"What lights?"

Joel's heart ached. He had hoped everyone else would see that. He turned to the family. "We need to get you all to the Kidron Valley."

Jacob widened his eyes. "East of the Old City? That's Palestinian territory. Why on earth would we go there?"

"Because it's next to the Mount of Olives." Joel pointed at the TV. "Because the Russians are coming from the other direction, and because Jesus..." He figured the Hebrew name would be more appropriate. "...because Yeshua *commanded* you to."

Hannah straightened and turned away.

Far in the distance, the faint sound of thunder rumbled.

Chapter 9

Jacob looked at his wife a moment before turning back. He drew his eyebrows together. "Joel...we are Jews...we are not—"

"Completed Jews?" Joel's sense of urgency overwhelmed any patience he might otherwise have had. "But your grandfather—"

Jacob suddenly looked stern. "My own father returned to Judaism, and I don't very much like your choice of terms."

"Jacob, you all must understand—for you, becoming a follower of Yeshua is not *converting*—it's fully realizing your *own* faith, your own Scriptures." His heart was beating quickly. He looked around. "I'm guessing you won't have a copy of the New Testament around." He remembered seeing Tom use a smartphone. "Tom, may I please borrow your phone?"

More distant thunder rumbled. It grew in volume and rolled across the sky.

Tom looked at his father, reached into his pocket, pulled out the phone, and handed it to Joel.

"Thank you." Joel opened the internet browser and pulled up a copy of the Bible as quickly as he could. "I can spend a lot of time showing you how Yeshua fulfilled the prophecies of the Messiah's first coming, how He's the Suffering Servant in Isaiah 53, but first—" He looked up for a moment. "I want to show you what's about to happen tomorrow. Are you familiar with the timeline of Daniel chapter 9?"

Their blank looks suggested the answer was no.

Joel sighed and looked to the side for a moment. *Alright.* He pointed at the screen. "Daniel 9, verse 27. '*He* will make a firm covenant with many for one week...'" Joel looked up. "Given the context of a 490-year period described as 'seventy weeks,' most people

Chronos: Revolution

recognize this week as seven years." He looked at the screen. "But in the middle of the week he will put a stop to sacrifice and offering. And the abomination of desolation will be on a wing of the Temple until the decreed destruction is poured out on the desolator."

A louder clap of thunder boomed and rolled across the sky.

Joel looked up again. "Tomorrow may be Wednesday, the middle of the week, but it is also the middle of that *prophetic* week of years. The antichrist will reveal himself tomorrow and desecrate the Temple, just as Antiochus Epiphanes did before the Maccabean revolt." He typed on the phone and swept his finger across the screen several times. "You need to hear the words of your Messiah next. In Matthew chapter 24, starting in verse 15, Yeshua said, 'So when you see the abomination that causes desolation, spoken of by the prophet Daniel, standing in the holy place . . . then those in Judea must flee to the mountains! A man on the housetop must not come down to get things out of his house. And a man in the field must not go back to get his clothes. Woe to pregnant women and nursing mothers in those days! Pray that your escape may not be in winter or on a Sabbath. For at that time there will be great tribulation, the kind that hasn't taken place from the beginning of the world until now and never will again! Unless those days were limited, no one would survive. But those days will be limited because of the elect.'"

Joel faced Jacob's family. "Starting tomorrow, the antichrist will sweep New Rome away and establish New Babylon, and then the greatest persecution in history will begin. This may be hard to believe, but it'll be far worse than the Holocaust was."

Jacob opened his eyes wide. "Two billion people have already died. I believe it."

Chapter 9

Joel tightened his lips for a moment. "It will start with you—with Jews. But after Yeshua intervenes on your behalf, the antichrist will attack the Church with a vengeance."

Jacob's eyes were fixed on Joel. "Intervenes? How?"

Two claps of thunder boomed from opposite directions. Tom looked in the direction of the first clap, then turned to the other. "That's strange."

Joel swept his finger across the screen several times. "Zechariah 14, starting in verse 4. 'On that day His feet will stand on the Mount of Olives, which faces Jerusalem on the east. The Mount of Olives will be split in half from east to west, forming a huge valley, so that half the mountain will move to the north and half to the south. You will flee by My mountain valley, for the valley of the mountains will extend to Azal.'"

Joel studied Jacob and his family. He didn't see anger on their faces. He saw angst. He looked at the phone and flipped forward through the Scripture. "Revelation chapter 12, verse 6, 'The woman—'" He looked up. "The woman here is Israel." He looked down again. "'The woman fled into the wilderness, where she had a place prepared by God, to be fed there for 1,260 days.'"

He swept his finger up the screen to move down the same chapter. "Verses 13 to 17 explain what follows: 'When the dragon saw that he had been hurled to the earth, he pursued the woman who had given birth to the male child.'" He looked up, "The male child is Yeshua." He continued reading from the screen, "'The woman was given the two wings of a great eagle, so that she could fly from the serpent's presence to her place in the wilderness, where she was fed for a time, times, and half a time. From his mouth the serpent spewed water like a river flowing after the woman, to sweep her away in a torrent. But the earth helped the woman. The earth opened its mouth and swallowed up the river that the dragon had spewed from his mouth. So the dragon was furious with the woman and left to wage war against the rest of her offspring—those who keep God's commands and have the testimony about Jesus.'"

Joel put the phone down. "Do you see now? Yeshua is your Messiah. He already came as the victorious sacrifice. In fact, He died at the very moment the priests sacrificed the Passover Lamb in the Temple." Joel paused to let that sink in. "Now, He is beginning His return as the Conquering King, and He will provide an escape for you, right here. He will protect you for the second half of the seven years." Joel extended his hands and clenched them into fists. "But only if you *obey* Him and *go*." He pointed at the television. "Don't you get it? This mysterious Russian leader will see Israelites as puppets of the American regime he is destroying. He's about to ravage this city and all the people in it. You *must* go now."

A clap of thunder shook the house and rattled dishes from directly overhead. Everyone shuddered.

Hannah covered her mouth with her hands. "The Russians are shelling the city."

Tom hurried to the window. "I don't think so, Ma." He ran out the door and beckoned everyone to follow. Joel followed them out.

They tilted their heads back and stared into the starry night sky. There wasn't a single cloud, and yet bursts of light like flashes of lightning dotted the sky from horizon to horizon. The rolls of thunder became nearly continuous, punctuated by what sounded like distant, percussive explosions.

Chapter 9

As dire as the situation was, Joel was relieved to see the others looking. "You can see *that*, right?" He peered over the hedges and saw dozens of people stepping out of their homes and staring into the sky. He spoke under his breath, "Now I know why Phanuel had to leave." He remembered the mighty angel's words at Hains Point: "*The war is coming.*"

In the sky to one side, a blinding burst of light flashed like burning phosphorous. The people staring at the sky squinted and turned their heads to the side, then shuddered with the explosive boom that followed. A distant ball of fire appeared at the site of the flash, carved a long, straight, slow path to the ground, and left a long trail of flame in its wake.

In the other direction, another blinding flash preceded an explosive crack and the appearance of another fireball that scorched its way to the ground.

Jacob muttered something in Hebrew, then glanced at Joel. "What is this?"

Joel dreaded the truth. "The war in Heaven. Satan and his angels are being cast out."

Another blinding flash and crack of thunder drew everyone's attention to the next fireball.

Jacob shook his head. "No. No. That war took place before Adam and Eve."

Joel shook his head. "Remember the book of Job?"

Jacob stared up again. "What about it?"

Several flashes and explosions rocked the sky. They became more and more frequent.

Chronos: Revolution

Joel had to raise his voice over the din. "Satan and his angels appeared before God's throne. We also know from the Apostle John in the book of Revelation that Satan has been accusing God's children before the throne day and night." Joel looked up. "They've had access to Heaven all this time—but no more." He took a deep, heavy breath. "This is going to complicate matters—a lot." Joel looked at Jacob. "Sir, you and your family need to prepare yourselves. You may see a *lot* of miracles. Angels—even angels who have been cast to the earth—may still have great power."

A man yelled, and a woman near him shouted. Joel jerked his head in their direction. They and others pointed up at an angle. Joel looked where they indicated. One of the fireballs was streaking straight toward them. Jacob's family crouched and stared.

The roar of the approaching flame grew louder and louder. Amidst the growing roar, a single, deep voice could be heard in a long, sustained scream. The fireball roared just overhead with a flash of heat. It disappeared over the house and silhouetted the building with a pink-orange burst of light and a clap of thunder that shook the ground.

Joel jumped through the hedge and ran around the house. Just down the street, smoke rose from a ten-foot wide crater. In the middle, a man in a dark tunic rose to his feet.

The orb! Joel ran around the house and through the back door. He grabbed his overcoat, made sure the orb was still inside, plunged his arms into the sleeves, and pulled the collar over his shoulders. He ran back out and to the front yard and grabbed Jacob's arm. "Which way to the Temple?"

Chapter 10

The roads were gridlocked. Horns honked, drivers shouted out their windows, and people ran in every direction. The sky flashed, cracked, and rumbled with the continued storm of falling stars. People couldn't seem to decide what to fear more: the approaching Russian army or the terrifying shower of meteors.

Joel watched from the back seat with Hannah and Tom's nephew. Tom struggled to drive them in short lurches through the pandemonium while Jacob switched channels on the radio. The frenzied reports were no help. Much of the night had passed as they struggled to make their way through the city.

Some distance ahead, the flashing night sky silhouetted the high part of the Old City, still dominated by the gold-topped Islamic Dome of the Rock.

Tom threw his hands out in frustration. "We aren't getting anywhere, Poppi." He looked at his watch. "And I'm supposed to report for duty in an hour."

The street around them grew brighter. People around looked up, pointed, yelled, and scattered. Passengers abandoned their cars and ran away with the doors left open. An ominous, crackling roar grew louder, accompanied by another deep, bellowing scream. Twenty feet ahead, a meteor crashed onto an abandoned car and crushed it with an ear-shattering boom and a blinding burst of flame.

Joel and the others in the car shielded their eyes. A moment later, a strong-looking man emerged from the scorched heap that was once a car, looked at his hands, and studied his own clothing. He wore a dark tunic and sandals.

"Father, he no longer gets to wear white linen, does he?" Joel prayed.

He has rejected My grace.

The man jumped off the car's wreckage and ran down the street.

Joel heard shouts from behind. He turned and saw a familiar, dark-haired man wearing jeans and a black leather jacket running straight for them.

Joel's eyes went wide. *Aphiel!* He ducked as the angel ran along the side of their car and stopped by the hood. Joel sat up and stared at the dark angel's back.

Aphiel clutched his leather jacket for a moment, then extended a hand and made a fist. He shook his fist over and over.

Joel watched with fascination. *He can't produce his scepter. I wonder if he's completely robbed of power.*

Aphiel screamed, clasped his hands over his head, and swung them down on the hood of the car. Like a piledriver on tinfoil, he crushed the engine. The motor stopped abruptly.

Okay, not completely robbed.

Aphiel stared at his hands, screamed, and sprinted down the street.

Joel heard a child crying. He looked in the seat next to him. Tom's nephew held on to Jacob's wife, pressed his face against her

Chapter 10

blouse, and sobbed. She cradled his head with one hand and clutched her armrest with the other, breathing hard. Joel looked in the front seat. Jacob and Tom were frozen. He guessed they were in shock.

Joel reached out with both hands, placed one on Tom's shoulder and the other on Tom's nephew, and gave them a firm squeeze. "Father, in the Name of Jesus Christ...in the Name of *Yeshua HaMashiach*...bless Jacob and his family with your peace right now." A cool breeze swept through the open windows. "And please deliver them safely to your rescue today. Let them look on their Messiah for the first time. We thank You, we honor You, and we trust You. Amen."

Jacob spoke for the first time since the angel had crashed onto the nearby car. "Why didn't we know this was coming?"

Joel drew his hand off their shoulders. "Because you weren't familiar with the writings of the Apostle John. Yeshua is the prophesied *Immanuel*, God with us. He is *Adonai*. Are you ready to call on your Messiah, yet?"

Jacob stared at the dashboard for a moment, then nodded quickly. "Yeshua...*Yeshua Hu Adonai*."

In the backseat opposite Joel, Jacob's wife echoed. "Yeshua." Tom repeated it.

Joel looked at Tom's nephew, placed a hand on the back of the trembling boy's head, and gently turned him so he could look into the boy's eyes. "What do *you* think?"

The boy nodded. "Yeshua...*Yeshua HaMashiach*."

Joel gave the boy a reassuring smile. "Then no matter what happens, you'll one day get to see Him smiling at you."

The heavenly cracks of thunder suddenly became louder and more frequent. The sky flashed with an intense storm of lightning. Joel leaned to his window and looked up. "Time to get out."

All four car doors opened as one. They hurried out and stepped in front of the car's crushed motor. Tom brought an old portable radio he had brought with them. Joel pointed toward the Dome of the Rock. "Is the Temple on the north end of the Temple Mount?"

Jacob stood next to him. "No, the Temple Mount, it turns out, wasn't the Temple Mount at all. It was Fort Antonia." He gently redirected Joel's arm to the right. "The Temple is just south of that, above the Gihon Spring."

Joel opened his mouth, huffed some air, and shook his head slightly. "No wonder Jesus said not a stone would be left on another."

The blasts from above grew deafening. Everyone shuddered, ducked, and looked up. A flurry of blinding flashes burst across the sky. A dozen fireballs appeared, then a hundred, then a thousand. Within seconds, the entire sky was dotted with fiery-tailed meteors streaking toward the earth. A final flash exploded above. It sent an expanding wave of light across the entire sky. Then with a deep, loud, bellowing scream the whole earth could hear, the largest fireball appeared and carved its fiery path to the ground.

Joel looked ahead of its path. It would strike west of the city. "Shining morning star, how you have fallen from the heavens! You destroyer of nations, you have been cut down to the ground."

Jacob watched the satanic fireball plummet. "From the prophet Isaiah."

The flashes in the sky abruptly ceased, even as the countless fireballs continued their long fall to the earth.

Chapter 10

Joel looked at Jacob and his family. "It's time to go."

The morning sun backlit the Temple and its broad, raised foundation. To its left, the long structure that was once called the Temple Mount lifted the Dome of the Rock and the Al-Aqsa Mosque slightly higher than the temple.

Jacob held Hannah's hand and led them along the crowded, cluttered road. Tom carried his nephew. The boy wrapped his arms and legs around his uncle and buried his face in his neck. Far behind them, the faint rumble of diesel motors and axle squeaks warned of the impending Russian occupation. To their left, throngs pushed their way to the Jewish-controlled area below the Western Wailing Wall. Hannah pointed. "Look, Jacob. We should go."

Joel looked at her and shook his head. "No, no. Please trust me. You must go around to the east side." She looked at Jacob.

Jacob gave her a reassuring nod. "We will go around. We will wait for our Messiah." She nodded and leaned against him as they continued to walk. He wrapped his arm around her. They made their way along the road that wrapped around the south end of the Temple's foundation. The crowd grew thinner the farther they went.

His nephew still wrapped around him, Tom scurried a bit to catch up. "Poppi," he gestured back toward the Wailing Wall. "If Yeshua is the Messiah, someone needs to tell them."

Jacob stopped. "But would they listen? Before tonight, I wouldn't have."

Out of nowhere, a deafening voice shook the earth. "Fear God and give Him glory!" People everywhere shuddered and froze in their tracks. The voice's echoes swept back and forth from horizon

Chronos: Revolution

to horizon before it continued, "Because the hour of His judgment has come! Worship the Maker of Heaven and Earth, the sea and springs of water...water...water."

Jacob leaned toward Joel. "The voice just said to fear God and give Him glory."

Joel was puzzled. "I understood it, Jacob. He's speaking English, after all."

Jacob blinked. "He's speaking Hebrew." They stared at each other for a moment.

The voice continued. "If you confess with your mouth, 'Jesus is Lord,' and believe in your heart that God raised Him from the dead, you will be saved...saved...saved."

Tom turned on the radio. The voice squawked from its speaker. "If you confess with your mouth"—he turned the knob—"*Si tu confesses de ta bouche le Seigneur Jésus, et si tu crois dans ton coeur*"—he turned the knob again—"*Innaka inna i'tarafta befemmika beyessou'a—*"

He turned it off. They stared at each other.

The voice finished. "Call on Jesus now—follow Him." The echoes faded into the distance.

The silence that followed was deafening. The entire world seemed frozen in place. The only sound was a gentle breeze.

Joel broke the silence. "This good news of the Kingdom will be proclaimed in all the world as a testimony to all nations. And then the end will come."

Tom looked at him. "Who said that?"

"Jesus."

Chapter 10

Hannah seemed much more at peace with what was happening. "Well—there can be no doubt about our Messiah *now*."

Someone shouted in the distance. It sounded like Russian. The motor sounds of the approaching army resumed and began to grow louder.

Tom's nephew pointed behind them. "Look."

They turned to see where he was pointing. In the distance behind them, the first tanks crawled over the hill, illuminated by the morning light. They cast long shadows behind, pushed abandoned cars out of the way, and crushed other cars underneath.

Still heading east, Joel led the family to where the western side of the Temple's foundation met the southern face. He peered around the corner along the southern side. Half a dozen fierce-looking men in dark tunics stood near the wall, right in their path. They had ripped the sleeves off their tunics, baring their muscular arms. Joel felt like he was looking at a gang of *sheddim*.

Tom shook his head. "Oh, that's not good."

Hannah pointed back toward the approaching army. "Rock." She pointed at the dark angels in their path. "Hard place." She looked at the others. "Now what?"

Joel had anticipated this. "I should be able to help." All he needed to do was to pause time, and they'd be home free. He reached into his overcoat pocket, placed his hand on the orb, closed his eyes, and felt for the orb's power.

He felt nothing.

He tried again. He extended a hand and tried to open a portal. Not even a spark. Joel looked down. "It isn't working." Jacob and the others stared.

91

Joel tilted his head. "Father, why won't it work?"

Without hearing anything, he knew in his heart. The fallen angels still had strength and power, but not their unique authority. They had sacrificed that by rebelling. Joel didn't understand why, but in like manner, the orb seemed to have lost its authority over time. "Then what am I to do, Father? Why bring it here if it's useless?" Joel considered what was happening. "Father, do you want me to bring the orb through the Mount of Olives with the fleeing Jews?"

No.

He blinked. "Okay, that's pretty clear. What, then?" Joel tried to listen. He heard nothing. His frustration began to grow, but he mustered all his will and pushed it aside. "No, Father. You're speaking to me, aren't you? I'm just not hearing you. Please help me listen."

The army was heading straight for them. People began to stream around the corner past them. Joel exchanged glances with the others. "We have to keep moving." He led the way along the south end of the Temple foundation. Even if he couldn't go with them, he needed to get Jacob and his family to the other side.

They couldn't avoid the gang of dark angels. Joel studied their faces carefully and felt at least one hint of relief. Turiel and Aphiel weren't among them.

One of the angels spotted them approaching, tapped the others on the shoulder, and pointed. They gathered like a gang of street thugs and formed a line. The one who saw them first stepped in front and folded his thick arms. "What do you want with us, humans?"

Jacob's voice trembled. "Shalom?"

Other people began to gather behind them. Three college-aged girls tried to get by after giving the angels a wide berth. One of the

Chapter 10

angels stared as they passed. He jutted his chest out and turned to watch them leave. One of the girls flashed a smile and slowed down. Her friends pulled her away.

Joel watched the covetous angel and kept his thoughts silent. *Nothing will stop them from having their way with people now...at least for a while.* He moved in front of Jacob's family and stared at the ringleader. "We just want to pass."

The angel scowled, shook his head, and clenched his right hand into a fist.

Joel was certain that would hurt. "Father, please help us."

As abruptly as before, a second heavenly voice shook the ground. "It has fallen!"

The angels shuddered, their eyes tense with fear. They bent their legs as if to distance themselves from Heaven, cowered, and stared into the sky.

"Babylon the Great has fallen!—"

Joel saw his opportunity. He gathered Jacob and his family and ushered them through the gang of terrified angels.

"—Who made all nations drink the wine of her passionate immorality—which brings wrath!"

Even the echoes startled the otherwise fearsome-looking angels. From an opening near the center of the Temple foundation's south wall, a long, shallow stone stairway spilled down to the street. As they walked past the bottom step, Joel had a sudden impression he should stop. "Father, do you want me to take the orb to the Temple?"

Yes.

Joel nodded. "Will you take it from me there?" Again, Joel heard nothing. "Okay, I'll obey first. Then I'll ask."

He looked at Jacob. "I have to leave you now." More people began to stream around the end of the Temple foundation, ahead of the approaching army. Others flocked in from the south.

Joel pointed farther along the wall. "You must go without me. Wait in the Kidron Valley between the Old City and the Mount of Olives. You'll have a head start."

Jacob furrowed his brow. "You won't come with us?"

Joel shook his head. "I'm not certain I can." He gestured with his head. "If I'm not mistaken, that means of escape is reserved for you. Since you are His chosen people, God has special things in store for you."

"You can't come with us, but you *can* go to the Temple? You're not a Jew."

Joel pulled his lips in and nodded. "I haven't worked that out, yet." He tilted his head to the side. "At least I can get to the Outer Court—the Court of Gentiles—right?"

Jacob nodded. "Will that be far enough?"

Joel took a deep breath. "Hebrews 10:19, 'we have boldness to enter the Sanctuary through the blood of Jesus.'" Jacob nodded silently. He stepped forward, planted a kiss on each of Joel's cheeks, stepped back, and stared at the ground.

Hannah leaned forward and kissed his cheek. "Thank you. Thank you." She stepped back. "God be with you."

Joel smiled and nodded. "He *is* with me. He is *in* me. Since you've called on Him, He is in you, too. He promised it." She nodded and smiled.

Tom approached with his nephew still wrapped around him. He extended his right hand. "Good luck, Joel. Thank you."

Chapter 10

Joel shook Tom's hand. "And thank *you* for your help, Tom." He looked at Jacob and Hannah. "Thank you *all*." He reached out and rubbed the boy's back. Then he pointed east. "Now hurry." They nodded, turned, and followed the thickening crowd along the wall and around the corner.

Joel looked back in the direction they had come from. The angelic thugs stared at the approaching army. Joel looked beyond them. A steady stream of tanks and troop carriers followed, crowding the narrow street. Further back, a polished black van with an extended top crested the hill. Small tricolor flags of white, red, and blue waved from their mounts above the fenders.

Joel's abdomen squeezed together. "That's him. No time to lose." He turned and lifted a foot to bound up the stairs. A strong hand grabbed his shoulder and yanked him back.

"Just where do you think you're going?"

Joel jerked his head toward the hand and slowly followed a leather sleeve to its owner. He stared into Aphiel's face.

Chapter 11

Aphiel pulled Joel's face inches from his own and sneered. "Where's the orb?"

Joel stared back. "Where's your scepter?"

Fear flashed in Aphiel's eyes. He let go, stepped back, and looked down. Then he looked up, tightened his lips, and glared. "Look around you, Seer. The world is *ours* now."

"Maybe."

He clenched his fists. "It *is* ours!"

Joel longed to see God's justice served right then and there. He gestured with his head toward the approaching army. "Your destiny is the same as your master's, and you know it."

"I don't *have* a master."

Joel gestured again. "Maybe you should tell him that."

Aphiel's glare melted.

"How did John put it? A time, times, and half a time?"

Aphiel's eyes darted back and forth.

"You have one thousand two hundred sixty days, Aphiel—that's forty-two months." Joel's indignation grew hot. "And the last part of it is going to be hell...on...earth."

By now, Aphiel was clenching his teeth and running his fingers through his hair. He dropped his hands. "Wait. Why am I afraid?"

Chapter 11

He jerked his head toward Joel and thrust his pointed finger out. "*You* should be afraid. Scepter or no scepter..." He seemed to savor his last words as he stepped slowly toward Joel. "I'm going to enjoy killing you."

Joel found himself repeating his earlier prayer, "Father, please help."

A third voice shook the stairway beneath them. "Be warned!"

Aphiel's bravado vaporized like water on hot oil. His eyebrows turned up, and he raised his hands next to his head. "No, no, not again."

"If anyone worships the beast and his image and receives a mark on his forehead or on his hand—he will also drink the wine of God's wrath, which is mixed full strength in the cup of His anger!"

Aphiel covered his ears and paced back and forth. "Make it stop. Make it stop."

Joel made his way up a few steps into the dark stairway and watched Aphiel.

"He will be tormented with fire and sulfur in the sight of the holy angels and in the sight of the Lamb"—Aphiel kept pacing—"and the smoke of their torment will go up forever and ever!"

Joel bounded up the steps. He emerged into the morning sunlight. He found himself at the broad Outer Court, facing the side of the main Temple structure. He ran to his right toward the east end.

"There is no rest day or night for those who worship the beast and his image, or anyone who receives the mark of his name!"

Joel reached the eastern end of the Temple foundation near the southern corner and looked over the edge. All along the Kidron valley and up the barren face of the Mount of Olives, neither cars

Chronos: Revolution

nor pedestrians moved an inch. Everyone stood in place and listened to the angelic warning. "This demands the perseverance of the saints, who keep God's commands and their faith in Jesus!" The final word, the Name of Jesus, echoed over and over.

A fourth voice shouted, "The dead who die in the Lord from now on are blessed!"

Joel surveyed the scene below and up the mountain. "Thank you, Father. At least no one will take the mark in ignorance." He turned around. The broad Outer Court ran along the eastern side of the Temple foundation. A tall wall with a broad opening in the center separated it from the Inner Court.

Joel studied the entrance to the Inner Court. If he was right, it wouldn't be safe for him to try to go in. Only Jews would be permitted to enter. A small group of people congregated some distance from the entrance next to a camera mounted on the eastern outer wall facing into the Temple. Another camera mounted high above the entrance faced east across the valley. Shouts drew his attention back to the stairway. A dozen soldiers wearing green digital-camouflaged tactical gear and armed with rifles emerged from the top and scattered in both directions. More and more emerged. Half of them ran straight for Joel.

The Inner Court suddenly looked like a safer option. Joel ran to the Temple entrance. As he approached, he recognized the gathered people as a news team. He turned and bolted through the entrance. Just inside, two guards surprised him from either side and grabbed his arms.

He stared at the view inside. In the middle of the courtyard, several steps led up into another broad opening to the Court of Priests,

Chapter 11

beyond which lay a roughly eight-foot wide bronze altar with raised corners that stood about four-and-a-half feet high. A thin column of smoke rose above it, and several men in white priestly attire were tending the flames. Beyond the altar on the left, a bronze basin filled with water was mounted on a marble pedestal. Just beyond that, a tall white marble structure, the Sanctuary, dominated the Inner Court, towering above the altar.

Joel squinted to see into the Sanctuary. Inside, a row of small flames on a set of gold lampstands lined the walls on the right and left. A small altar stood in the middle with smoke rising above it, and behind that, a richly ornate, wall-to-wall, red, purple, and blue cloth draped from the ceiling, illuminated by the golden glow of the lampstands and obscuring what lay behind.

Joel couldn't pry his eyes away. Behind that ornate veil lay the *Holy of Holies*, the *Most Holy Place*, the point where God's very Presence had abided in the first and second temples, the place entered only once a year by the high priest. Paul's words to the Church in Corinth suddenly took on new meaning. "Don't you know that you are God's sanctuary and that the Spirit of God lives in you?" Joel suddenly felt ashamed for taking those words so lightly. For the first time, he began to apprehend what Paul was telling the Church. *You are holy, so live with that in mind.*

The guards pushed him back. Once he was outside the entrance, they let go and returned to their posts on each side. Joel was exhausted, parched, and at the end of his rope. "Father, "what do you want me to do? Please show me something."

Something hit Joel in the middle of his back. A hand grabbed his shoulder and yanked him around for a second time. It was Aphiel, his teeth bared in a fierce growl. He grabbed the lapel of Joel's overcoat with his left hand, clenched his right fist, and drew it back.

"Stop!"

The voice came from behind Aphiel. Two soldiers aimed their rifles at the angel. Half a dozen more stood nearby and stared at the spectacle.

Aphiel froze with his arm flexed and turned his head to the soldiers. His voice was calm. "What did you say?" He released Joel's lapel, made a show of dusting off his jacket, and turned to face his challengers.

The young soldier who had spoken looked like it was his first time holding a rifle. His arms trembled. "I said, stop!"

Aphiel walked slowly toward him. "Are you sure you want to say that?"

A deep voice made Joel's chest vibrate. "*I* am quite sure."

Aphiel looked to the side. Joel followed his gaze, and his heart sank. A dark-haired man, easily nine feet tall, wearing a dark navy-blue overcoat with shiny brass buttons and a navy-style wheel cap strode along the Outer Court toward them. An older man of average height walked with him, the hem of his red priestly robe fluttering in the breeze.

Joel took several slow steps backwards into the Inner Court. This time, the guards didn't object.

Joel's heart pounded. Fear and anger swirled around his chest. *So, this is the man who led the bloody Russian coup.* Even as his hands shook, Joel found himself half-chanting, half-praying, "I will fear no evil. I will fear no evil." He ran through verses in his head. *Do not be anxious about anything...You will not fear the terror of the night or*

Chapter 11

the arrow that flies by day." He reached behind to feel his way and kept stepping slowly backwards into the courtyard. He drew back to one side, out of view of the camera, and watched.

The modern-day giant stared at Aphiel just long enough for the angel to shrink back and disappear around the corner into the Outer Court. The entrance to the court was more than tall enough to accommodate the man as he took several long, deliberate strides into the courtyard and turned to face the entrance.

Dozens of soldiers raced into the courtyard in two lines, ran around the outside, met in the middle, and stopped in front of the steps that led up to the Court of Priests. They formed a line and faced the camera with their rifles across them in ready position, forming an impressive military backdrop. A handful of priests with white robes and turbans emerged from the entrance to the Court of Priests. Another priest emerged with them. He wore a blue tunic over his white robe and a square ephod over his chest with twelve variously colored stones. He pointed into the air and opened his mouth to say something.

The giant snapped his fingers. "Your Temple sacrifice is over."

A handful of soldiers surrounded the priests and ushered them into the Outer Court. The giant watched them leave. He looked at the civilians just outside in the Outer Court and pointed to the camera facing the Temple. "Is that on?"

A woman among them nodded. "Yes, sir. You're live. The world is watching...and listening."

"Why don't you introduce me."

She shifted back and forth. "You...need no introduction, sir."

Chronos: Revolution

"I don't suppose I do." The man cleared his throat, looked directly into the camera, and spoke in a loud and pronounced authoritative tone. His deep voice resonated off the marble walls. "New Rome is no more. I have swept it away. Today, you witness the birth of New Babylon, and together, we will rebuild. From the ashes of Rome," he pointed to the sky, "we will rebuild our kingdom until it is a mighty tower that reaches into the heavens."

Joel had heard those words before. What God had stopped on Nimrod's tower by confounding human language, this man was doing again. But this time, he had technology to overcome the language barrier. Joel knew the man's words were being translated live into every language on earth.

"I have raised the Russian Federation to become the foremost of our kingdoms, and what I did for them, I now do for you. We will build an economy that serves everyone, where no one goes hungry, where no one lives in poverty. We will control distribution and see to it no one is forced to do without." He spread his arms in a grand gesture. "Today, I bring you a new order where everyone can be rich, where everyone can have whatever they can dream of. And in return," he turned his right fist out toward the camera and pointed at a mark on the back of his hand, "you will take one of these—a symbol of your worship of me."

He opened his arms again. "There is room for everyone in my kingdom—in my empire," he spoke in a low voice. "so long as you worship...me." He shook his fist. "I know what you just heard—the *lying voices* of the old order." He pointed up. "You saw the battle in the skies last night. You saw with your own eyes how we—" he jabbed his thumb in his chest, "how *we* have conquered the very

Chapter 11

heavens and taken them for ourselves." He slapped his hand at his side and bellowed. "Don't listen to those voices! Don't listen to those lies! They don't want you to be happy. They don't want you to realize your dreams."

He gestured behind himself into the Court of Priests. "The Temple sacrifice ends today." He pointed to himself with both thumbs. "After all, you have really been sacrificing to *me* all these years."

He combed his fingers slowly through his hair. He pointed to himself again. Each sentence was louder than the previous. "*I am* the one who cares about your dreams. *I am* the one who will fulfill them for you. *I am* your just king...*I am* your righteous emperor...*I am* the Grand Mahdi...*I am* Maitreya...*I am* the true son of God!...*I am!*" He shook his fist and sneered. "*I am!*" He shook it again. "*I am!*"

He fell silent and dropped his hand to his side. He stared at the camera for a long moment. "And I will prove it." He paused again. "I know...some of you may be wondering to yourselves,"—his tone was mocking— "but that other guy rose from the dead." He pointed indignantly into the camera. "If you were *His* follower, then don't you forget that He was supposed to take you away by now." He swept his arms around. "You've been waiting for some great, divine rescue from the sky." He pointed at the camera again. "But guess what? He's not coming. He has *left you* here with everyone else, so stop believing in Him just because of some...*parlor trick* like rising from the dead."

He extended his right arm and placed it on the shoulder of the man in the red robe, only about half his height. "We will show you

Chronos: Revolution

that for us, such things are child's play." He spread his arms. "*We* are among you now. We will show you miracles like you've never seen."

He dropped to his knees and angled himself slightly away from the camera. "I will show you how a *real* son of God rises from the dead."

The red priest reached out to a nearby soldier, who handed him a semi-automatic pistol. The priest brandished it for the camera, turning it back and forth to give the viewers a clear look. Then he stepped behind the kneeling giant, stretched his arm out, and aimed for the back of the giant's head at pointblank range.

The civilians near the camera began to mutter. The soldiers stared.

The giant stretched his arms straight out to each side.

The red priest fired.

Chapter 12

The gunshot cracked and echoed. The bullet's impact jarred the giant's head forward, and an unmistakable, bloody exit wound blew out of his forehead. Everyone jumped in shock. Several people screamed.

The giant's arms fell limp, and his corpse toppled face-down onto the stone floor.

Joel held his hands against the wall behind himself and stared. He felt a deep, sickly chill. Someone—*something*—was there.

The giant's soul stood up, stared at his own body, and smiled. "Now we'll show them." He watched the red priest.

The red-robed priest, the *false prophet*, walked alongside the corpse, knelt beside him, extended his right hand out of his flowing sleeve, placed the ends of his fingers on the giant's wounded head, and closed his eyes.

A dark shadow fell over the courtyard's entrance. Joel looked up. A huge spirit, strangely familiar and at least fifty feet tall, stepped over the outer wall.

Joel couldn't keep his body from shuddering. He hadn't seen such unmitigated evil since Nimrod's tower. The thought jarred his memory. *That's the spirit that inhabited Nimrod. He must be the first son of Semyaza, the chief of the Titans.* The huge spirit became steadily smaller until it reached a height of about nine feet. It stood near the corpse.

The giant's soul knelt beside his own corpse, seemingly oblivious to the titan's spirit behind him. Then he jerked around. "Who are you?"

The spirit cackled. "We won't be needing you anymore. There's only room for one of us." He lay face-down inside the corpse.

The soul stood. "What are you doing? That's *my* body." He tried to scream into the priest's ear. "You can't do this to me. You promised."

The priest ignored him, if he heard him at all.

The chill Joel felt grew colder. An ominous, dark pit opened in the stone floor. The soul drew back and screamed. "No! You promised!" He looked at the priest. "I *let* you kill me, because you promised."

The dark gullet of Hades moved beneath the terrified soul. He raised his arms to shield his face and plunged in with a blood-curdling scream that descended in pitch and volume as the pit swallowed him, closed, and disappeared without a trace.

Joel's heart was trying to beat out of his chest.

The red priest removed his hand from the giant's head, stretched his arms out to each side in a grand gesture, and stood.

On the stone floor, the giant drew air in an abrupt, deep gasp.

Several soldiers jumped back. The woman with the news crew covered her mouth.

The giant pulled his hands up to each side, slapped his palms on the floor, pushed himself up, and slowly rose to his feet. The exit wound on his forehead had closed, leaving a bloody mark. He

Chapter 12

pressed his right fist against his jaw and popped his neck to the left. Then he repeated the act with his left fist, popping his neck to the right. He stared into the camera, spread his arms, and formed a cross with his body. "Who is like me? No one! I am your king! I am!...I am!...I am!"

Joel was incredulous. *This isn't a resurrection. It's a demonic reanimation.*

A dozen imp spirits bounded into the courtyard, jumped onto the giant, and latched on. They began to slither around his spine and neck. The image made Joel sick.

The red priest extended an arm toward the giant. His voice was shrill and piercing. "Who is like your king? Who is like your emperor?" He moved back two steps and gestured into the Court of Priests toward the white-marble Sanctuary that towered above.

The soldiers parted and provided a clear view of the entrance to the Court of Priests and the Sanctuary behind them.

The priest continued. "Now, watch your emperor...your *god*... stand where he belongs, in the Most Holy Place."

His arms still stretched out, the giant turned and made his way toward the steps that led up to the Court of Priests, the altar, and the Sanctuary. A shout from just inside the Court of Priests appeared to surprise him. "You will *not* enter the Sanctuary!" A man with a long, white beard, laced sandals, and a crude, sackcloth tunic tied with a rope at the waist stepped out and stood on one side of the entrance. A second man in sackcloth with a white-and-gray beard emerged and stood on the other side.

The giant dropped his arms to his side. He turned toward the camera and laughed. "No one stands in my way." He raised his arms

107

Chronos: Revolution

again. "After all—*I am!*" He turned back, looked at his soldiers, and pointed. "Kill them."

Joel knew what was coming. *No, no, no. Don't do it.*

A dozen soldiers quickly formed a line across the front of the entrance and stood with their left sides directed toward the Sanctuary, their rifles pointed up. An officer stood in the middle, just behind the line, and raised his hand. "Ready!"

The soldiers grabbed their rifles' bolts and chambered a round with a quick series of clicks.

Joel forgot to keep his thoughts silent, "Don't do it!"

"Aim!" The soldiers pressed the butts of their rifles against their shoulders and aimed for the men in sackcloth.

Joel couldn't watch. He slid down against the wall, ducked his head to face away from the soldiers, and placed his arms over his head.

"Fire!"

Joel heard a roaring inferno and felt a blast of heat. The soldiers' shrieked in pain and terror. Their screams were interrupted only as each soldier gasped breath to shriek again.

The pitiful sound ripped Joel's heart in two.

They fell abruptly silent. The roar of the inferno ceased, and a dozen rifles clacked onto the stone floor.

Then Joel heard something he imagined no one else could. The men's souls muttered in confusion, yelled in fear at the unmistakable roar of Hades' gullet, and screamed again as they fell in. Then came absolute silence. The only sound came from Joel's heart thumping in his chest.

He lifted his head and turned around slowly. The giant had drawn back and crouched, his arms over his head. In front of him,

Chapter 12

twelve rifles lay on the ground. There was nothing, not even ash, to indicate anyone was ever there to hold them.

The rest of the soldiers in the courtyard shook violently, staring with terrified eyes. A steady stream of urine dripped from one man's pants.

The giant stood up straight and stared at the two men in sackcloth.

The second man at the entrance gestured out into the first half of the Inner Court and shouted, "This courtyard has been given over to the Gentiles for forty-two months, but you will not enter the Sanctuary."

The giant stared. Everyone watched in silence.

The giant clenched his fists, snarled, and bellowed at the top of his lungs. His arms shook as he yelled. He pointed at the bearded men. "You want to protect your...Jewish relic? You think you can show *me* wrath?" He practically spit the words. "If you want to see wrath,"—He spun around to face the camera—"I'll show you wrath!"

He turned to an officer nearby. "Order the rest of the army in from Tel Aviv and demolish this city. Kill every Jew and Christian you find. Make no exceptions. If you find a pregnant woman, get a knife, and deliver the baby for her. If you find a woman nursing her baby—use your imagination."

He spun toward the entrance, flipping the tails of his overcoat behind, and rushed out of the courtyard. His soldiers followed.

The anchorwoman turned to the camera and raised her microphone to her mouth. Her jaw quivered. After a moment, she pushed out her first words. "Ladies and gentlemen. What you've seen here says it all. If you're in Jerusalem...be warned. We leave you with the view from the Temple." She dropped the mike to her side, hung her head, and stepped away.

Screams and shouts began to echo from below the temple. The news crew and the Temple guards hurried toward the outer wall. Joel stepped out and looked down with them. More and more people ran into the valley below. A man shouted, "That's right! We have seen the abomination that causes desolation. We must flee for the mountains."

Joel spotted Jacob and his family in the middle of the mob. They looked worried, but otherwise safe. Next to Joel, the anchorwoman shook her head. "They're fools. They'll be trapped down there like fish in a barrel. It'll be a massacre."

More and more people gathered below. Others sprinted around from the Temple's south side, pointing behind themselves and screaming. "The soldiers are coming! The soldiers are coming!"

The crowd began to stir. People cried out.

Joel ran to the corner of the Temple complex so he could look around the south side. A vast army of soldiers approached on foot, and the stream of tanks and troop carriers followed behind.

A thunderous sound began to rumble across the sky. The rising sun became dark gray and plunged the earth into deep shadow. The entire army stopped in its tracks. The soldiers drew back.

Joel hurried back along the eastern wall and stood in front of the entrance to the Inner Court. The fear he had felt earlier was eclipsed by anticipation. "Father, oh my goodness, Father. I get to see you!" He placed his hands on the outer wall to brace himself and looked up. His eyes went wide with wonder.

Chapter 12

The rumbling grew louder, and the earth began to shake. Soon, Joel realized only the Mount of Olives was shaking. People on the giant slope ran out of buildings and sprinted down its face. The sound of cracking rock echoed from its summit. A crevasse formed, pulled soil and pavement apart, and stretched from the peak all the way to the valley below. Buildings crumbled and collapsed into the earth. Then, as if two, giant hands ripped something as frail as a tissue, the two sides of the mountain pulled apart and formed a chasm. Rocks rolled down into the center, and a massive cloud of dust rose into the sky.

With a mighty roar, the chasm formed a broad, straight valley with high walls through the mountains. The dust settled. On the far end of the long valley, a glorious light shone back into the darkness surrounding the Temple.

Joel looked up again, dropped his jaw, and fell to his knees.

Dressed in a glorious, glowing white robe with a hem dipped in deep, red blood, the Lord Himself placed one sandaled foot on the north side of the Mount of Olives with an earth-shaking impact and the other foot on the south side. He looked down on His chosen people as He provided their means of escape.

Joel gazed up into His eyes—*His eyes!* Like lightning, they shone the deepest, most intense love Joel had ever seen or felt. The heart-piercing compassion in His glorious eyes melted Joel's heart and left him completely undone.

Shouts drew his attention below. Joel pried his eyes away from his Lord and stood to look over the wall. The throng in the valley stared up with awe. Some pointed and shouted. "It is the Messiah! Jesus is the Messiah! *Yeshua HaMashiach! Yeshua Hu Adonai!*'"

Chronos: Revolution

Like the ancient Hebrews trapped by the Red Sea who saw their safe passage through the water, the first people ran into the broad chasm. Soon, an endless throng pushed their way toward the opening. Once in, even the eldest among them ran toward their salvation with reckless abandon.

Joel searched for Jacob's family and quickly found them, the only people looking in his direction. They waved over their shoulders and ran into the valley. Joel returned the wave. He looked back and forth and watched the people flee. He was struck with the memory of Lamech and his followers fleeing west from the City of Enoch all those years before. The parallels were remarkable, save for one mighty difference.

Joel looked up again. He stepped back against the wall around the Courtyard, slid down, rested his forearms on his knees, and stared at his Lord and Savior, his Captain and King, his Father, his *Abba*, his Friend, his *Love*.

Jesus turned His head in what looked like slow motion from one shoulder to the other, smiling on His flock as they ran through His gate.

Joel's head and heart rushed. He bathed in Jesus's glorious and overpowering love. He remembered Jesus's words. "Jerusalem, Jerusalem! . . . How often I wanted to gather your children together, as a hen gathers her chicks under her wings, yet you were not willing!" Joel realized God, after a painfully long wait, was getting exactly what His heart longed for.

From high above, Jesus's eyes met Joel's. Joel's heart leapt. His Maker was looking at him. His tears made his voice quaver, "I love you, Jesus. I love you so much." Jesus slowly nodded and drew His

Chapter 12

lips up into a more intense grin. Then His head slowly swung down to watch the fleeing Jews.

Joel had no idea how long he had been watching. Dehydration began to make his head throb. His neck was in agony from craning toward the sky, but he didn't care. He would have willingly starved; he would have happily died of dehydration, rather than take his eyes off his Divine Rescuer, his Eternal Father.

A clear, plastic cup of water blocked his field of vision.

Chapter 13

Joel's neck hurt too much to move quickly. He slowly turned so he could follow the arm bearing the cup of water. It was the white-bearded man in sackcloth.

The man nodded, pointed at the water, and then to his own mouth. The message was clear: *drink*.

Joel nodded, "Thank you, sir," and took a drink. It was cool and sweet. His body took over, and he chugged the entire cup in a few gulps. He suddenly remembered how exhausted he was. He struggled to move his head and grimaced from the pain.

The old man reached down and placed his hand on the back of Joel's neck. It felt like hot coal. The heat seared through Joel's neck, and the pain disappeared. He moved his head back and forth, looked into the man's eyes, and smiled. "Thank you again."

The man extended an open hand, his thumb pointed up. Joel reached up and allowed the man to pull him to his feet. He followed him through the entrance to the Inner Court.

The guards were gone.

Joel spoke under his breath. "I wonder where the guards went?"

The man turned back, smiled, and pointed into the valley where the Jews were fleeing.

"Oh. Makes sense. *I* would go if *I* could."

Chapter 13

The gray-and-white-bearded man joined them. "Escape for the rest of the world—the rest of the *faithful*—is coming." He frowned. "But not before a painful period of trial."

Joel thought about that. "Paul did warn us. He said in Second Thessalonians that our being gathered to Jesus would not come until after the man of sin is revealed, and Jesus said in Matthew 24 that He would gather His elect *after* a terrible tribulation of the same elect—a severe persecution that corresponds to the breaking of the Fifth Seal in Heaven." He shook his head. "I'm afraid many people have failed to recognize those warnings."

"The Fifth Seal has been broken. The persecution has begun."

Joel's heart was heavy again. "Then we must wait and hope for the breaking of the Sixth Seal, when Jesus said He would gather His elect."

"The Day of the Lord. Rescue of the redeemed—followed by wrath on the rest."

Joel couldn't suppress half a grin. "Nice alliteration. You would have made a fine twenty-first century preacher." Joel stared at the rifles that littered the stone floor.

The white-bearded man stared with him. Then to Joel's surprise, he covered his eyes with one hand and wept aloud.

Joel remembered the soldiers and thought he should feel more compassion for them. By now, though, he was getting overwhelmed by the wild, emotional swings. He had gone from fear and near despair to overwhelming joy. Now he was swinging back to grief. His heart was more exhausted than his body.

The gray-and-white-bearded man wiped his own eyes as they stared at the rifles. "We take no pleasure in that," he gestured toward the camera. "But the world must understand who their Savior is..." He narrowed his eyes. "...and who their enemy is."

The white-bearded man wiped his eyes, sniffed, grabbed Joel's empty cup, and disappeared into a structure along the outer wall. A moment later, he emerged with more water.

Joel accepted it gratefully. He drank it and looked up again at Jesus. "Why, Lord? Why did you bring me here, especially if I'm not to give it to you?"

The white-bearded man spoke for the first time. "Give Him what?"

Joel looked down. He couldn't imagine needing to keep the orb from these men. They were clearly prophets of God. That thought struck him. *Prophets*. He looked up. "May I ask you something?"

They looked at each other and nodded.

"Who are you?"

The white-bearded man grinned slightly. "Who do you think we are?"

Joel stuck his lower lip out for a second and scratched his head. "Well...I know you're the two faithful witnesses who will guard the Sanctuary for forty-two months." A sober thought hit him. "After that, they'll kill you, won't they?"

They nodded slowly.

"I'm sorry."

"Thank you, but don't be. It will need to happen as a testimony."

The gray-and-white-bearded man interjected. "You should have enough information now to guess who we are."

"Really?"

Chapter 13

"Really. What does the Scripture tell you about the relationship between mankind and death?"

That was *not* the question Joel expected. "Well...the author of Hebrews told us that everyone dies once, though Paul also told us that we will not *all* die."

"Mm-hmm. Those who will *not* die will be those who live through the persecution to be gathered."

"Okay, which means everyone in the past has died *once*." Joel put it together. "Ahhhh...I see. There are only two men in all history who never died...Elijah, who was taken in the whirlwind..." The gray-and-white-bearded man nodded.

Joel's gut surged with the realization. He turned to the white-bearded man. "And *Enoch*."

Enoch smiled, nodded, and spoke in the pre-Flood language. "I was wondering when you would put it together."

Joel reached out and shook Enoch's hand. "It's an honor to meet you, sir. I've been sort of...tangled up in your legacy, you could say."

"I should say so. What is your name, young man?"

"Joel."

"It's a pleasure to meet you, young Joel." He stepped closer, looked into Joel's eyes, and tilted his head. "You have the gift of seeing, don't you?"

"Gift and curse."

"Yes, indeed."

"I think it may be because your grandson, Lamech, blessed me. He didn't get to finish saying what the blessing was, though."

Enoch nodded. "That was a difficult time...much like now." He extended a hand. "May I see it?"

Chronos: Revolution

"Of course." Joel whipped the orb out of his pocket and handed it over.

Enoch accepted it, stared, frowned, and shook his head. "Yomiel, Yomiel. I'll bet you wish you could be celebrating with your friends, right now."

"Who's Yomiel?"

Enoch raised the orb an inch to draw attention to it. "*This* is Yomiel." He lowered the orb to his side. "It's just as well. They know their days are numbered," he looked at Joel, "which will make their fury against believers all the worse."

"I wish I could have warned more people."

Enoch raised the orb in front of him again. "You're a custodian of this orb, young Joel. You may yet have just such a chance."

Joel liked hearing the man call him young. It felt paternal. "I guess I would seem awfully young to you, wouldn't I?"

Enoch grinned. "You're even younger than this young pup with me,"—he pointed to his comrade with his thumb—"Elijah, here. Why, he's less than...what?...three thousand. Just a kid."

Elijah shook his head. "That's hardly fair. You got a two-thousand-year head start on me."

Joel felt a little awkward about his next question. "So...if you've both been, you know...in Heaven all this time, then why don't you look more—"

Enoch finished the sentence for him. "Heavenly?"

Joel nodded.

Enoch gestured with both hands as if to indicate the clothes he was wearing. "Trust me, these aren't our resurrection bodies. We have to drive around in these old models for a while."

118

Chapter 13

"Drive around. You know about cars?"

He pointed out the gateway. "And cameras, too."

Joel smirked. "That's good." He rolled some of the sackcloth from Enoch's robe between his fingers. "Because I'd hate for you to come across as...you know...provincial, or anything."

Enoch and Elijah bellowed with laughter.

Elijah shook his head and sighed. "Oh...thank you, young Joel. It's nice to have something to laugh about here." He exchanged a sober glance with Enoch, whose laughter was just waning. "Our mission here is a heavy one."

They stood silent for a moment.

Joel felt the weight of his childhood return. His memories taunted him. *Joshua, Christina, and Joy.* It made the heaviness around him seem appropriate. He was paying for his failure. He turned and looked up at Jesus. "I'm sorry I failed, you, Jesus. I'm so sorry."

Enoch and Elijah stood on each side of him and looked up.

Joel glanced at them. "Would you do anything different?"

Elijah spoke first. "Of course, I would." He gestured up. "Once you've seen Him face-to-face...once you've..." His eyes watered.

Enoch continued, "Then you realize just how naïve you were... how much you failed to realize just how *wonderful* He is."

"How do you cope with the regret?"

Enoch turned to Joel. "Grace, young Joel. Grace."

Elijah faced him from the other side. "You can never deserve His grace. You can never earn it, but he *showers* you with it."

Joel whispered, "His grace is sufficient for me."

Chronos: Revolution

Enoch nodded. "I think that's a grievous understatement. His grace is not just *sufficient*—it's *overwhelming*." He placed a hand on Joel's shoulder. "Accept His grace, Joel—all of it. Recognize that *all* of your sins are forgiven."

Elijah stepped closer. "Only then will you be able to live a life worthy of Him." He looked up.

Joel tried to apprehend that. "I guess that means I have to forgive myself."

Enoch poked Joel in the chest. "Who are *you*, young Seer, to refuse to forgive anyone *He* has already forgiven? Refusing to forgive yourself is *pride*, Joel, not humility."

Joel hadn't thought of that. "Wow...I guess you're right."

Enoch blinked. "You guess?" He looked at Elijah. "He's a tough audience. What will it take to convince him?"

Shouts in Russian echoed over the courtyard wall. They walked to the Outer Court and looked down into the valley. Only a few dozen people remained, running into the long mountain valley.

High above, Jesus watched them run through, then raised His head and looked toward the enemy's army.

Joel expected to see an angry scowl. Instead, Jesus looked sad. He stared and waited. The sun grew bright again, and for the first time in hours, daylight returned.

A little while later, Joel heard deep, bellowing shouts in Russian. He hurried to the southeast corner of the Outer Court and looked over the side. The giant had climbed to the top of the high-topped van he had arrived in. He waved his arms, pointed around the Temple, and shouted over and over.

Chapter 13

His shouts threw his army into complete turmoil. Joel was struck that they weren't staring into the sky. "Why wouldn't they be looking at Him?" He looked above the split mountain.

Jesus was no longer there.

"Uh, oh." Joel turned back to the army below. A green, all-terrain vehicle zoomed past the giant's van and swerved through the crowd of tanks and soldiers. An officer with a wheel cap stood out of his open door, waved, yelled, and called his troops forward.

Vehicles revved their engines. Men began to shout. Within moments, the entire formation—troops, tanks, and personnel carriers—pressed forward and made its way past the giant's van, around the Temple, and toward the mountain valley.

Chapter 14

Joel ran back along the Temple's east side and stared into the long chasm. The last stragglers were a long distance ahead, but the vehicles, even the tanks, would overtake them in no time.

The vehicle with the officer leaning out the door was the first to drive in. Some of the quickest trucks followed first. Then a long series of tanks bounded over bumps and zoomed into the valley, surrounded by countless hundreds of troops carrying rifles.

In the distance, faint screams from some of the last of the fleeing civilians echoed out. They knew the army was pursuing them.

More and more tanks and troops filed in and flooded the high-walled chasm. Hundreds grew to thousands. Joel wondered if he might even be seeing tens of thousands. He didn't trust his judgment of such vast numbers. One thing was certain, though: what was once a throng of fleeing civilians quickly became a vast sea of green.

Once again, Joel knew what was coming. His gut churned, and his palms became sweaty. "All these men, Father. All these foolish men following their false messiah." His heart ached for them.

The entrance to the chasm became a bottleneck, and soon, the congested traffic got the better of them. The valley below became clogged with a traffic jam as troops and vehicles fought to be the

122

Chapter 14

next to file in for their easy victory over a mob of unarmed civilians, an act they probably expected to earn them great favor from their false messiah.

A faint, deep rumble began to grow. At first it was hard to hear over the engine noise and pandemonium, but it crescendoed quickly. The mob of troops and tanks fighting to enter the chasm froze. A final pair of vehicles pulled away from the mob and zoomed in.

The split mountain began to vibrate with the rumbling. The vibration grew until the chasm shook. Truck brake lights illuminated. Tanks rolled to a stop, and troops turned around and tried to run for safety.

The mountain's shaking became violent. The chasm lurched back and forth. Vehicles struggled to turn around. Their tires screeched over and over as the ground beneath them heaved from one side to the other. They struck the rock walls and collided with each other with a long series of honks and crunches. Men yelled, struggled to run, and tumbled helplessly on the ground.

Then far in the distance, tanks, trucks, and men plunged out of view into a huge, growing explosion of dust that flooded through the chasm like an iconoclastic cloud. As the ground fell away, the walls on each side tumbled in. The plunging ground raced from the distance toward the chasm's entrance. More and more tanks, honking trucks, and screaming men plunged into the earth as the walls fell in like a wave rushing to shore. The rumbling became an overpowering roar.

Outside the chasm, complete panic set in. Soldiers jumped over vehicles and trampled each other to get away. The last of the troops in the chasm screamed at the top of their lungs and plunged into the

Chronos: Revolution

earth. The cliffsides fell in with a final roar, and the churning cloud of gray soot burst out, flooding the Kidron Valley.

The roar grew silent. Rocks rolled down the face of the scarred mountain, and the dust cloud grew. It rose toward the Outer Court. A strong wind blew from the west and drove it back over the heap of rubble that was once the Mount of Olives. Slowly emerging from the gray cloud below, grown men screamed and cried in terror, their voices shaking.

The giant's deep voice bellowed from the south. Too numb to run, Joel walked to the southeast corner and looked down.

The giant yelled at his surviving troops. He pointed west, thrust his hands out in quick gestures, whipped them to his side, and shouted in fury. Joel was immediately struck by how much he resembled recordings he had seen of Adolf Hitler. *Could that be the same spirit that occupied him?*

Tired of the spectacle, Joel turned away.

Elijah disappeared into the Inner Court. Enoch walked over to Joel, reached out, and pulled the bewildered young man with him.

Joel walked with him into the Inner Court and up the stairs into the Court of Priests. They followed Elijah around the altar. He didn't have words for what he had just seen. He stumbled a few more steps toward the Sanctuary, stopped, and stared at the ground. He thought of what was still to come, the Great Tribulation of the Church—a second Holocaust, greater than the first. Their rescue would come, yes, but not before many, many martyrs died.

He knew what would follow that, too. After Jesus rescued His believers, the unrepentant earth—everyone who refused to call on Him—would suffer the Day of the Lord, the trumpet and bowl

Chapter 14

judgments leading to the climactic Battle of Armageddon and the final earthquake to end all earthquakes—the one that would destroy every building, level every mountain, sweep every island away, and, in essence, reverse much of the damage of the Great Flood.

Joel tried to look past that to what he knew would be a glorious, wonderful reign of Jesus Christ right here on earth, but he couldn't see that far. The violence and suffering, the unmitigated evil all around him clouded his vision like the dust in the valley, and he couldn't see past it. Despite the sunlight around him, all was darkness.

He looked up. Elijah was sitting on one of the steps leading into the Sanctuary entrance, his face buried in his hands. Enoch walked up to his comrade and patted his shoulder.

Joel looked beyond them into the Sanctuary. He longed to run in, pull the shroud aside, climb onto the Ark of the Covenant, and jump into Jesus's arms, but he knew that wasn't the answer. As he had told Hannah, God lived inside him.

He turned around and stepped away from the Sanctuary. "Holy Spirit, please...please comfort me."

Joel thought about the orb. He looked into the sky. "This is it, Father, isn't it? I've finished my mission. Enoch has the orb, now." He gazed out of the Courtyard at the demolished mountain and the dust cloud blowing over it. "The orb is useless, too, so I'm trapped here, right?" The thought made his despair even heavier. "And if there's no point in me staying here, then I need to make my way... somewhere out there."

Joel felt completely lost. The odds of him finding his way back home were slim to none, if there was still a home to find.

Chronos: Revolution

Enoch surprised him from behind. "Why so downcast, young Seer?"

Joel's shoulders hung like lead weights. He turned to the kind, old man. "You have to ask?"

Enoch put his arm around Joel's shoulder. "Come with me." He led Joel back to the steps that led into the Sanctuary.

Joel's feet dragged with each step. He hadn't slept the night before. The angelic war and their long, tedious trip through the congested city had prevented it. His eyes were heavy and dry.

Enoch stopped. "You're exhausted, aren't you?"

Joel nodded.

Enoch placed a hand on Joel's chest. Joel felt the familiar heat and a rush of energy. Enoch drew his hand back. "We need to get you some rest, then...but not here." He held the orb out in his hand.

Joel was surprised to hear that. He stared at the orb. "I thought that...well, since you have the orb..."

The reality of his circumstances fell on him like a brick wall. He hung his head to the side. "You have *one* orb."

Enoch watched him.

Joel felt apologetic. "We recovered the first orb and returned it to your Guardians, but this..." Joel pointed to the orb in Enoch's hand. "This orb was discovered some years ago and more or less fell into my family's hands." He looked into Enoch's face. "The Seer was my mentor, Karl Aufseher. He hid it for me to find, and that's what brought me here." He wondered how much Enoch already knew. "The Guardians told me Aufseher had a mark from you...a mark you told them to look for, but he's gone now. He said he had"—Joel made quotation marks in the air—"'passed the mantle' on to me."

126

Chapter 14

Elijah lowered his hands from his face and pulled his head up. "Sounds like your mentor was borrowing some of my terminology."

Joel thought about it and nodded. "Just as you passed your mantle on to Elisha."

"A fine man...not unlike you."

Joel was grateful for the approval. He suddenly remembered the question he had always wanted to ask. He looked at Enoch. "Why on earth did you make a second orb?"

Enoch took a deep breath. "I've done what I had to do, Joel, just as you have done what you had to." He set the orb on the ground. "If Karl Aufseher passed his mantle on to you, then we need to finish the job." He reached out. "Your hand, please."

Joel extended his hand. Enoch pulled Joel's arm out, turned his hand up, and pushed his overcoat and shirt sleeves back. He placed his own hand on the inside of Joel's forearm and closed his eyes.

Joel felt a third instance of searing heat, though it didn't hurt. Enoch pulled his hand away, leaving a pronounced mark behind.

Joel stared at it. "Is this a tattoo?"

Enoch shook his head. "No, it's a mark, and not the kind our enemy is using, I assure you. The Guardians can now be certain you have inherited the Seer's responsibilities. When you return, you will be responsible for their orb, too."

Joel felt a rush of hope. "When I return?"

Enoch nodded.

Joel's sense of relief surprised him. He let out a breath that trembled hard. "I thought the orb would no longer work."

"It will work for me." Enoch placed a hand on his shoulder. "Persevere, young Joel. This is a heavy burden, I know, but with the Holy Spirit's help, you will overcome. I am certain of it."

Joel furrowed his brow. "I thought His yoke was supposed to be easy…His burden light."

Enoch's expression brightened. "It is, Joel. It is. Salvation is absolutely free. No strings attached other than your faith—your trust in Him," he pointed a finger in the air. "But His anointing, His power, will cost you everything."

Elijah stood next to Enoch. "But you get much more in return, and you get to enjoy His blessings in the meantime," he smiled. "*Wonderful* blessings, and when you cast your cares on Him, you can trust Him to bear the burden for you. Just remember—His blessings have a purpose."

Joel looked at him. "And what purpose is that?"

"To equip you, Joel. To empower you to bring about His good, pleasing, and perfect will."

Joel still felt weary, and his heart was still numb, but he was grateful for the renewed sense of purpose and direction.

Enoch bent over, picked up the orb, and handed it to Joel. "Don't worry, my friend." He gestured around them. "Soon, the revolutions will be complete."

Joel accepted the orb and glanced out of the Courtyard. "And what a revolution we've seen here."

Enoch followed his glance. "Yes."

Joel looked around. "Before I go…"

Enoch looked at him.

"May I see the Sanctuary?"

Chapter 14

Enoch huffed a laugh. "What do you think?"

Joel shrugged. "I'm torn, to be honest. On the one hand, Ezekiel wrote of the Millennial Temple that no foreigner, uncircumcised in heart and flesh, may enter the Sanctuary."

Elijah leaned in. "Of course, your heart *is* circumcised because of your faith in Jesus."

Joel nodded. "But I haven't been *ritually* circumcised in the flesh." He swung his head from one side to the other. "On the other hand, the New Testament says, 'Let us approach the throne of grace with boldness...'" Joel shrugged, "and 'we have boldness to enter the Sanctuary through the blood of Jesus.' Both passages are from the author of Hebrews."

"Another fine man...one of Paul's greatest disciples. You should meet him some day."

Elijah gestured out into the Court of Priests. "Tell us, Joel...what do you see as you approach the Sanctuary?"

Joel looked back. "Well, first you pass the altar of Sacrifice." He looked at Elijah. "Jesus's sacrifice paid for my sins, makes me righteous, and makes me holy, enabling me to approach the throne." He gestured to the basin of water. "Then you pass the Laver of Cleansing. He washes my sins away, making me clean, also to permit me to approach His throne."

Elijah gestured up the steps into the Sanctuary.

Joel walked up slowly, his eyes wide. He stood on the top step and stared into the Holy Place. He gestured to His right. "The table of showbread...Jesus, the Bread of Life...with one important difference." He held his arms out and crossed them. "Ever since He ascended, He has been sitting at the right hand of the Father, not the left."

Joel gestured to his left. "The golden lampstand...God's seven-fold Holy Spirit." He gestured straight ahead. "The altar of incense...the prayers of the saints, going up before the throne as a pleasing aroma."

Joel stared at the thick, red, blue, and purple veil that spanned the room behind the altar of incense. "The veil, torn from top to bottom when Jesus died, to remind us that we now have direct access to the Father because of the Son...and beyond the veil...the Ark of the Covenant...the Mercy Seat...an image of God's throne in Heaven...with two seraphim stretching their wings over Him."

He glanced over his shoulder. "Now that I'm here, I don't think I want to go in."

Enoch looked surprised. "Why not?"

Joel looked down. "Because I'll see the real thing one day...and I think I want to respect the Jewish tradition. Besides, I don't think I want to take my weak flesh in there with me."

Elijah nodded. "All good reasoning."

Joel took one last look and imagined the real thing. He turned and stepped down to the stone floor. "Would you really have let me go in?"

Enoch smiled. "We'll never know now, will we?"

Joel wanted to laugh. He just didn't have it in himself. He looked at Elijah. "It has been an honor, sir, to meet you."

Elijah nodded. "The pleasure has been ours, young Joel. We'll meet again, I'm certain."

Chapter 14

Joel looked at Enoch. "And you, too, sir." He looked at the orb in his hand. "I'm honored that you would trust me with this."

Enoch squared himself in front of Joel. "When you see the elders, tell them I am pleased. I know they have gone to great lengths to keep this safe."

"I think they'll be happy to hear that. I don't think things have gone exactly as they were supposed to."

"A great deal has happened that is against God's *will*, Joel, but you may trust that in His *providence*, He will work—even through the bad—to bring about His good."

"I beg to differ!" Aphiel's voice surprised them from the Outer Court. He drew his shoulders back, strode in, and looked around. The angelic thugs from the street followed him.

Joel looked at Enoch, who threw an urgent glance at the orb, then at Joel's pocket. He discreetly slipped the orb into his overcoat before turning to face the invaders.

Elijah pointed at them. "Get out. You have no authority over us."

"Maybe not..." Aphiel pointed at Joel. "But nothing's stopping me from doing whatever I want to *him*."

Enoch spoke under his voice, "Time for you to get in the Sanctuary."

Elijah stepped closer. "Yes, we defend the Sanctuary, not the Courtyard."

Aphiel appeared on the Sanctuary steps. "Not so fast."

Enoch faced Aphiel, extended his arm, and drew Joel behind him.

Elijah shouted, "You will not—"

"Don't worry, human. I won't go into your precious tabernacle." He glanced over his shoulder. "It's a tiny room, really. You can keep

Chronos: Revolution

it." He glared at Joel. "Now..." He formed fists and cracked his knuckles. "I think you have something that I want."

Enoch held Joel back and kept his eyes on Aphiel. "Farewell."

Aphiel shook his head. "I'm not going anywhere."

"I wasn't talking to you."

A portal opened under Joel's feet. He plunged in.

Chapter 15

THE DAY OF THE *CHRONOS* LAUNCH

Karl Aufseher crushed his hat against his chest and gazed down at the polished marble headstone.

The dedication on the stone was etched beneath a line of Hebrew characters and a round symbol carved within a laurel wreath:

Righteous Among the Nations
ANNA G. AUFSEHER
Beloved Wife–Devoted Mother–Courageous Rescuer

Karl bathed in bittersweet memories. "How I miss you, dear Anna." He turned his eyes to the sky. "I wish you could be here to see all this." He enjoyed visiting, as if they were sharing a cup of tea together. "Little Karl and Joanna are doing well...of course, he hasn't been little for years. Joanna had to turn down an offer to be university president. Between you and me, I think she's ready to retire." He brightened. "And you'd be so proud of Jamie. She has grown to become a priceless ally."

Chronos: Revolution

He tightened his lips. "Today's the day, Anna. I can't believe it's already here." He looked at the empty plot next to hers. "Only a few more years, Anna. Only a few short years."

An hour later, he sat in a busy café, sipped coffee, and watched the entrance. He checked his watch after every other sip. A wall-mounted large-screen television played a news broadcast behind him. "*We'll be back after this break for continued coverage of today's historic launch from Cape Canaveral.*" A brief fanfare played before the feed cut to an investment commercial.

The bell over the front door chimed, and a tall, sturdy man with a dark beard stepped in with a thick canvas bag over his shoulder. He scanned the room until his eyes fell on Karl.

Karl lifted his cane in one hand and nodded. He pushed his chair out, rose to his feet, watched the man approach, and extended his hand. "Kemuel, thank you for coming, especially so soon after your loss. Adinah...was a lovely woman. It's good to see you again."

Kemuel shook his hand and took his seat. His deeply concerned look was heart-warming. "It's good to see you again, as well. I heard about Anna, too, and I'm so sorry."

Karl tightened his lips, burdened with knowledge.

Kemuel leaned his head down and looked up into Karl's eyes. "How *are* you?"

Karl was grateful for the concern. "I suppose we can relate to each other's circumstance, then. I'm doing well, thank you," he grinned. "But not as well as you, clearly. It's been what...the better part of eighty years? And you look just the same. You and your friends really don't age much, do you?"

134

Chapter 15

"You look pretty good for your years, too, all things considered. Care to share *your* secret?"

Karl pulled his lips into a faint grin.

Kemuel tilted his head and spoke quietly. "The new location you recommended for us has turned out to be much better in that respect. We can much more easily maintain a cozy two atmospheres of pressure inside." He smiled. "I think the elders were kind of ashamed they didn't think of it, themselves." He shook his head and gazed into the distance. "I'm often impressed by American ingenuity."

"That ingenuity has been part of America's blessing. America is in many ways founded on the gospel."

"And a lot of darker things."

Karl nodded. "Tares among the wheat. You'll find them everywhere." He smiled. "I'm glad the new location worked out." He pointed to Kemuel's bag. "Did you bring them?"

"Yes, tunics and boots for two men and one woman, as well as an appropriate change for myself. Your message was cryptic. Just where are you sending me?"

The news fanfare played again.

Karl gestured with his head toward the TV behind himself. He kept his eyes fixed on Kemuel's.

Kemuel furrowed his brow and leaned his head slightly to look around Karl.

The broadcast resumed. "*Welcome back for our continued coverage of the countdown and launch of the historic Chronos spacecraft...*"

Kemuel's eyes widened. He looked back at Karl and practically whispered, "You've *got* to be kidding."

135

Chronos: Revolution

Karl slowly shook his head.

"Why?"

Karl thoughtfully measured what he should say. It was clear the other Guardians had been cautious about sharing what they knew—even with Kemuel. After all, by now they would have realized Kemuel was the man they had met in the pre-Flood past.

Karl chose his words carefully. "There's more to their mission than meets the eye. They have a second...*you know what*. They have what you all have." He waited for that to register.

Kemuel's eyes became saucers. "Do you mean they're..."

Karl waited for him to connect whatever dots he knew about.

Kemuel craned to watch the TV. "They're the ones the elders told us about...the ones who came to them way back..." Something else appeared to register. "That's why they named their ship after the Greek god of time."

Karl raised his hand in a gesture for him to stop. "I'll fill you in on the way...there is much to share...but the short of it is..." He scratched his neck and took another breath. "I'm preparing to hand off my ministry."

Kemuel forgot to be discreet. "Hand it off? But you're..." He looked back and forth, leaned closer, and spoke quietly. "But you're the Seer. Can you even hand that off?"

"Elijah did."

"You're not exactly Elijah."

"True enough, but it has to be done." He gave Kemuel a sober look. "I won't be around forever."

Kemuel stared for a long moment. "That must be heavy knowledge to carry around."

136

Chapter 15

Karl chose not to respond to that. It *was* heavy.

"So, all this is about what...raising up your own, personal Elisha?"

"Something like that."

Kemuel looked down, drew a long breath, and ran both hands over his scalp. "And what if I refuse?"

"You can't refuse, Kemuel."

"What, I don't have a choice in the matter?"

Karl diverted his eyes and nodded. "You're right. You're right. Okay..." He stared across the table. "You *mustn't* refuse, Kemuel. If you do...all will be lost." He recognized how melodramatic his own words were. "No pressure."

Kemuel snickered. A serious look swept back over his face. He folded his hands on the table, looked through the wall on his left, and sighed. "You're the Seer. Of course, I won't refuse." He looked at Karl. "I need to notify the councils and get their instructions."

"I understand."

"Just how do you plan to get me on board?"

"Once I'm close enough to the...*you know what*...it won't be a problem."

Kemuel raised his eyebrows. "And just how do you plan to get close enough to the *you know what?*"

The bell over the door chimed. Karl gestured toward it with his eyes.

Kemuel turned around in his seat.

Jamie Michaels stood at the door and pointed at her watch.

Karl stood. "We need to hurry. She has a plane to catch, and you have a spaceship."

Chronos: Revolution

Karl's heart was beating hard. *I'm too old for this.* More than any other time in his life, he felt like he was meeting his destiny. Everything, his entire life, had led to this moment, and everything else hinged on it. He tugged at the one-piece technician's uniform Jamie had provided for him, rested his other hand on the large, rolling cart at his side, and gazed through the window at the sleek, delta-winged *Chronos* spacecraft.

He shifted his throbbing ankle and leaned on the cart. Without his cane, the cart was providing valuable support. He soon found himself watching the lead astronaut, Will Stark, and the woman next to him, Kat Dalton. He felt comfortable enough doing it. With their helmet visors down, it was unlikely they'd realize anyone was staring. He glanced at the thick, metal attaché case in Stark's hand that housed the gold-encased orb, but an instant later, he was staring at Stark and Dalton again. He had expected it to be easy to see them, but it turned out to be much harder.

Karl wanted more than anything to talk to them. There was so much to share. They didn't know it, but he had followed them discreetly from the shadows their entire lives: every football game, every graduation, every military ceremony. *Father, I just wish I could get a message to them.*

A television aboard the ground shuttle played a news broadcast. Karl distracted himself by listening. *"For the historic launch at Cape Canaveral of the Chronos spacecraft, a technological leap forward in time..."*

Karl mused at the irony of the statement. *It's a leap all right, just not forward.* His own personal commentary ran through his head.

Chapter 15

"*The brave crew of Chronos One will conduct the first-ever horizontal space launch and then spend a record three months in deep space—*"

No, they won't.

"*After which they will reenter the earth's atmosphere and glide to a landing at Edwards Air Force Base.*"

Glide is such a kind word. He looked up and realized the lead astronaut had lifted the visor of his helmet.

Their eyes met.

Karl was nearly ripped in two by conflicting impulses. In a split second, he knew what he had to do. It was one of the three hardest things he had done in all his life, overshadowed only by his twin sacrifices all those decades before: leaving Anna in Marseilles, and leaving the orb in Tunisia. He mustered all his willpower.

He pried his eyes away...and kept them there.

Their ground shuttle inched its way to a side hatch on the spacecraft a short distance from the front of its fuselage. As it docked, a hiss indicated a successful, hermetic seal. Karl's adrenalin rushed. He watched the hatch and felt for the orb's power.

A technician opened the hatch. Karl looked for his chance. The technician was in the way. He stepped away. Karl began to raise his hand and concentrate. Another technician blocked the hatch. Karl lowered his hand and sighed. "Criminy."

The three-member crew stood, made their way to the hatch, and ducked through one-at-a-time. Karl kept his hand on the cart and watched.

Two technicians still stood in the way. If the crew closed the hatch from the inside, his opportunity would be gone, and he was sure to be caught when the ground shuttle returned. Karl murmured, "Move...move...move." At last, the technicians moved to each side.

Karl raised his hand and concentrated. Everything went silent. He pursed his lips and slowly exhaled. He opened the side of the cart. Frozen in time, Kemuel crouched inside, his arms wrapped around the canvas bag. Karl touched his arm. He jumped a bit, apparently startled, then climbed out of the cart. He twisted his neck back and forth. "That's not comfortable at all."

Karl closed the cart and led the way to the hatch. "Be careful not to touch anyone. You could injure them." He ducked through the hatch to find the crewmembers dangerously close. He had to crawl on all fours to get by. He stood and stared at them again while Kemuel followed.

Once Kemuel stood, Karl led him down the passageway to the aft compartments. "Jamie made sure to leave some space for you... as well as a relatively comfortable place to sit. You'll be there for a while, I'm afraid, before they discover you."

"I'm a bit concerned about what will happen when they do find me."

"Well, this isn't a pirate ship. You won't walk the plank."

"I should hope not."

Karl reached out and squeezed Kemuel's arm. "Don't worry, Kemuel. When they find what they're going to find, they'll be glad you're with them." He stepped into the adjacent compartment, opened the door to a tall storage bin, and moved out of the way.

Kemuel looked in and took a deep breath. He tightened his lips and nodded. "Alright, then." He climbed in, sat, lay the canvas bag

Chapter 15

on the floor between his legs, and leaned on a conveniently cushioned wall. "How will *you* leave?"

"Portal."

Kemuel nodded. He seemed nervous. He rolled his eyes to scan his temporary home. "Alright, then."

Karl reached out, squeezed Kemuel's shoulder, and stared into his eyes. "God is with you, Kemuel."

Kemuel suddenly looked more peaceful. He nodded back. "Thank you."

Karl felt a surprising wave of emotion. Kemuel was taking quite a risk based merely on the weight of his testimony. "Thank you, Kemuel. You have no idea what this means to me. Thank you."

Kemuel reached up and squeezed Karl's shoulder. "It's an honor, Seer. Grace and peace, Brother."

Karl grinned. "Grace and peace." He gently closed the door to the storage compartment, raised his hand, concentrated, and resumed time.

Voices echoed down the passageway. "Did you feel that?"

"I felt a gust of wind."

"Yep, me too."

Karl raised his hand and stopped time again. He opened the compartment. Kemuel was frozen in time. He had closed his eyes in an apparent effort to relax. Karl smiled, closed the compartment, and made his way forward.

He stopped and stared at the crew again. He stared into their eyes, and his heart ached. This would be the last time he would ever see them, and as the Seer, he knew what they were in for.

Chronos: Revolution

"Father, I haven't been able to talk to them all these years. I just wish I could tell them. I wish I could get a message to them. I wish I could make up for what they're..."

A new thought hit him. His eyes widened. "Oh, my goodness, Father, I could totally do that...and Jamie could help." He looked up. "May I? I know this is kind of...above and beyond, but Father, may I please?"

He listened carefully. He didn't want to be wrong about this one. *Yes.*

His heart leapt. He placed a hand on his forehead. "Okay, this is gonna be a challenge. I'll need to open a portal...there...while keeping time stopped...here." He formulated his plan and nodded. "I can do it."

He stepped back to make room. He raised his hand and concentrated. A blue field popped open in front of him.

Chapter 16

Modern Day

Kemuel stepped through the portal out of the station's control room, stood on the pre-Flood hilltop and savored the fragrant, gentle breeze. He closed his eyes as the air wafted against his face and tousled his hair. The cloudless, glare-free, deep azure sky cast a golden glow. In the distance down the hill, a massive sauropod trumpeted a call to his herd.

Kemuel opened his eyes, sauntered several steps to one side, looked back toward the portal to ensure some measure of privacy, and finally gazed down at the headstone. "I miss you, Adinah...so much." He looked at the ground. "I can't talk to my father about this. I haven't been able to talk with him about anything...not for a long time." He closed his eyes. "You have no idea what he has done."

He took a deep breath and tried to shake that off. He shook his fist. "We're so close, honey...so close. We're almost done, I can feel it." He looked around. "One way or another, I'll be joining you here soon...I hope." He gazed into the sky, then looked down again. "I wish you were here. I need you."

He plopped onto the grass with his legs flexed wide, wrapped his arms around his knees, and buried his head in his hands. "God's calling her away, Adinah. I've been trying to avoid it, but I've seen it coming for some time." He almost whispered the next words. "I don't think she'll be coming here with the rest of us." He drew a tense breath. "And I don't know how I can live without her, too."

He stared at the headstone. "I know what you'd say. You'd tell me that in every father's life, there comes a time when he has to let go." He cupped a hand over his forehead and sobbed quietly for a moment. "I don't know how I'll do it." He squeezed his eyes shut. "I'm losing everybody."

Moments later, he re-emerged from the portal and walked straight up to Gemaliel. "Thank you. I know we aren't supposed to open any portals right now."

Gemaliel nodded. "I'm certain no one will object to this one." He nodded to a fellow elder who stood opposite the orb. The other elder returned the nod, and Gemaliel closed the portal.

Kemuel made his way to the closest thing to outdoors they had. As he emerged into the station's crisp light, he found Grace waiting for him. She was staring at the ground, grinding her foot into the stone pavement. As he approached, she looked up and brightened.

She fell in next to him as he walked. They strode quietly along the path as it gently curved up between rows of red crape myrtles and raised patches of lush, green grass. Kemuel wrapped his arm around her shoulder.

She leaned her head against him. "Dad, do you think he doesn't trust me? Is that why he pushed me away from the portal?"

Kemuel stopped and looked into her eyes. He had a stock answer, but he didn't want to diminish her feelings with some trite

Chapter 16

response. He looked to the side for a moment. "No...that isn't it. You've earned his trust, I'm sure of it."

"Then why? Why wouldn't he trust me to go with him?"

Kemuel shook his head. "I don't think it has anything to do with trust. I think it has more to do with guilt."

"Guilt? What makes you say that?"

Kemuel sat on a bench under the shadow of a broad oak tree. "I see it in his eyes."

She sat next to him.

"He's afraid of getting you, or anyone else, hurt."

Grace shook her head. "Of course. It's his brother and sisters, isn't it? He told me they died because of him." She closed her eyes for a moment. "He also told me he was only eight. I can't even imagine." She looked at her father. "Do you know how it happened to them?"

He shook his head. "I was in the middle of a seventeen-year time jump, and they never talk about it...none of them." Kemuel could hear his daughter's heart in her words. He dreaded where this was going, but he knew she needed him. "You're really falling for him, aren't you?"

She pulled her lips into a sad smile. "Yes...Are you okay with that?"

Kemuel spread his arms along the back of the bench and stared at a flowerbed on the other side of the path. "When Professor Aufseher introduced the two of you, I approved wholeheartedly. Joel is a fine young man, and I respect his parents."

"But?"

Kemuel hadn't really taken the time to figure out how he felt about this or why. He took a deep breath. "He's getting more and more caught up in…"—he turned his eyes up—"all of this…and now, he's inheriting the Seer's abilities."

"Isn't that good? I mean…who wouldn't want the ability to see what he does?"

"You might be surprised." Kemuel looked intently into her eyes. "Being the wife of a Seer won't be an easy life."

"I don't want easy. I want God's will for me."

Kemuel smiled. "Your mother would be *really* proud."

Grace smiled sweetly. "I miss her."

"Me too."

They took a moment to enjoy the station's constant breeze, listening to distant conversations and children's laughter.

Kemuel stood, reached down, and took hold of Grace's hand. "Let's go home. It's late. Yesterday was exhausting, and we didn't really get any sleep last night."

She stood but didn't walk. "How can we go home, Daddy? They've been gone for more than a day with no news whatsoever. What if they need our help? How can we just sit around?"

Kemuel gently pulled her along the path. "Well, first, my little Grace from God, we won't help them by worrying, especially about things we don't know about. When you get a chance to rest, *take it.*" He swung their interlaced hands playfully.

She giggled.

"And second, we won't be just sitting around. We'll be doing the most important thing we can."

She nodded. "Praying."

Chapter 16

"That's my girl." He led her into their home's entrance. They ducked and descended the spiraling ramp. She stood at the bottom of the ramp and stared across the room.

"Daddy?"

Kemuel turned back.

"Is it wrong if I'm still worried about him?"

"Well, right or wrong, it's human." He settled to his knees. "Come on. Let's take our anxieties to Jesus."

"I just hope we don't have to wait long to hear from him."

There was a loud pop near the ceiling. They both looked in the direction of the sound. Kemuel stood.

The second pop pushed on their eardrums. They both winced and covered their ears. A blue spark appeared, grew, and crackled in a growing circle. A blue field opened.

Joel fell through, landed on his feet, and stumbled to his knees. The field closed with a crack.

Joel slowly pulled himself to his feet. He still wore the overcoat from the funeral, unbuttoned and dusty. His hair was disheveled.

Grace hurried to him. "Joel! Are you alright?"

His voice sounded weary. "I saw...Enoch." His eyes rolled up. Kemuel jumped in front of him, and Joel collapsed into his arms.

wwwwwwwwww

Joel woke up in a strange, very dark room. He had no idea where he was. The only thing he was certain of was that he was on a bed, under a thick, warm comforter.

He felt a rush of near panic. *The orb! Where is it?* He whipped the comforter to the side, swung his legs off the edge of the bed, and

147

Chronos: Revolution

swept his hands across the covers. He blinked the dry sleep from his eyes, squinted hard to convince them to moisten, and rubbed them clear.

The faint glow of a globe on a nightstand provided the only hint of light. He saw a round shadow next to the light source. He hurried to it and felt it.

It was the orb.

He sighed through pursed lips and looked around. The walls were hewn from rough stone. A soft rug covered the floor. Still, his feet were cold. He looked down and realized he was wearing shorts and a t-shirt, and they weren't his.

The warm fragrance of sweet bread wafted in from the other side of a sturdy door. He heard two cracks, followed by a sizzling sound. The warm, rich aroma of freshly brewed coffee followed soon after. His stomach rumbled. He realized he was so hungry he was dizzy.

He walked to the door and slowly pushed it open. Light flooded into the cozy bedchamber.

Kemuel looked up from setting a small table. "There he is."

Joel felt safer already. He looked around and realized he had seen that place once before, after retrieving the other orb. "Have you heard from my parents?"

Kemuel shook his head. "I'm afraid not."

Movement drew Joel's attention to the side.

Grace finished slicing a loaf of bread, stepped behind a hot stove, and looked up. "We thought you might like breakfast, American-style. I'm a master at eggs. How do you take them?"

Joel's mouth watered. "Wow...thank you both. I'm starving. Umm...I'm pretty easy with eggs...soft-boiled, over-easy, scrambled."

148

Chapter 16

She smiled. "Good taste. Over-easy it is."

Kemuel ushered Joel into the kitchen. "Coffee drinker?"

Joel nodded.

He gestured to a coffee station that would put a barista to shame. Within minutes, they sat around the table and Joel warmed himself with a hot mug. Grace set a plate in front of him with two eggs over-easy and took a seat.

Kemuel reached out, took their hands into his own, and closed his eyes. "Father, thank you for bringing Joel back to us safely. We are truly grateful. Please continue to bless and protect him as he serves You. We seek Your good and perfect will. Please guide our every word and deed. In Jesus's Name...Amen." He let go of their hands, then grabbed them again. "Oh, and thank you for the food. Amen." He looked at Joel. "Dig in."

Joel laughed quietly.

Grace passed him bread, bacon, and potatoes. "I know you probably eat healthier than this most of the time, but I figured you needed the sustenance...and some comfort."

He nodded. "Yes, thank you." He shoveled in his first bites and gulped them down. "Umm...*when* are we?"

Kemuel rested his fork on his plate. "It's 9 a.m. in DC, three days after Aufseher's funeral. You tumbled into our living room and fell unconscious about twenty-four hours ago."

"Who knows I'm here?"

"No one." Kemuel looked at Grace. "Well...we do."

Joel thought about that. "I'm surprised you wouldn't have standing orders to report...you know...me or the orb...right away."

"We do, straight from the councils."

Chronos: Revolution

Joel was surprised at that. "Don't get me wrong, I'm glad to have some peace and quiet, but why didn't you report it?"

Kemuel exchanged a glance with Grace. "Because there's one person who suddenly outranks the councils."

"Who?"

"You." Kemuel nodded toward Joel's arm.

He looked down and remembered. He turned his forearm over to reveal Enoch's mark.

"We figured we'd let you decide when and how to share whatever news you have."

Grace was watching Joel. "When did you last see your parents?"

Joel lowered his head. "Mom should be okay. We left her on the Metro. She was planning to contact Jamie."

Kemuel leaned on the table. "And your father?"

Joel shook his head. "I don't know. He fell onto the deck of the *Timekeeper*. The last I saw of him..." Joel turned his eyes to look into Kemuel's, "your father was pointing a gun at him."

Kemuel stared at the table. "I'm so sorry, Joel. I don't know what to say."

As worried as Joel was about his parents, he hated seeing Kemuel hurting. The man was beginning to feel like a second father. "You don't need to apologize. You're not him."

Grace sounded indignant. "I still don't believe it. Grandpa wouldn't do anything like that."

Joel felt sorry for Grace, too. He wondered when she would be able to cope with the harsh reality of the situation. "So, you haven't heard from the *Timekeeper,* either?"

Chapter 16

Kemuel shook his head slowly. After a moment, he pointed across the room. "You'll find some of Kenan's...a friend's clothes over there. His wife was kind enough to lend them to me."

"Does she know?"

"She probably suspects, but I trust her. She's one of the finest, most gracious persons I've ever met." He swallowed hard. "Her husband was, too."

Joel saw the grief in Kemuel's eyes. He let that subject pass.

They ate in silence for several minutes. Joel relished the moment. He hadn't enjoyed a good, quality family time with his parents for months.

A thought came to him. "Can the *Timekeeper* get here without using a portal?"

"Yes."

"How long does it take?"

"Not quite four-and-a-half days at one G.

"Can they go faster?"

Chapter 17

The round auditorium that served as a council chamber was packed. News of Joel's arrival spread like wildfire, and even the youngest children sat in their parents' laps. The frenzied conversations echoed at such a high pitch people had to shout to the person right next to them. The result was deafening.

Joel heard the uproar from quite a distance. He walked slowly toward the council chamber, Kemuel and Grace by his side, the orb slung over his shoulder in a leather pouch, the tunic of a noble, fallen warrior covering him like a shield of honor. He didn't feel worthy of it.

The last stragglers darted up the ramp and looked back at him curiously. Kemuel led Joel up. As they neared the top, he gestured for Joel to enter first. Joel stood just outside of the entrance. Inside, Kadmiel shouted at the top of his lungs, trying to get control over the noise. The poor man wasn't making a dent. The whole station was electrified by the hope their mission might—just might—be over.

Joel lowered his head. All the Guardians' responsibility—and the elders' authority—was about to fall on his shoulders, and he had no idea what to do with it. *Father, you've brought me this far. Please help me finish the job. Please show me what you want me to do with the orbs.*

Chapter 17

He looked over both shoulders at Kemuel and Grace. They each gave him a nod of encouragement. He looked forward, took a deep breath, and walked inside. Within seconds, the room fell silent. Joel stood at the top of the steps and scanned the large chamber.

Every eye was on him.

He walked down the stairs toward the council table. Each step reverberated off the stone walls. The council members stood to receive him. A loud rush sounded as the crowd followed suit and rose to their feet. Kemuel sat Grace in his usual seat on the front row and followed Joel.

Kadmiel stepped around the table to receive Joel. He extended his hand. "It's a pleasure to see you again, young Seer."

Joel lowered his head and returned the handshake. "It's good to see you, too, sir."

Kadmiel led Joel to an empty seat next to his own. Joel looked at the high-backed chair with wide eyes. In his youth, he had seen the combined councils many times as they sat high above the floor of the chamber that had been carved into the mountain near Lamech's house. He had always been a little awestruck by their authority. Now he was being invited to sit with them.

Kemuel pulled the seat out for him and gave him a reassuring smile. Joel stood in front of the chair. Kadmiel stood next to him, extended his arms, and waved his hands down in a gesture to sit. The room roared again as everyone settled into their seats.

Kadmiel gently grasped Joel's arm to encourage him to remain standing. He looked across the room. "I call this meeting to order. Let us open with prayer."

The crowd slipped from their seats and knelt in front of them.

"Father in Heaven, we call upon your holy Name, Jesus Christ. We ask that Your will be done among us this day. We remain ever hopeful that we may complete the weighty tasks set before us, and we ask for your blessings, protection, and guidance to that end. Amen."

The crowd climbed into their seats.

Kadmiel looked around the chamber seats above him. "We have been grieving the loss of our friend, the Seer, who has been a priceless ally. His loss has been particularly painful because of our hope that he was the one...the one Enoch commanded us to entrust with his orb...or rather, his *orbs*, as we have come to discover."

He gestured to Joel. "The eldest among us will remember young Joel Stark, who grew up with us in the City of Enoch...who recently returned the orb that had been stolen from us...and who, just three days ago, went in search of the damaged orb that the Seer had hidden somewhere in history."

The room broke out in polite applause. Joel got the impression they were grateful but sitting on pins and needles. The applause dissipated quickly.

"Not as many of you know that the Seer passed his abilities on to young Joel, here." The crowd began to murmur. Kadmiel raised his hands for silence. "I know what you're thinking and no...he does *not* have Enoch's mark."

The disappointment in the room was palpable. Joel wondered if now was the time to reveal his new mark from Enoch.

Kadmiel turned to Joel. "I may owe our friend an apology. I'm afraid we've caught him off guard today." He spoke in a lower voice. "I never intended to call a plenary session, but everyone...and I mean *everyone*...wants to hear your news."

Chapter 17

Joel nodded. "I understand, sir."

Kadmiel raised his voice for the room again. "As I said, three days ago, we sent Joel and his parents in search of the lost, damaged orb." He looked at Joel. "We await your news, young Seer." He sat down and watched.

Once again, every eye remained fixed on Joel, and he felt the full weight of their attention. He wasn't afraid of public speaking, so much, but he had no idea where to start. He remembered the Washington Monument, the battle at Hains Point, and the overwhelming events from the future. He turned around and looked at Kemuel.

Kemuel seemed to read his mind. He glanced around the room, took a deep breath, and walked forward. He raised his voice for all to hear. "Before you hear anything else, if I may..." He looked directly at Joel. "If I may...," he waited.

Joel nodded quickly.

He nodded back. "You need to know that Joel Stark—" He reached for Joel's right arm and raised it like a referee declaring the winner of a prize fight. "—has seen the patriarch, Enoch." He pulled down the sleeve of Joel's tunic and revealed Enoch's mark.

Everyone who could see the mark gasped. His eyes fixed on Joel's, Kemuel held his own forearm out and turned it from side to side, inviting Joel to do the same. Joel recognized the cue, raised his arm over his head, and slowly turned to reveal the mark to everyone present.

A man from the crowd shouted, "Then he *is* the one."

A woman followed, "But has he found the damaged orb?"

Kadmiel stood. "Ladies and gentlemen, *please*. Remember your—"

Chronos: Revolution

Joel interrupted, "It's alright, sir."

Kadmiel nodded and sat. Joel cleared his throat, still trying to formulate what to say. Then he decided to start by communicating without words. He reached into the leather pouch, retrieved the damaged orb, and held it up.

The crowd stared in silence. Joel thought they might all be collectively holding their breath. Then one pair of hands clapped slowly, followed by another, then another. Within seconds, the entire auditorium erupted with jubilant cheers and applause.

Joel knew what they were thinking. *Our mission is over. Our rescuer is here.* He placed the orb back in the pouch and allowed them to enjoy their celebration. He placed his hands on the table and waited.

Kadmiel seemed to read the sobriety in Joel's expression. He stopped applauding. The rest of the councilmembers followed his example in short order. After a moment, Kadmiel stood and raised his hands. The jubilation slowly quieted. Soon, the crowd was silent once more. Kadmiel and the councilmembers watched Joel.

Joel nodded his thanks before looking up at the crowd. "I had expected to report this only to the elders, but you all deserve to know. Enoch *did* tell me I would be responsible for both orbs, but I fear that your mission may not yet be over." He began to turn slowly to address everyone. "One of the reasons for your success over the centuries has been secrecy. The rebellious angels, in particular, have been ignorant of the orbs and the power they wield." He tried to be delicate with what followed. "Because of the...betrayal you recently experienced...an angelic *ruler* named Turiel learned about one of the orbs four thousand years ago on Nimrod's tower. I can

156

Chapter 17

only guess that he followed Professor Aufseher for years, hoping to find it, because three days ago, immediately after the funeral, Turiel began to pursue me. That led to an angelic battle, which led me to find Enoch."

Joel stopped. He was flooded with too many memories.

Seated next to Gemaliel, Zemirah leaned in. "And so, instead of coming here with the orb, you decided to travel *back* to see Enoch?"

He looked at her. "No. The angel who helped me escape advised me to travel *forward*...as far as I could. I found Enoch guarding the Temple Sanctuary with Elijah. Enoch gave me this mark and sent me back here."

"And what did he tell you to do with the orbs?"

Joel looked down. "He didn't get a chance."

Kadmiel looked puzzled. "But why didn't he just keep the orb you had with you?"

"He and Elijah will be martyred after forty-two months in the Temple. He won't be able to keep it safe."

The chamber was silent. The mood was sober. Kadmiel looked up at Joel. "Do you have any recommendations, Seer?"

"Yes. Keep your orb under double guard. No one person is to be left alone with it."

"We've been doing that ever since you returned it."

"Good. There's one more thing." He looked around the table. "I think Joachim might be on his way here. You should prepare."

Uruk jumped to his feet. "He's coming here?" Joel had never seen him so agitated. "We must not permit him to come. He cannot be trusted."

Kadmiel raised a hand in a gesture for calm. "Now, now, Uruk. We have due process for such things. We will take him into custody and hear his testimony."

Uruk shook his head. "But you know he cannot be allowed even to get close to the orbs." He looked around the table and held his hands out imploringly. "He has always been the most skilled at using them, and he has proven that he'll do *anything* to get them to the enemy." He pointed to his own chest. "I should know. I've been paying for his betrayal for decades."

"Uruk, you're advising us to break our own rules."

"These rules *must* be broken, Kadmiel. Trust me."

"Uruk, *please* sit down. You do not have the floor." Kadmiel looked up at Joel. "What would you have us do, Seer?"

Joel's eyes darted back and forth as he thought. He looked at Kadmiel. "Convene both councils...everyone who is not guarding your orb...to confront him. He'll be much less apt to do anything with everyone here."

Kadmiel nodded. "Wise advice."

Uruk slapped the table. "If you're going to put the Seer in charge, then he has to make the tough choices." He stared at Joel. "You need to destroy the *Timekeeper* before he arrives, and you know it."

Joel blinked, aghast. "There are innocent crewmembers on board. *My father* is on board."

"In war, people die. It's unfortunate but true."

"This isn't war."

"Then what do you call it?" Uruk pointed at Joel. "If you don't destroy them now, before it's too late, you'll kill us all!" He thrust his pointed index finger onto the table. "Mark my words."

Chapter 18

Joel sat at the council table with the orb pouch slung over his shoulder, his elbows on the table, and his head buried in his hands.

The chamber was completely empty.

He found himself thrust into a leadership position with no idea what to do next. He had single-handedly taken the station's entire population from elation to near despondency. He first earned their praise, then their derision.

He shook his head. That was too harsh. The crowd in the chamber had dispersed in near-total silence, but Joel didn't get the impression they blamed him. It was just that their greatest hope had been dangled in front of them and then deferred, maybe indefinitely, and their hearts ached for it.

To add insult to injury, one of the most trusted members of the councils was advocating the *Timekeeper's* destruction, and Joel thought some of the elders might agree with him.

He couldn't have been more caught off guard by Uruk's behavior. He had always been so kind and thoughtful. Now he was completely given to fear. Joel wondered what must happen to such soft hearts when awash with anxiety.

It reminded him of Joachim. In Joel's father's eyes, Joachim had become the exemplar of fear unchecked, of cowardice leading to

Chronos: Revolution

cruelty. Joel wondered what his father would do in the same situation. Would he sacrifice the *Timekeeper's* crew—a dozen men and women—to protect an entire station full of men, women, and children? The thought made him shudder. The question seemed so Machiavellian. Killing the enemy in war was one thing, especially an enemy bent on killing you or those you were commissioned to defend, but this was completely different. This was cold-hearted calculation—playing God with human lives.

"No." Joel pushed the chair back, stood, and shook his head. "I cannot agree to this. Whatever Uruk might say, this is not like killing in war. This is murder."

He walked into the dark tunnel that led from the auditorium floor. From the tunnel's end, the angry words of another debate ricocheted off the stone walls in a confusing series of echoes.

Joel rounded the corner into the station's control room and almost collided with a man running straight for him. The man blinked. "Oh...Seer...I was just coming to get you." He pointed behind. "The *Timekeeper's* approaching and trying to make contact."

Uruk shouted at the young man who was working what Joel guessed must be the communications console. "I said...*do not* allow them to say anything. He'll do whatever he can to get to the orbs."

A second elder stood near Uruk and shook his head. He looked conflicted.

Joel was worried about his father. Was he even alive? He steeled himself. *All right. When in command...lead.*

He walked past the mounted orb to the console. The young man sitting in front of it looked back at Joel. Joel leaned down and

Chapter 18

looked over the man's right shoulder. "Is this the first time they've tried to communicate?"

The young man shook his head. "I honestly don't know, sir. I just discovered a short while ago that our system had been disabled at our end."

Joel furrowed his brow. "Let me speak with them."

He seemed relieved. "Yes, sir."

Uruk's voice shook. "You'll kill us all, Seer."

Joel looked at him and shook his head. "By *talking* with them?"

By his tone, it was clear Uruk thought his meaning should be patently obvious. "He's just buying time so he can get close enough to the orbs to destroy us."

Joel's insecurity was evaporating in the heat of anger. "I will not make decisions based on fear, Uruk, and I will not murder."

Uruk huffed and turned away. Joel turned back and nodded to the console's operator. The second elder approached and looked over the young man's other shoulder.

Within seconds, Seth's voice squawked through the speaker. *"This is the Timekeeper . . . do you copy?"*

Joel's pulse quickened. He looked at the young operator. "How do I speak to them?"

"It's voice-activated, sir. Just talk."

Joel nodded. *"Timekeeper*, this is Joel Stark, do you copy?"

"Oh, thank goodness. This is Seth."

"Is my father with you?"

"Yes, he's safe. One moment please."

Joel heaved a sigh of relief. There was a brief pause.

Will's voice followed. *"Joel, this is your father—"*

161

Chronos: Revolution

Joel felt a searing pain behind his forehead. A burst of energy popped his ears. Through the speakers, a roaring impact and shouts from the crew hissed, followed by static.

Joel spun around. Uruk stood with his open palm raised toward an open portal. The *Timekeeper* was visible on the other side of the blue field.

Joel's adrenalin spiked. "What do you think you're doing?"

Uruk jerked his free hand toward the field. Another searing pain struck Joel's forehead. A second blast of energy shot from the orb through the portal. The blast pushed the orb back and cracked its mount. On the other side of the portal, the *Timekeeper* lurched with the impact.

The second elder shouted, "Uruk, you'll destabilize their batteries and detonate the ship."

Uruk's voice shook. "That's the idea."

The *Timekeeper* began a slow, wobbling spin. A jet of mist burst from the side of the hull and blew an increasingly long cone of white crystals that spiraled with the ship's slow turn. Uruk drew his hand back to fire again.

Joel sprinted forward and tackled him hard. Uruk grunted with the impact. The portal slammed shut. They hit the stone floor with another grunt. Kadmiel and Gemaliel ran in with a group of guards.

Joel jumped to his feet, yanked Uruk off the ground, and shoved him toward the guards. "Take him into custody, now!" The guards restrained him and stared, clearly confused. Joel spun back to the console. "Can you raise them again?"

The young man shook his head. "They're not responding, sir."

162

Chapter 18

Joel faced Kadmiel and pointed to the mounted orb. "We need to evacuate the *Timekeeper,* quick."

Kadmiel didn't ask questions. He glanced at the orb and made a double take. It was leaning over in its shattered mount. He pulled Gemaliel with him, retrieved the orb from its mount, raised a hand, and opened a portal. It opened to the *Timekeeper's* transporter room. The room was empty, and the door to the bridge was sealed.

Gemaliel stuck his arm through the portal. "Ouch." He whipped it back, shook it, and looked up. "Cold...the room is decompressed. You should try the bridge."

Kadmiel nodded quickly. He closed the portal and reopened it. The crowded bridge appeared on the other side. Crewmembers grasped whatever wouldn't move as their legs floated in the air. One of them pointed. "Look!" The crew cheered.

Seth's voice echoed through. "Go, go, go!"

They began to push themselves through the air toward the portal. They floated head-first, penetrated the field, and rolled onto the stone floor. Two guards ran to the portal, helped the crewmembers up, and ushered them away to make room.

Joel counted. "Eight...nine...ten." His father wasn't among them.

Seth was the last to emerge. He rolled to his feet and looked at Joel and Kadmiel. "Two hands unaccounted for...Joachim and Commander Stark." He looked at Joel. "They were trapped aft when the compartments sealed."

Joel grabbed his shoulders. "*Where* aft?"

Seth shook his head. "Either the conference room or the galley."

Joel threw an imploring glance at Kadmiel. Kadmiel closed the portal to the bridge and opened a third. The *Timekeeper's* conference

Chronos: Revolution

room appeared. Chairs floated above the table. Joel stood just in front of the field and craned his neck back and forth. The room was empty. He looked at Kadmiel. Kadmiel nodded and closed his hand into a fist.

The instant before the field closed, a shock wave blasted out with a blinding flash. It slammed everyone away from the portal and onto the ground as the field disappeared. Joel gasped and pulled himself to his feet. "It can't be."

Kadmiel sat up on the stone floor, exchanged a sober glance with Gemaliel, and raised his hand to open a fourth portal.

Gemaliel grabbed his arm. "Better open this one from a distance." Kadmiel nodded slowly and raised his hand.

The portal opened into space. A distant fireball grew, and debris flew outward. A large chunk flew straight toward them, spinning slowly. It was the *Timekeeper's* stern, the ship's name still legible on the surface.

Kadmiel closed the portal. No one said a word.

Joel fell back, thudded onto the floor, and buried his head in his hands.

His father was dead.

Chapter 19

Joel sat on the cold, stone floor with his face buried in his hands as wave after wave of emotion crashed over him. First shock, then grief, then anxiety, then anger. A dull fog rose from within. Once again, his heart couldn't keep up.

One of the guards holding Uruk broke the silence. "Um, where should we take Councilman Uruk?"

Joel felt the lonely burden of leadership. He didn't have the luxury of selfish anger. Without looking up, he spoke in a low, restrained tone. "Away from here, please." The shuffle of footsteps told him Uruk was gone.

As they left, Gemaliel whispered to Kadmiel, but the room's rock-hard acoustics permitted no secrets. "What recourse do we even have for such a crime?"

Kadmiel spoke in a low voice. "The only recourse possible...banishment...if all councilmembers agree, of course."

"That doesn't seem likely."

Joel heard the sniffs of a man weeping quietly. He felt an arm wrap around him and pull him to his feet. He turned to see its owner.

It was Kemuel, his face wet with tears.

Chronos: Revolution

Joel had almost forgotten; Kemuel had just lost his father, too. He knew his own tears would come. But not yet. "Where can we go to get away and...grieve?"

Kemuel and Grace led Joel on a long walk to the center of the station and halfway around its cylindrical surface. They passed lush, flowering trees, rich crops, and cozy, inviting homes along the way. The council chamber was directly above and far to one side.

Joel was surprised at how the walk had refreshed him. When he was eight, right after his siblings were killed, a well-intentioned neighbor had told him God ministers to a heart's grief through beauty. His experience that day seemed to confirm it. Beauty was the only thing that penetrated the fog in his heart.

Straight ahead, a long set of steep, interlocking, silver spires rose high above the station's beveled-glass chapel. At its base, two cascading waterfalls trickled among lush flowers and framed a pair of thick, mahogany doors.

Kemuel heaved one of the doors open and ushered them in. Joel stepped in. His eyes were immediately drawn up. The beveled glass between the spires refracted the station's light into a dazzling array of spectra and rainbows. On each side below the glass, lush foliage spilled onto a blue-carpeted floor with long blue-cushioned pews arranged to face the altar. High above the front, a stained-glass image of Jesus gazed down onto the pews, His arms spread as if drawing the worshiper in for a warm embrace.

Joel mused aloud. "It doesn't really look like Him."

Kemuel stood next to him. "Well, it is an abstract."

"At least you got the skin right."

Chapter 19

"We based it on Scripture. Ruddy-gold, like jasper and carnelian."

Grace stood on his other side and took Joel's hand into hers.

Joel gave her hand a squeeze. He took it all in. He was too worn out emotionally to pray words, but he was getting much better at simply inclining his heart to the Holy Spirit. He allowed the Everlasting Father to immerse him in comfort and strength.

He felt the Holy Spirit's peace, but at the same time, a sense of urgency grew. He had made up his mind during their walk, and he was determined. He gave Grace's hand another squeeze and led her down the center aisle.

Kemuel followed.

When they reached the front, Joel was pleased to find a broad open area between the front pews and the altar. He unslung the pouch from his shoulder and pulled out the blue-and-white orb.

Kemuel furrowed his brow. "What are you doing?"

Joel managed to smile. "What do you think I'm doing?"

"I think you're about to open a portal, and you need to be careful. You can't change the past. You'll create an anomaly."

"Trust me." Joel held the orb in his left hand. "Father, please help me get this just right." He extended his right palm and concentrated. A blue field rose smoothly from the carpeted floor. A short distance beyond the field, Will and Joachim sat in the *Timekeeper's* galley, grasping a floor-mounted table to steady themselves without gravity.

They saw the field right away. Will nodded to Joachim, who swung his legs over the table. Will jammed his knee under the table and reached out with one hand to steady the elder. Joachim lay prostrate across the table, wrapped his fingers around the table's edge

Chronos: Revolution

with his arms extended, and then flexed his elbows to launch himself through the air. Will gave him a push to help.

Kemuel stepped in front of the portal and reached through. Joachim sailed toward him. Kemuel grabbed his arms and pulled him up. Joachim's legs fell under him. He landed smoothly on the floor, stepped away, and turned around. "Hurry, Will. Hurry."

Will followed suit quickly. He swung himself over the table and launched himself through the air. Joel clutched the orb under his left arm and reached out with his free arm to help his father. Will grabbed Joel's arm and opposite shoulder and settled onto the floor with little difficulty.

Joachim's tone was urgent. "Close it quickly."

Joel extended an open hand and squeezed it into a fist. The portal closed just as the blinding flash and shock wave burst out. They raised their arms and shielded their faces. For an instant, the chapel glowed bright with a fierce blast of hot air.

All was quiet.

Joel set the orb on the ground, opened his arms, collided with his father, and squeezed him in a fierce, tight hug. A new wave washed over him, a wave of relief. With the tension gone, the tears came. Joel buried his head against his father's neck and wept. He remembered his father tumbling onto the *Timekeeper's* deck, Jacob's family, the angelic war, the hapless antichrist's soul, and the thousands of soldiers buried alive.

And yet, eclipsing all the pain was the memory of *Jesus's face* looking down, *His eyes* piercing Joel's soul with love beyond measure. Joel clutched his father's shirt with white-knuckled fists and heaved sob after sob with bursts of laughter in between.

Chapter 19

Sometime later, his tears subsided. Joel still didn't want to let go. He was making up for lost time. "I love you, dad. I love you so much."

Will squeezed him tight. "I love you too, Son. Thank you." He rocked gently back and forth. "Thank you."

Joel finally remembered he and his father weren't the only ones in the room. He let go, stepped back, and wiped his face.

Kemuel and Grace were arm-in-arm. She leaned her head on his shoulder and smiled.

Joachim stood alone.

Kemuel didn't look at him. Instead, he stared at Joel. "Just how is it that you didn't create an anomaly? You just changed the past."

Joel picked up the orb and placed it back in the pouch. "Yes, but I didn't change the outcome that stimulated our actions. The *Timekeeper* was still destroyed." He slung the pouch over his shoulder. "I worked that out while we were walking here."

Joachim stared at Kemuel's side. Kemuel dropped his gaze to the floor.

Grace walked around her father and hugged Joachim. "Welcome back, Grandpa. I've missed you."

He hugged her back. "Thank you, little Grace from God."

Kemuel spat the words. "Don't call her that."

Grace spun around and looked at her father, her eyebrows squeezed together.

Will tried to interject. "Kemuel, you need to—"

Still facing away from the man, Kemuel raised his arm to the side and pointed at his father. "You don't *deserve* to call her that."

Joel stepped forward. "Kemuel...stop."

Kemuel blinked and dropped his hand. "Why?"

Chronos: Revolution

"Because...I think we've been terribly wrong about something." He faced Joachim. "I worked a few other things out, too, while we walked here, like how Uruk said he had to touch the orb to use it... and how every time Uruk uses the orb to fire a blast, it thrusts the orb back."

Joachim nodded. "Uruk never got that right."

Joel took a step forward. "Which means...you helped us in Kansas City, didn't you? I mean, it must have been you who took out the *Nephilim* in the plaza. Those shots were smooth and precise."

Joachim nodded slowly.

Kemuel's eyes were wide. "But...he *stole* the orb."

"Are you sure?"

Will stepped in front of Kemuel. "What did you see that day? What *exactly*? Did you see your father?"

Kemuel's eyes drifted up. He shook his head. "I didn't see *him*. I heard Uruk scream my father's name, and I saw Uruk disappear into the portal."

Joachim clasped one fist in his other hand and rested it against his mouth. Joel thought he might be praying.

Kemuel jerked around to face his father. "But...if you didn't take the orb...why did you leave? Where did you go?"

Joachim spoke over his clasped hands. "Uruk sent me on what he said was a secretive mission..." He gestured toward Will. "...to help *them*."

"The *Chronos* crew?"

Joachim nodded. "He sent me to Germany, 1945, to establish Aelter Aerospace. He joined me..."—he scratched his head—"oh, about 1950, I think. Decades later, I liquidated my interest in the

170

Chapter 19

company and took my experience to work for the American government. I built the *Chronos* spacecraft."

Will interjected, "And did a great job. She flew like a dream."

Joachim beamed a bit. He looked at Kemuel. "I made sure there were extra seats—*on the bridge*—for you and Joel. I designed the onboard computers with your experience in mind, knowing you would help program the system. In Kansas City, I even encouraged Dr. Sekulow to insert his own tracking system within the hull of the orb, so no one could ever take it from us." He shook his head. "I have to admit, I wondered why I never heard from anyone else all those years, but Uruk kept telling me it was necessary."

Will looked down. "Dr. Vollstrecker. Jamie recognized him in Kansas City."

Joachim nodded. "Yes, Erik Vollstrecker. He helped me build *Chronos*. I'm surprised you never saw him." He looked at Kemuel. "Only recently, at the Kansas City facility, I got the impression he was using the orb for his own purposes, but I didn't realize you suspected *me* of anything until that last incursion destroyed the place."

Joel looked up. "Of course...that jibes with what Professor Aufseher told me. He said he knew our enemy as Dietrich Engel, but he also told me Engel changed his name after the war." He pointed in the air. "But what about your Aelter Aerospace vans with the creepy goons?"

"Like I said, I sold my shares. You can probably guess to whom."

Will looked at Joel and Kemuel. "There's something else you both need to know about Joachim. That day on the mountaintop tower above the City of Enoch...the day the Guardians escaped to the future..."

Joel tensed his eyebrows and nodded. "When Joachim promised to keep the portal open for us, but instead—"

"Abandoned us?"

Joel nodded.

Will looked at Joachim. "We left him in charge of the portal, but he didn't abandon us."

"Didn't you look up the tower and see him jump in?"

"I saw *a man* jump in. I assumed it was Joachim."

Joel opened his eyes wide with the revelation. He looked at Joachim.

Joachim's clasped fist was still in front of his mouth. "Uruk came back through the portal and insisted on taking over." He looked at Will. "I was terrified, I admit it, which is why I let him do it. I am sorry, Will. If I would have known he abandoned you, I wouldn't have destroyed the tower...I would have gone back to get you."

Will nodded. "I forgive you, of course, Joachim. You didn't know. I'm sorry, too."

"For what?"

"For passing my misunderstanding on to your son. I'm afraid I poisoned him against you."

"Maybe, but you did it innocently."

Kemuel stared at the floor and spoke in a low voice. "You didn't poison me. Uruk did." He shook his head. "All those years..." He spoke louder. "*All those years*...he acted like he cared, like he was concerned for me...but all the while he was just turning me against you."

Joachim was still staring at Kemuel's side.

"Why? Why would he do that?"

Chapter 19

Joel folded his arms. "He must have been planning this for years... for centuries." He looked at Joachim. "He feared the *Nephilim*, and when he saw that Joachim was scared, too...he must have figured he was the perfect mark. That's why he was so hell-bent on destroying the *Timekeeper* just now. He knew if Joachim came here, we would all know the truth..." He closed his eyes. "That Uruk was the man in the hood, all along."

Will looked down. "I'm sorry, Joachim. You must have been so lonely."

Joachim pulled one side of his mouth into a faint smile. "Not completely lonely. I've been keeping an eye on you all...from a discreet distance."

Joel looked at Kemuel. He expected to see their friend reconcile with his father right there. That wasn't what he saw.

Kemuel slowly drew his lips into a snarl. He squeezed his hand into a white-knuckled fist. "I'm gonna *kill* him." He turned to charge up the aisle.

Joachim jumped forward and grabbed his shoulder. "Son." Kemuel froze and stared at the ground, his fists clenched. "Son, I understand now. This wasn't your fault."

Kemuel looked up, still frozen in place.

"I saw our relationship sour after the *Chronos* mission, but I never talked to you about it. I never asked why. I was such a fool."

Kemuel's voice was barely audible. "You weren't the fool...I was." He turned around and looked his father in the eye. "I was a fool for letting him trick me. I should have known better. I should have honored you."

Chronos: Revolution

Joachim stood a little straighter. He looked like a burden had been lifted.

Kemuel's voice softened. He pointed at his father. "Actually, you and I made a pretty good team. You are truly...unmatched...as a warrior with the orb, and as far as I'm concerned, you got over your fears long ago." He shook his head. "I even let Uruk trick me into thinking you were somehow responsible for Kenan's death."

"That's the enemy's spirit, Son...deceptive...subtle...but don't worry about that, now. That's all behind us." Joachim reached out and squeezed Kemuel's shoulder. "A father's greatest joy is to see his son grow into a man—" he looked at Grace, "or a granddaughter grow into a mighty woman." He looked at Kemuel and grabbed both shoulders. "And what a man you've become. Every mission I went on with you...was an honor. I'm so proud of you."

"And I'm proud to be your son." Kemuel looked down. "Forgive me?"

"Of course, Son."

They embraced each other with their fists squeezed tight. Grace looked on with her hand covering her smile.

Joachim let go of his son. "Oh yes." He reached into a jacket pocket, pulled out a small, sealed, brown-leather binder, and handed it to Kemuel. "When I realized what was happening, I began to *really* pray in earnest. I felt led to write this. You can read it later."

Kemuel nodded. He stared at it like it was a priceless treasure, then slipped it into a pocket in the side of his tunic. He closed his eyes and heaved a breath. "This reminds me of something else I must do." He pulled a red binder from under his jacket.

Chapter 19

Joachim watched him pull it out. He gestured with his eyes. "That's for her, isn't it?"

Kemuel nodded slowly. "You know about that?"

Joachim nodded back.

"I learned it from the Seer. How could you know?"

Joachim took a deep, slow breath. "The same way I know young Joel, here, now has Enoch's mark."

Joel blinked.

"You'll have to figure that out when the time comes."

Kemuel tightened his lips. "Okay." He looked at Will and Joel. "Would you excuse the three of us for a moment?"

Joel looked at his father and nodded to Kemuel. "Of course." He walked to the side of the sanctuary with his father and took a seat. "What do you suppose he's doing?"

Will sat next to him, stretched his arms along the back of the pew, and shrugged. "I don't know...but look at them."

Joel turned.

"Three generations of legacy, finally being made right."

"Don't worry, Dad. You'll get that, too. You'll see your own father again one day."

Will placed his arm around Joel's shoulder and gave it a firm squeeze. "I know, but I'm already satisfied. I have *you*. You are my legacy. I take a lot of comfort in knowing you'll carry on after I'm gone."

Joel looked at his father. He was grateful. Those words meant the world to him, but the torturous singsong returned. *Joshua... Christina...Joy...Joshua...Christina...Joy.* He tried to push it down.

175

He didn't want to poison the moment, but the idea weighed on him. *You'd have even more legacy if I hadn't gotten them killed.*

After a moment, he and his father turned to watch the others.

Kemuel handed the red binder to Grace and spoke in a low voice. She looked at it, then looked into her father's eyes. She nodded. Joel could just make out her words. "Okay. I trust you."

Joachim's voice carried better. "You mustn't tell him...okay?"

The three of them drew together into a tight hug, then stepped back and turned to Will and Joel.

Joachim took a deep breath and sighed. "God is good. No matter how much evil the enemy unleashes, you can count on God's providence to work through it." He looked at Joel. "Now...we have an elder to confront."

"No, you don't." The loud voice surprised them from directly above.

They looked up. His white robe flowing beneath him, his wings flapping gracefully, his golden scepter bearing a brightly glowing orb, Turiel hovered just below the beveled-glass roof.

Chapter 20

Joel jumped to his feet. His first impulse was to protect Grace. Turiel seemed to apprehend that. He folded his wings and dropped to the floor—right next to her. He grasped his scepter with both arms and pointed the orbed end against her head. She tightened her jaw and stared at him with a harsh squint.

Kemuel jumped forward to tackle him. An invisible force blasted him back. He rolled up the center aisle and stopped on one knee. Joachim extended an arm across Grace, pushed her back, and placed himself between her and the rebel angel.

Turiel stared at him. "Following your flying boat was easy enough, but when it was destroyed, I found myself a bit lost, I must say. It took me a while to find this..." he looked around, "fascinating place." He looked at Joachim again. "So much trouble you've gone to—and for what?" He stared at Joel. "To protect your little orb." He flexed his arms and shook his scepter. It glowed brighter. "Now hand it over."

Joel clutched the pouched orb under his arm. He was at a complete loss. *Father, please help. I'm no match for him. What should I do?*

Just wait.

Joel figured he should buy time. He stared at Turiel. "What do you want our orb for? You already have one."

177

Turiel slanted his head and glared.

Joel took one step forward. "Your days in Heaven are numbered, Turiel. I've seen it."

"Who says I even want to be there? Earth holds so many more..."—he took a deep breath and smiled— "possibilities."

Joel steeled his countenance. "When you're cast out of Heaven, Turiel, you'll need to enjoy your time on earth quickly."

"And why is that?"

"Because you'll have only a short time before a thousand years of imprisonment with your master...and after that, your ultimate destination—"

Turiel's malevolence melted.

"The lake of fire...for the rest of eternity."

Turiel's eyebrows slanted. He blinked, narrowed his eyes, and gritted his teeth. "Nice try, human...but when we *win* our war, your threats will be pointless."

Okay, Father, I've bought some time, and I'm running out of ideas.

Turiel pushed Joachim to the side, raised his scepter so its staff was horizontal, and pointed it at Grace's head. "Now, unless you want to watch your girlfriend die—"

A bright light flashed outside of the chapel. It streaked between the spires and struck Turiel head-on. He dropped his scepter and tumbled back with an *authority* in golden armor grasping his robe at the shoulders. They rolled across the floor, their wings flexed taut.

Turiel threw him off and jumped to his feet. The *authority* lunged forward with an arm flexed to punch. Turiel spun around and struck his jaw with a flexed elbow. The *authority* grunted, fell back, and shook his head. Turiel crouched and extended his hand

Chapter 20

toward his scepter. It shook for a moment and launched toward his open hand.

A second light streaked between the pillars. Another armed *authority* landed on Turiel's scepter, grasped it with both arms, and held it to the floor. Turiel shouted and tightened his open hand. His scepter slanted up from the floor. The *authority* kept his full weight on it, grimacing as he fought against its force. It dragged him slowly toward Turiel.

The first *authority* jumped from behind, wrapped his arms around Turiel's at the elbow and pulled him back. The second *authority* fell to the floor with the scepter and heaved a quick sigh. Turiel struggled against the winged warrior's grasp and grimaced, "You'll pay for this."

The *authority* behind him looked at Joachim. "We can only buy you time. More are coming. You must evacuate the station *now*."

Joachim bounded to the front of the sanctuary and slammed something behind the podium. A deep, intermittent horn echoed outside. Grace ran to Joel, grabbed his hand, and pulled him up the chapel's long aisle. The others followed. She shouted over her shoulder, "The people will gather in the auditorium."

They pushed through the chapel's heavy doors. The intermittent horn was much louder from outside the chapel. They stared at the far end of the station. There, opposite the long, cylindrical, heat-and-light apparatus that formed the station's axis, the auditorium structure hung down, from their perspective, from the top surface of the station's cylindrical interior.

For the third time that day, Joel's forehead felt like an icepick pushed out from inside. He gritted his teeth and squinted.

Chronos: Revolution

The long tube that stretched from the station's control room to its glowing axis pulsed with a flash of energy. The station's axis tube flashed. Sparks popped from its surface and disappeared.

Joachim pointed. "Uruk must be firing pulses from the orb. He'll detonate our battery stores. We have to stop him."

Will watched the glowing axis assembly with interest. "But if he can do that from anywhere on the station, how will you stop him?"

"Get me close enough, and I'll stop him."

Joel shook his head. "That's a long run."

Grace took a few steps forward and looked over her shoulder. "I can get us there in thirty seconds. Trust me?"

Kemuel joined her. "I know what you have in mind. Lead the way." He looked back. "Follow us...and do just as we do."

Grace sprinted across the grass on the balls of her feet. Joel was impressed with her speed. She ran straight for a short, landscaping wall, jumped onto it with both feet, flexed her knees, and launched herself into the air.

To Joel's surprise, she aimed considerably to the right of the auditorium. She stretched her arms out and soared. Kemuel followed, leapt onto the bench, and launched himself behind her.

Joachim shook his head. "Oh, my poor knees." He jogged, jumped onto the short wall, and leapt into the air. He rolled slowly forward.

Joel grimaced. "I'll bet he didn't want to do that."

Joachim tucked into a ball to speed his roll. As his head rolled back around, he stretched out again to slow his roll and see where he was going. Then he repeated the process.

Joel was impressed by the elder's agility.

Chapter 20

Will looked at him. "You go next, Son."

Joel nodded. He rubbed his hands together, took a deep breath, and sprinted for the landscape wall. He jumped, planted his feet on its surface, flexed his knees, and launched himself, hoping to pull an impressive Clark Kent.

He was close. Without the station's rotating floor constantly pushing up against his feet, he immediately felt the weightlessness of zero-gravity. He rolled slowly forward and to the side. He tried to mimic Joachim by curling into a ball, but since he was both rolling and yawing, it only sped his out-of-control turns. He stretched out to slow the spins. The result was a slow, sweeping, panoramic view of the entire station while he sailed through.

Everywhere on the station's cylindrical interior, people emerged from their homes and hurried toward the auditorium.

He saw his father flying behind him, then the others flying ahead. As they soared past the ship's glowing axis assembly, he realized why Grace had aimed so far to the side. The station's slow rotation was steadily bringing the auditorium directly into their path.

Far ahead, Grace, reached the ground, curled into a ball, rolled to her feet, and grabbed a shrub to steady herself. Kemuel's landing was equally impressive. Joachim approached next, still controlling his forward roll by curling occasionally into a ball. Kemuel reached up and helped him land as smoothly as possible.

Joel tried to figure out how to time his spins to land on his feet. As the ground approached, he turned helplessly away, struck the earth with an oomph, and bounced off. The ground moved past him underneath, and he floated slowly away from the surface. Kemuel grabbed his shirt from behind and pulled him down. Once there,

Chronos: Revolution

the station's spin pulled him to the side. An instant later, the centrifugal force pressed him against the ground. He heaved a sigh of relief. Nearby, Will fell onto a shrub, grabbed its branches, and let it pull him along with the station's spin. He swung his legs around and lowered himself to the ground.

Joel's head throbbed. He grimaced.

A blast of light flashed up the tube to the axis assembly and pulsed from one end to the other. More sparks flew out.

This time everyone seemed to notice Joel's pain. They stared at him for a moment.

People hurried past them toward the auditorium structure. Parents carried infants and led children by the hand. Most adults had a single bag slung over their shoulders. They streamed up the ramp to the entrance.

The images reminded Joel of the day the Guardians fled up the tower to escape the *Nephilim* attack. For him, that was only a few years before. Now, it felt like an eternity had passed.

Two streaks of light flew overhead. Joel's gaze followed them straight to the chapel. Inside it, light flashed, and a cluster of wrestling angels crashed through the beveled glass and spun with a flurry of wings and limbs. The glass flew out, streamed through the air, and curved in an unexpected arch as the station rotated around it.

More angels streaked in, hovered, identified targets, and tackled each other. Joel couldn't tell which side they were on.

A robed, scepter-bearing *ruler* with a gold breastplate struck the ground next to Joel and rolled to his feet. It was Phanuel.

Joel heaved a sigh of relief. Phanuel wasted no time. "Joel, evacuate the people from the auditorium. I'll meet you in the control

Chapter 20

room." He turned to Kemuel. "You need to do it now." He aimed his scepter up, fired a blast at a passing *authority*, and leapt into the air.

Joel looked at Kemuel. "Do what?"

Kemuel's eyes watered. He turned to Grace. "I love you." He kissed her cheek, pulled her into a tight embrace, and stared over her head with a deeply pained look. "Never forget...your daddy loves you."

She rested her head against his chest. "I love you too, Daddy. I always will."

Joel hated the sound of this. They were saying goodbye, forever.

Kemuel held her tight. "Dearest Anna, my little Grace from God."

Joel couldn't hide his shock. "Anna?" He stared at her and seemed to recognize her for the first time. The implications struck him hard, and his heart sank. He was about to lose her, too. "You're Anna Aufseher."

Still hugging her father, she looked at Joel. "Not yet."

Joachim looked apologetic. "She didn't know. We just explained it to her in the chapel."

Anna seemed conflicted. "My name *means* Grace, so that's what everyone always called me."

Joachim pointed to Joel's pouch. "I need to use your orb, Joel."

The idea tormented Joel. He was about to send Grace—Anna, it turned out—away forever. He grasped the pouch and debated whether to give it to Joachim.

Joachim shook his head. "You can leave it in the pouch." He leaned over and kissed Anna's cheek while she hugged her father.

Chronos: Revolution

She drew back from Kemuel and turned to hug Joachim. "Bye, Grandpa." Then she hurried to Joel and looked mournfully into his eyes.

Joel shook his head. He wanted to say something, but he was at a complete loss for words. He wanted to keep her with him, but if she was such a critical part of history, they could never be together.

She wiped a tear with one hand. "I have to go." She threw her arms around him and hugged him tight. "I love you, Joel."

He hugged her back. "I love you, too…Anna."

"I'm so sorry."

Joachim extended his open palm. A portal opened next to Grace.

She looked into it, then glanced at Joachim and her father one last time. She leaned toward Joel and kissed him on the cheek. She turned around and ran through the portal.

Joachim closed his palm. The portal disappeared.

Joel wanted to yell. He stared at Joachim. Kemuel stepped in front of Joel. "She's safe, Joel. Trust us."

Joel stared where the portal had been.

"Joel, you've more than earned my blessing. I would have been proud to call you my son-in-law." He tightened his lips. "I'm sorry I won't have that pleasure."

A blast of energy detonated on the ground nearby and blew a cone of topsoil into the air. Phanuel flew past. "Hurry, Joel!"

Joel grimaced from another brief, splitting headache. The axis assembly pulsed and sparked. On the far end, a small part of its surface ruptured with a flash of red.

Joachim and Kemuel ran toward the auditorium entrance.

Will squeezed Joel's shoulder. "We need to go with them, Joel."

Chapter 21

Joel pushed his personal torment aside. There were too many lives at stake. He ran behind Joachim.

They had to file in with the crowd that was climbing the ramp. The people ahead of them entered the auditorium and hurried to either side, quickly making room for others to enter.

As Joel climbed the ramp, he ran his hand along the railing and glanced behind. From one end of the station to the other, families hurried across and around the station's interior surface toward the auditorium while scepter-wielding *rulers* and sword-bearing *authorities* fired blasts, struck each other, and wrestled in the air. Joel turned and entered the auditorium. Inside, people streamed around the rows of seats.

Around the table below, elders—both men and women—looked up into the seats and gathered people into groups. Kemuel ran past the elders and ducked into the tunnel to the control room.

Joel followed Joachim down the steps and around the table. He spotted Kadmiel just as Joachim approached him.

Kadmiel's eyes looked like they might pop out of their sockets. "Joachim! How?"

Joel shouted ahead. "I did it."

Kadmiel blinked. Joachim grabbed Kadmiel by his shoulders. "No time, brother. Where's the orb, and where's Uruk?"

Kadmiel pointed into the tunnel. "The orb is in the control room. As for Uruk, I haven't seen him."

Shouts echoed from the tunnel. Joachim hurried around the table and ran in. Joel paused next to Kadmiel. "Make sure everyone's accounted for. Then we'll evacuate from here." Kadmiel nodded.

Joel glanced back at his father and ran into the tunnel. He could hear his father's footsteps right behind. Light flashed from around the corner with a deep boom. Joel hurried around and stopped next to Joachim. His father joined them.

On the other side of the chamber, Uruk held the gold-encased orb over two elders and two guards who lay on the floor, groaning. Near the entrance, Kemuel shook his head and pulled himself to his feet.

Joachim helped Kemuel stand. "Son, get the others out of here."

Kemuel nodded, "Yes, Father." He helped the first elder get up and ushered him toward the door.

Will pulled one of the guards off the floor. Together, they helped the other elder to his feet. Joel found the last guard unconscious. He grabbed the material of his tunic under the man's shoulders and dragged him toward the entrance. The other guard tapped Joel on the shoulder. "I'll take him from here, sir."

Joel stepped aside and looked into the control room. Uruk clutched the gold-encased orb under his arm. Joachim stared at him with his fists clenched at his sides. "This ends now, Uruk."

Uruk stared back, trembling. He shook his head. "No...no."

Joel heard a strange voice. *Shut up, you fool!*

Chapter 21

Uruk raised his hand toward Joachim. "Leave us alone. Just leave us alone." He looked terrified.

I said shut up! You have the orb...use it!

Joel blinked. He squeezed his eyes closed and opened them. A strange shadow writhed within Uruk, slithering up his spine. "How did I miss that before?"

Uruk extended a palm. Nothing happened. He drew his hand back and pushed it out again. He stared at Joachim. The fear in his eyes morphed into intense hatred. His voice became raspy. "Stop that! Let me portal!"

Joachim shook his head. "You're coming with me, Uruk."

Uruk shook his head slowly. His lips drew into a sinister grin. "You may be able to keep me from portaling, but you can't stop everything." He extended his hand toward Joel.

Joachim raised his hand. "No, Uruk!"

Splitting pain pushed against Joel's forehead. He grimaced and pushed the butts of his hands against his temples. Uruk drew his hand back and shoved it out. A blast of energy shot from the orb toward Joel. The recoil shoved Uruk back.

Joachim thrust out a hand. The energy arced away from Joel and exploded into the wall. A shower of dust and rocks settled to the floor.

Will dove to the side to avoid the blast. He hurried behind Joel and tried to pull him away. Joel's head hurt again. Still pressing his hands against his temples, he grunted and fell to his knees.

Uruk fired another blast. Joachim diverted it again. This one struck the ceiling and showered the floor with another blast of rocks and dust. Will leaned over Joel and sheltered him from the debris.

Chronos: Revolution

Kemuel reemerged from the tunnel. Joachim glanced at him. "I love you, Son."

Uruk followed Joachim's gaze to Kemuel, grinned, and extended his hand toward him. Joel's head split again, and Kemuel raised his arms to shield himself. Joachim charged straight for Uruk. He extended his left palm as he collided with Uruk and shoved him back. A portal opened ahead of Joachim's open palm. Uruk screamed as Joachim tumbled through the portal on top of him.

The portal closed. The chamber was silent.

Kemuel ran to where the portal once was, breathing hard. "Father."

Will reached down and pulled Joel to his feet. They watched Kemuel.

Kemuel looked down. "Father. I just got you back." He fell to his knees and slumped. "It's happened. I've lost everyone." He stared through the floor and whispered, "I'm alone."

Joel's heart ached for him. He knew it must be a father's worst nightmare to grieve a parent and an only child at the same time.

Will stepped behind Kemuel and placed a hand on his shoulder. He gestured toward the chamber's entrance. "Come on, Kemuel. We have a station to evacuate."

The floor shook. Dust fell from the scarred ceiling.

Still kneeling, Kemuel heaved one foot under himself, then the other. Will helped him stand, placed an arm around his shoulder, and tried to pull him toward the tunnel.

The floor shook again. The lights dimmed for a moment. Kemuel turned toward one of the consoles. He stepped in front of it and read the displays. He ran his hand over his hair and looked back. "The battery stores are destabilizing."

Chapter 21

Joel had hoped they wouldn't have a deadline. "How long do we have?"

Kemuel spoke in a low voice. "Impossible to say...seconds, or minutes." He reached out and tweaked some controls. "There... that'll help." He looked up. "I'll stay here, disconnect the mains, and shunt power to the more stable of our battery stores. That'll buy you"—he looked from one display to another— "a few minutes, at best. You need to hurry."

Joel nodded. He had no doubt Kemuel was willing to sacrifice himself for the others. In his grief, he probably preferred it. He glanced at his father, who gave him a sober nod. They ran together into the tunnel. As they ran, the auditorium's pandemonium grew louder. Joel hurried straight to Kadmiel.

When Kadmiel saw Joel, he raised his hands and turned around. "Silence please, ladies and gentlemen. Silence."

The room became quiet. All eyes were fixed again on Joel.

The floor shook. The lights dimmed again.

Kadmiel stood in front of him. "All but ten are accounted for."

Will hurried past them. "I'll go check outside." He bounded up the steps and pushed the auditorium doors open.

Joel didn't think he had ever seen them closed before. He watched them swing shut behind his father. He had to swallow his anxiety over his father's safety. He looked at Kadmiel and gestured to the orb in his pouch. "I assume you have a place to go. Can you open a portal while this is still in the pouch?"

Kadmiel blinked and nodded. "Of course."

Chronos: Revolution

Joel remembered Uruk in the C-130 when they were fleeing from Kansas City, insisting that he hold the orb to open a portal. Just one more deception.

Joel gestured toward the tunnel. It was the perfect place for Kadmiel to open the portal. Kadmiel seemed to read Joel's mind. "If you want to go help your father, the orb must remain within view of the portal." He pointed up the stairs. "You cannot take it past the entrance."

Joel swallowed and nodded.

An explosion outside made the entire building lurch. Joel grabbed the back of a chair to steady himself.

Kadmiel extended a palm toward the tunnel. A dozen feet beyond its entrance, a blue field rose from the floor and filled the opening.

Joel peered through. Tall grass waved gently next to a wooden chapel.

Kadmiel shouted toward the seats above. "Families stay together. We'll start with the bottom row." Parents and children at the floor level began to shuffle toward the tunnel entrance and file in from each side.

Joel walked past them and hurried up the stairs. He pushed the door open to utter chaos. Outside, hundreds of white-robed *rulers* and armed *authorities* collided and wrestled in the air. Swords clanged with crackles of lightning. Blasts of energy flew in each direction, demolished homes, and incinerated trees. Angels tumbled through the air and collided with the ground with bursts of soil and rock. Across the cylinder's interior, homes, crops, and foliage were ablaze. The station's axis assembly pulsed brighter and brighter

Chapter 21

as sparks flew out and red-hot chunks burst off its surface. Gray smoke and floating debris filled the interior with a dull haze.

Joel stood in the open doorway and looked everywhere for his father. "Dad! Dad! Where are you?"

"I'm here, Son!" His shout came from some distance to one side. Joel followed the voice and cupped his hand over his eyes.

Through the haze, Joel spotted his father leading what looked like two sets of parents and their children toward the auditorium. Joel counted them carefully. There were eight of them, plus his father. That meant there were two more out there. Joel squinted and scanned in all directions. He could see no one other than the battling angels.

Will reached the bottom of the ramp and ushered the families past. They grasped the rail and ran up, holding their youngest children by the hand. Joel held the door open and made way for them.

Kadmiel joined him at the top of the stairs. "Oh, thank the Lord." His eyes darted from person to person as they entered. He looked at Joel. "We're still missing two."

Joel watched his father step in and turned to Kadmiel. "Do you know who? What do they look like?"

Keturah hurried up the stairs to his side. She looked at her husband. "It's Kenan's family."

Kadmiel shook his head. "Dear Lord." He looked at Joel. "It's a woman and her seven-year-old son."

Chapter 22

Joel looked across the auditorium. The top rows were just beginning to file down their aisles toward the portal.

Joel unslung the pouch from his shoulder and handed it to Kadmiel. "Stay here. Get everyone out. We'll go find them."

Kadmiel and Keturah nodded together.

He started for the door and turned back. "Where do they live?"

Kadmiel pointed almost straight up. "Opposite us."

"Near Kemuel's home?"

"Right next door."

Joel looked at his father. "I know where that is." Will nodded.

Joel burst out the door and sprinted down the ramp. As he ran, he suddenly felt much heavier. He had to push up hard for each step. He paused and shook his head. "I don't understand."

Will paused next to him. "We must be running with the station's spin. It's increasing the centrifugal force against our feet."

Joel looked up. Angels streaked and spun in every direction. "Well...leaping across isn't an option." He steeled his eyes forward. "My quads can take it if yours can." He lunged forward, kept to a pace he could maintain, and led his father between smoldering gardens and under flaming branches.

Chapter 22

The dense, high-pressure atmosphere helped, but the smoke began to choke his breaths. He wheezed and gagged. He slowed to a stop, doubled over, and bellowed a series of hacking coughs. He gasped for air and looked behind. The smoky haze hung like a dense fog. He couldn't see more than a couple dozen feet. "This is no good."

Will paused next to him and placed a hand on his shoulder. "Wait...listen."

A faint, high-pitched voice cried out in the distance. "Help! Somebody please help us."

Joel pointed to the side. "They're on the next path."

"Help!"

Joel jumped over a landscape wall, bounded over a smoldering patch of grass, pushed through a set of bushes, and emerged onto another paved path.

The voice now came from his right. "Help us please!"

Joel heard his father push through the bushes behind him. He hurried toward the young voice. Within seconds, the boy's faint image emerged from the smoky haze.

The boy pointed behind himself. "Help my mom, mister, please."

Just beyond him, a young-looking woman with long, dark hair leaned her hand on a landscape wall and jumped forward one step, holding one foot off the ground. She looked up. "I've broken my ankle. I tried to get him to run ahead, but he wouldn't leave me."

Joel ran to her side.

Will joined them and looked at the woman's son. "Good boy. You were smart to stay with her and call out." He looked at the mother. "We'll carry you and run to the auditorium."

She shook her head. "No, no, no. Don't run that way."

193

Chronos: Revolution

Joel put it together. "We'd be running against the station's spin. We could float off the surface, and then we'd be helpless."

Will placed an arm around the woman's waist to help support her. "But walking will take too long."

Joel shook his head. "We could run the other way."

"That's even farther, and I'm sorry, but running with the station's spin while carrying someone...my legs don't have it in 'em."

Two yelling angels spun past overhead. A blast struck the ground nearby.

Joel wiped his brow. "I'm out of options."

A baritone voice surprised him from behind. "Will this help?"

Joel spun around.

Kemuel jogged up the path with the pouched orb slung over his shoulder. "The others are gone. Kadmiel told me where you went." He looked at the woman. "I wasn't about to let Kenan down again."

Leaning on Will, she grimaced, hopped forward, and shook her head. "You didn't let him down, Commander Kemuel. We all know that."

Kemuel unslung the orb's pouch and held it out for Joel.

Joel accepted it and slipped it over his shoulder. "Do you know where...or *when* the others went?"

Kemuel stepped to the woman's opposite side and wrapped an arm around her waist. He and Will lifted her a few inches off the ground. He looked at Joel. "Kadmiel said you should be able to... how did he put it...*reopen* the last portal."

Joel nodded. "Father God, please help me." He extended a hand, closed his eyes, concentrated, and turned his head to the side. He didn't know what he was feeling for, but he felt for it, nonetheless.

Chapter 22

A blue field stretched above the path a dozen feet ahead. On the other side of it, grass waved. A large gathering of the Guardians pointed from the other side and shouted. They waved their hands in frantic gestures to approach. "Come in! Jump in!"

Turiel shouted from directly above, "*There* they are!"

Joel looked up. *He must see the portal's glow.*

The young mother looked at her son and spoke urgently. "Go in, Jared. Quick."

On the other side of the blue field, Keturah knelt with her arms wide.

Turiel's feet struck the ground like thunder just in front of the portal. He held his scepter with both arms and blocked their way. "Not so fast." An armed *authority* streaked toward Turiel from above. He raised his sword and yelled.

Turiel pointed his scepter and fired a thunderous blast. The winged warrior grunted and flew back. A long, orange flash pulsed above with a burst of sparks, bright enough to be seen through the haze. The ground shook. The armed *authorities* Joel had seen before with Turiel landed on each side of him. They raised their swords and glared.

Will and Kemuel pulled the mother back a few steps. Kemuel moved in front to shield her. Joel put his arm around the boy's chest and pulled him back. "Let the others go, Turiel. Your beef is with me."

Turiel looked incredulous. "I don't care about them, boy. Why should I?" He pointed his scepter at Joel. "Now give me the orb."

Joel shook his head. "Not a chance."

The ground lurched back and forth with a loud rumble.

195

Chronos: Revolution

"And just how do you plan to *keep* me from taking it for myself?"

A deep, electronic hum pierced the air from above. Joel looked up. Glowing through the gray haze, the axis assembly pulsed bright. A shower of sparks burst in all directions from the far end. The burst traveled quickly across the entire length of the axis in a long, quick series of flashes. When it hit the end near them, a large chunk glowed orange, exploded off the end, and struck the round ice wall that formed one end of the station.

A cone of ice fragments exploded back from the point of impact. The surface cracked. The axis assembly's glow became a blinding glare. Joel felt its heat like the hot summer sun. He looked at the trio of angels in front of them. His eyes landed on Turiel. "I don't have to stop you."

Turiel furrowed his brow. A sword-wielding *authority* spun out-of-control above and collided with the ice wall. A white-robed *ruler* streaked after him with his glowing scepter raised. The *authority* whipped his feet against the icy surface and pushed away just as a scepter blast struck his point of impact. The ice cracked again. A chunk disappeared as if it fell through the surface. A loud whistle grew. The gray, smoky haze streamed toward the point of impact and disappeared. A stiff breeze pulled toward the opening and grew into a gusty wind.

Joel dropped to one knee and placed an arm around the boy's shoulder. "Father in Heaven, we call on your holy Name, Jesus Christ."

The little boy folded his hands in front. "Yes, Jesus."

The wind became a gale. It roared past them toward the fractured ice wall.

Chapter 22

Turiel shook his head. "You fools. You accomplished nothing. I'll pry the orb from your dead hands."

A deep yell grew from one side. Joel looked in its direction. Shouting with his teeth bared, Phanuel streaked through the gale across the station's surface. He struck the *authority* next to Turiel and tackled the whole trio to the side like bowling pins.

Keturah was still visible on the other side of the portal. The boy's mother shouted, "Run, Jared! Run!" Joel pushed the little boy forward. He sprinted through the portal into Keturah's arms.

Phanuel growled. The two *authorities* grabbed his arms. He flexed them hard and grunted. They spun through the air as their wings waved furiously. Turiel pointed his scepter at Joel and streaked forward. His scepter glowed.

Joel knew a blast was coming. "What do I do, Father?" A thought swept across his mind's eye. *The shield of faith*. Joel raised an arm and took a deep breath. "I trust you, Father."

A blast ripped from Turiel's scepter. It struck an invisible shield that seemed to emanate from Joel's arm. It reflected straight back and struck Turiel. The white-robed *ruler* shouted and tumbled away.

Joel threw an urgent glance at Kemuel and his father. "Carry her through, fast."

They picked her up and hurried forward. Turiel screamed and shot toward them. He didn't raise his scepter.

Joel watched him approach. It was clear the angel was going for brute force this time. "Dad, look out!" Will let go of the woman and extended a hand while the wind buffeted his back.

The orb in Joel's pouch grew hot.

Chronos: Revolution

Turiel froze in the air as if in the grip of an invisible force. His robe flapped in the wind. "What is this?"

Will gritted his teeth, fell to one knee, and shouted over the gale. "I can't hold this long!"

Turiel glared at the portal and snarled.

Joel's head suddenly felt like it would explode. He felt the angel trying to close the portal. He grimaced in pain, extended his own hand toward the portal, and concentrated. He leaned into the storm-force wind and shouted, "Kemuel, take her through. Now!" His feet slid slowly across the ground.

Kemuel picked the woman up, leaned into the wind, and forced his way forward, step-by-step. Her long hair pulled in a straight line up toward the wind's point of escape.

Still gripped in the invisible force, Turiel flexed his arms and grunted. His scepter began to glow.

Will raised his second hand with the first and turned his head away. He bared his teeth and yelled. The pain in Joel's head was excruciating. He fell to one knee and focused everything he had on keeping the portal open.

Kemuel was steps away. The wind blew him to the side, and he stumbled away from the portal's opening. The woman held her arms around his neck and clung to him with all her might. He bent his knees, pushed his way back in front of the portal, and heaved his feet forward.

The axis assembly's loud hum became a dissonant growl. The bright glare began to flash. Sparks flew and the ground shook.

Men appeared on the other side of the portal. Kemuel reached its surface with the woman in his arms.

198

Chapter 22

Turiel clenched his fists, looked up, and screamed at the top of his lungs. Veins popped out of his neck. A blast of energy blew away from him in a growing sphere.

Will dropped his hands and fell back to the ground.

Turiel aimed his scepter straight at the portal.

Joel looked at him and shouted, "No!"

Kemuel stumbled and fell with the woman into the blue field. The men on the other side caught them and pulled them away. The field slammed shut with a crack of thunder. The pain in Joel's head disappeared. He blinked and shook his head.

Turiel landed with a thud. Steady as a rock in the fierce wind, he stared at Joel. He seemed to recognize the source of Joel's pain. He grinned and raised his scepter. It began to glow. Joel's head hurt again.

Will crawled against the wind toward Joel. "Son!"

Turiel stepped toward Joel, his glowing scepter aimed at the pouched orb. Joel held his head, doubled over, and yelled.

Phanuel shouted from the distance, still struggling in the grip of the two *authorities*. "Joel!"

Will reached Joel and placed an arm around his shoulder. "Son, how can I help?"

Joel's ears popped. The air was growing thin. "I can't open another portal. He's stopping me."

The icy wall above them cracked again. The dissonant buzz of the axis assembly sputtered. The glow grew blinding.

Phanuel shouted over the din, "Joel, he can't stop what he doesn't know about!"

Joel didn't know what he meant. "Father, what is he saying?"

199

Chronos: Revolution

The ice wall's crack spread in a dozen directions. More fragments disappeared around its hole. The far end of the axis assembly exploded in a red-hot inferno. Its flames incinerated the ground around it. A second blast exploded nearer, then another. The fiery explosions grew closer and closer.

Joel felt their approaching heat. He raised both hands and bellowed, "*Stop!*"

Everything grew silent.

Joel was breathing hard. He stared with wide eyes at the most recent explosion of flame, twenty yards away. All around, angels were frozen in the air in the throes of battle. A few feet down the path, Turiel stood with a snarl like a malevolent statue, his scepter pointed at the pouched orb.

Will gave Joel's shoulders a squeeze, "Good thinking, Son."

Joel looked at him. He looked at his father's hand on his shoulder with one finger on the skin of his neck. Touching him had kept his father animated.

In the distance, Phanuel pushed the two rebel angels away and flew up to Joel and his father. He knelt on one knee beside them and folded his wings. "You know, you don't have to shout to pause time."

Joel looked at him. "I was kind of caught up in the moment. Why weren't you affected?"

Phanuel glanced back at Turiel. "We're bound by time just like you are."

"But you?"

He grinned. "A gift from the Holy Spirit. He sometimes gives me the Father's eternal perspective from outside of time. He obviously knew I would need it."

Chapter 22

Joel suddenly remembered. "The other orb! Joachim and Uruk disappeared with it."

Phanuel shook his head. "Don't worry about that one. You can trust Joachim." He pointed at Joel's pouch. "You only need to concern yourself with this one." He looked at Will. "It's time to send your father home."

Will squeezed Joel's shoulder. "I'm not leaving without my son. We'll go together."

Phanuel shook his head. "I'm sorry, but no. He's bound to the orb. You need to let him go."

Joel could see the pain in his father's face. The man was about to lose his last surviving child. The noxious guilt in Joel's heart boiled over. No matter what he did, he couldn't escape the consequences of his own childhood failure.

Will tightened his lips. He opened them and blew out a shaking breath. He shook his head and barely got the words out as his eyes watered. "I can't lose him, too. I can't."

Phanuel reached out and placed his hand on Will's shoulder. "You must let him go, Will. If you don't, all will be lost."

Tears streamed down Will's cheeks. "Do you mean to tell me that the only way to end all this...is for me to sacrifice my own son?"

Phanuel surprised Joel by shedding his own tears. "You'll be in the best company, my friend...the best." The fierce angel gazed into the distance. "I've never seen the Father weep like He did that day... the day His Son was on the cross."

Will stared at Phanuel.

Joel watched resignation sweep across his father's face.

Chronos: Revolution

Will nodded, wiped his eyes, and stood. He pulled Joel to his feet, drew him into a tight hug, and wept. "Now it's my turn to cry on your shoulder." He drew back and swatted one of Joel's arms. "And a mighty pair of shoulders at that." He stared into his eyes. "You've grown into a fine man, Son...a fine man. I'm so proud of you."

Joel's guilt weighed heavily on his heart. He shook his head. "I'm sorry, Dad. I'm so sorry."

"Don't be sorry, Son. You're doing just what I've prayed for you... all your life."

Joel tensed his eyebrows and shook his head.

"You're fulfilling God's perfect will for your life." Will looked at Phanuel. "Will I ever see my son again...this side of Heaven?"

Phanuel shook his head slowly.

Will took a deep breath and nodded. He pulled Joel in for one final hug. "Goodbye, Son. Go with my blessing, and I'll see you on the other side." He drew back.

Phanuel pointed to Joel's pouch. "You need to open the portal, Joel."

Somehow, Joel knew just where to send his father. He nodded, took a breath, raised his hand, and opened a portal. He looked at his father. "I love you, Dad. I'm proud—" his voice choked, "very proud...to be your son."

Will nodded and turned to the portal. He seemed to hesitate. Then he tensed his arms and jumped through.

Joel closed the portal behind him. He stared where the portal had been. Then he turned to Phanuel. "Alright. Where now?"

Chapter 23

Joel stared at the frozen pandemonium around him, then looked at Phanuel. He had a foreboding sense he was about to go somewhere terrible.

Phanuel looked into his eyes. "You need to seal the orb's timeline. It needs to go where it was always meant to."

"And where is that?"

"The Abyss."

Joel's stomach rolled. He didn't like the sound of that. "And how am I supposed to get it there?"

Phanuel tightened his lips. "You won't like it. I'm about to send you into another battle."

"A human battle?"

Phanuel shook his head.

"Are you high? Because I think you might be."

"No, my friend. You can trust me." He looked to the side. "I'll help you open the portal."

Joel unslung the pouch, retrieved the orb, and held it out for Phanuel.

The angel drew his hands back with his palms facing Joel. "No, my friend, no. I cannot touch it. No angel can touch it."

Chronos: Revolution

Joel drew it back. "All right." He dropped the pouch and looked to the side. "Let's get this over with." He held the orb in his left hand, extended his right hand with an open palm, and concentrated. He could feel himself guided to the right point. A blue portal stretched up from the ground.

He looked back at Phanuel. Phanuel gave him a reassuring nod. "Have courage, my friend."

Joel nodded. He looked into the portal, took a breath, and walked through.

He emerged onto rocky soil. The sky above was deep azure, just beginning to dim into evening twilight. A rocky surface sloped up to one side. Joel looked the other way and realized immediately he was high on the side of a mountain. At the foot of the mountain far below, a broad, desolate, scarred canyon stretched into the distance. It more resembled a quarry than a canyon. Beyond its far wall, a large, familiar stone structure rose above the ground. The faint shouts of a *Nephilim* throng echoed across the canyon from the distant structure.

Joel heaved a sigh and shook his head. It was Semyaza's citadel amphitheater. That meant he was on Mount Taneen Sharr. He turned around and looked up. The Two Hundred would be gathering at its summit, and the last thing he wanted was for them to realize what he was carrying.

He scanned the horizon. "There must be righteous angels, too, right? They should be here any second."

Something struck the ground behind him. He spun around and slumped his shoulders. "But not yet."

204

Chapter 23

A white-robed *ruler* held his scepter over Joel and stared down. He spoke with quiet, malevolent arrogance. "You've come a long way, little human."

This angel looked familiar. Joel slanted his eyebrows and pointed. "You led the *Nephilim* army against Adrok...You're..." He uttered the sounds slowly as they came to his memory. "B-a-r-a-q . . ."

The angel spat back. "Get the name right, boy. It's Baraqiel. And you're standing on a holy mountain." He grabbed Joel's arm.

Joel clutched the orb against him.

"No human is to set foot on the holy Mount Sharr. The penalty is death." He smiled and looked down. "A painful one." He stretched his wings up with Joel's arm in his vice grip.

Joel knew that would hurt. "If it's all the same to you,"

Baraqiel looked down with his eyebrows raised.

"I'd rather walk."

The angel released his arm. He whipped his hand out in a gesture up the hill. "Well, get started, then. You'll have a special place among our gathering."

"Oh, I wouldn't miss it. Trust me." Joel stepped forward and pushed himself between craggy rocks up the slope. He knew he was marching to his own death. He mused to himself, *Not many people get to see what I have.* He remembered the battle at the Guardians' asteroid home in space, the army buried in the Mount of Olives, the angelic war in Heaven, and the skirmish at Hains Point. He remembered their quest for the hidden orb, landing on a river in a C-130, and the last incursion in Kansas City.

He remembered Anna, her bravery, and the loss he felt when she left. *I wish you every happiness, Anna. I never deserved you, but*

I will always love you. He remembered his dear mentor, Professor Aufseher, and his brave sacrifice. He glanced at the orb under his arm. *I won't let you down, Professor.* He glanced back across the canyon and remembered his escape with his parents in the *Chronos* spacecraft. He shook his head. *I won't be escaping this time.*

Then he remembered his sweet childhood in the City of Enoch. But most of all, he remembered his siblings. Their laughter and sweet smiles floated across his mind's eye. He spoke their names under his breath. "Joshua, Christina, Joy." He could think of no greater penance that what he was facing now. It seemed appropriate. He looked up where the angels would be, and indignation welled up in his soul.

Baraqiel sailed above and landed just ahead where the slope began to level near the top. Joel ignored him and walked past. He emerged onto the bald summit to a splendid array of glowing *authorities* with golden armor and fearsome swords. They surrounded twenty *rulers* with white robes and golden scepters.

Fury shook every muscle in his body. These two hundred rebel angels had wreaked so much havoc, destruction, and death. Only Lucifer had outdone them.

His foot shuffled against a high spot on the ground, and one of the warriors turned to look. The angel narrowed his eyes and placed a hand on the shoulder of his nearest comrade. The warriors parted and formed a clear path to their center, staring with cold malevolence as Joel walked through.

He met their glares courageously. He knew the power they wielded, but he also knew their destiny. He walked straight up to their leader and stared into his eyes.

Chapter 23

The warrior next to him—Joel knew he must be Azazel—seemed just a bit flustered. He turned slowly to his leader. "Shall I... destroy him, Semyaza?"

Semyaza's response seemed equally tentative. "No, Azazel, not yet. This is only the second son of Adam to transgress our holy mountain. I'm sure he has a good reason." He stared down at Joel with his eyebrows raised. "Do you have something to say before you die?"

Joel's voice shook with anger. "Your days on earth are over, Semyaza."

"Threats won't save your life, human."

"I don't care."

Semyaza's eyes widened for just a moment. He scoffed and shook his head. "If you're speaking of Noah's prophecy, you needn't fear for our sakes." He glared down. "Angels can't drown."

"I don't speak of his prophecy. I speak of his great-grandfather's prophecy. I speak of Enoch's."

Semyaza swallowed. "And you're here to carry it out?"

A deep, booming voice made him shudder. "No, Semyaza. *I'm* here to carry it out."

The assembly turned as one to the speaker. A mighty archangel landed firmly on the mountaintop. The crowd around him spread to make way.

Semyaza's eyes widened. "Raphael."

Raphael walked through the crowd. "The Seer is right, Semyaza. The Lord of Armies blessed you with power, responsibility, and honor, but you have traded it all for shame. You have chosen to serve yourselves, corrupting and murdering His beloved image-bearers." He stood a head taller than Semyaza, shook his head, and

Chronos: Revolution

practically whispered. "You were warned, Semyaza." He turned slowly and spoke in a loud voice for all to hear. "You have watched your sons, the Titans, fall under judgment and murder each other, and despite that—you have encouraged their *Nephilim* descendants to continue their wickedness, raping, murdering, stealing, and destroying. Instead of love and fellowship, you taught God's image-bearers warfare. Instead of worship and redemption, you gave them sorcery and witchcraft. You even perverted God's creation, breeding murderous beasts and engineering sickly viruses." His eyes landed on Semyaza. "Your judgment comes today."

Semyaza grasped his scepter with both arms and aimed it at the archangel. "No, it won't. Our master will rise up and come to our aid."

"Lucifer has abandoned you, Semyaza. He's languishing in the heavens even now, contriving his next plot."

Fear swept across Semyaza's face. Joel took great satisfaction in seeing it. Then the angel appeared to spot the orb under Joel's arm. His eyes narrowed. "That was in a gold case, before, wasn't it?" He pointed. "You must have taken that from the Gatekeeper." He drew his lips into a smile. "I have a feeling that orb of yours will change everything." He glared at Raphael. "With such power, even you won't be able to stop us."

Joel clutched the orb a little tighter.

Semyaza shouted to his company of angels. "It's time to fight, brothers." He looked down at Joel. "You can start by killing this one." He aimed his scepter at Joel. The orb at its end glowed. A blast of energy shot out.

Chapter 23

A white-robed angel struck the ground just in front of Joel and took the hit on his breastplate. He turned around and winked. It was Phanuel.

Some distance outside of the angelic gathering behind Semyaza, two *authorities* struck the ground with claps of thunder. Then two more. Like lightning bolts, a series of angels struck the ground with explosive blasts in a broad circle, and a ring of righteous *authorities* surrounded the rebels, their swords raised in flexed arms, their fierce expressions hard as flint.

Semyaza raised his scepter and shouted.

The rest of the Two Hundred raised their scepters and swords and shouted with him. The white-robed rulers charged at Raphael. The rest of the rebel *authorities* ran out with swords raised and collided with the righteous warriors who surrounded them. Swords clanged with streaks of lightning, and orbs blasted bright flashes of energy.

Joel stayed behind Phanuel. He spotted something from the corner of his eye coming straight for him.

It was a charging *authority*, his sword raised.

Joel shouted, "Phanuel!"

Phanuel spun and blasted the attacker with his scepter. Someone grabbed Joel from behind and pulled him up hard. Joel dropped the orb. His attacker dropped him from six feet off the ground. He landed hard, spotted the orb, and ran for it. Phanuel dove for it as well. Two of the white-robed *rulers* struck him from both sides and yanked him back.

Before Joel could reach the orb, Semyaza plucked it off the ground. He lifted it high above his head. "Ha!"

Chronos: Revolution

The battle stopped.

Semyaza shouted his victory. "I have it! I have the power of time." He glared at Raphael. "Now you cannot stop me, Archangel."

Raphael shook his head. "You have no idea what you're holding, Semyaza."

In his hand, the orb began to glow with an ear-piercing ring. It grew brighter.

Semyaza cried out, dropped the orb, and shook his hand. He stepped back and stared.

The orb grew into an intense, blinding sphere of light. A screaming voice rose in volume from within. When the sphere reached seven feet across, Yomiel became visible inside, still screaming. The sphere around him disappeared.

Yomiel fell silent. He looked around with wide, bloodshot eyes. His scepter—the one he had been imprisoned in—toppled to the ground beside him. Instead of picking it up, he shrunk away from it, trembling like a leaf. Every angel on the mountaintop stared at him.

Yomiel screamed again and stared at his hands. They became black and morphed into narrow appendages with two joints. His hair grew long and swept over his shoulders, and his teeth became long and sharp. His eyes darted back and forth in terror. He doubled over, and his back turned into a long, faceted shell. He bent over further and stood on four straight appendages as a horse might, if it looked like a locust. A tail grew behind him with a huge stinger like a scorpion.

He turned in every direction, prancing as if on hooves. Then an ear-piercing ring drew his attention to the ground beside him. He looked down at his scepter.

Chapter 23

Every eye looked at it, as well.

The orb at its end began to glow. Its light became more intense and traveled the full length of its staff.

Phanuel hurried next to Joel, wrapped his arm around his waist, stretched his wings up, and launched into the air. Raphael and the righteous company shot up with him.

Semyaza pointed up and screamed. "Stop them!"

The mountain's entire summit burst out in a cataclysmic explosion, spewing meteoric arcs of molten rocks in all directions. Phanuel curled into a ball and wrapped his wings around Joel to take the full force of the blast. He cried out as the impact blew them forward.

Safely cocooned by his guardian, Joel heard a second blast and felt another impact rock them forward. Phanuel loosened his grip, fell limp, and spun to the side.

Joel found himself plummeting alone. A beam of light shone up from the mountain. Joel shielded his eyes. Bolts of lightning struck from above onto the demolished peak. Beneath Joel, the cratered mountain pulled apart, and a pit appeared. It opened its deep gullet and caught the first of the rebel angels in its pull.

The helpless *authority* flapped his wings furiously but was powerless against its force. He reached up and shouted as he was pulled down.

Still plunging straight for the bottomless pit, Joel watched as angel after angel struggled in vain to escape the irresistible force. Something struck him from behind and knocked the wind out of him. He wondered which of the righteous angels had come to his rescue. Instead, Semyaza growled in his ear. "If I go, you go with me, human."

Chronos: Revolution

He aimed straight down and swung his wings to speed their fall.

Chapter 24

Joel plunged helplessly with the rebel angel straight into the gullet of Hades. The shaft surrounded them and sped past at blinding speed. Cold air assaulted Joel's face as the rock walls sped by. Every muscle tightened. He had to force his belly to draw breath through his tight throat. The air became warmer, and soon it began to grow hot.

Semyaza shouted in his ear, "Enjoy hell, human!"

An impact from behind jolted them hard. Semyaza lost his grip.

Phanuel gripped the rebel angel by the collar and stared into his eyes. "This isn't hell, Semyaza—it's Hades—and you're going farther." He punched Semyaza, grabbed Joel from behind, pulled him against his chest, and stretched his wings to slow their fall.

Semyaza flapped his wings, but they shriveled into his back. He flailed, screamed, and tumbled away.

Phanuel looked up. Joel followed his gaze.

A brightly glowing scepter tumbled straight for them. Phanuel plucked it out of the air. In his grip, its glow diminished and disappeared. He swung his wings with mighty rushes of wind, pulled them over to the side of the shaft, and continued to slow their fall.

The shaft opened abruptly on each side. The pit continued straight down into darkness. The Two Hundred continued their

Chronos: Revolution

long fall, flailing, screaming, and transforming into hideous creatures.

On one side, a huge, cavernous space overlooked the abysmal pit. It was dark, barren, hot, and dry. Countless hundreds of thousands of men and women looked out with desperate eyes. They watched the tumbling angels and stared at Joel.

Joel's stomach turned again. He was grateful for Phanuel's protection, but the prospect before him was frightening. Mercifully, Phanuel turned around and flew in the opposite direction. There, another vast, open space looked out over the pit, but this one was bright and pleasant. From there, more people looked out with fascination.

Phanuel carried Joel in and descended toward the ground. A group of onlookers parted to make room. With a series of flaps, Phanuel settled onto the surface and folded his wings behind.

Joel wanted to throw up. He settled onto his hands and knees and was surprised to find cool grass. Immediately refreshed, he looked around. There was pleasant light, but he could find no obvious source. Water trickled nearby.

Dozens of people approached him with looks of fascination—men and women with a wide array of facial features, skin tones, and hair color. Several tilted their heads. One finally spoke. "Are you alright?"

Joel looked into his eyes. He had no idea how to answer.

"We haven't seen a physical body here, well...ever."

Joel pulled himself to his feet. He extended his hand toward the man, palm up. The man who had been speaking reached out, extended a finger, and lightly touched Joel's hand. Joel wasn't sure

Chapter 24

what he felt, but it wasn't exactly a touch. The man drew his hand back and smiled.

Joel was growing confused. "What are you?"

Phanuel stood next to him. "They are exactly what you are, Joel." He gestured toward them with his hand. "Souls."

"So, this is the part of me that—"

"Not *part* of you, Joel. *You*. It's a common misconception. You don't *have* a soul. You *are* a soul, and you *have* a body...and *have* a spirit. That's one of the greatest things that sets you apart from me, for example—and from your enemies. We angels—even the rebellious ones—are spirits who can take physical form. Demons are disembodied *Nephilim* spirits who *cannot* take physical form. They can only attack the mind or, in extreme cases, *possess* bodies of defenseless victims. You, on the other hand, are made in God's image. Just as the Eternal Father interacts with His creation in time and space through His Son and His Spirit, you interact with the physical and spiritual realms through your own body and spirit." He poked a finger just below Joel's sternum. "And you are certainly not defenseless against the enemy, because His Spirit lives with yours."

A man interrupted. "Not here."

Phanuel looked at him and nodded. "True enough. When you died, you left your body to come here, and your spirit returned to the Father who gave it. Here, you are sustained by His Holy Spirit."

Joel was intrigued. "So, this is Heaven?"

"Goodness, no. This is Hades...or at least that's the Greek name for it. The Hebrew name is Sheol."

"But I thought Hades was...you know..." he pointed across the cavern, "hell."

Chronos: Revolution

Phanuel looked mournfully across the cavern and shook his head. "No."

Dozens of pitiful, terrified souls screamed and plummeted down the shaft and into the dark cavern. Hundreds more followed, then thousands. Phanuel watched with a heavy look of compassion. "Even that isn't hell...not in strict terms, anyway."

Joel watched the cavern fill with more and more victims of the catastrophe above. "I don't understand."

"Hell describes the final judgment." Phanuel turned to Joel. "You know what Jesus taught."

A cool, refreshing breeze wafted through, and the souls gasped in delight. Joel marveled. Jesus's Name had such power.

Phanuel smiled. Then his expression became sober again. "He taught that after His Millennial Kingdom, every man and woman from all history will appear before His white throne...which is distinct from His Father's sapphire throne in Heaven...for the final judgment." He swept his right hand toward the souls around him. "He will gather the sheep on his right..."—he looked across the cavern— "and the goats on his left...those who rejected His redemption. Without that redemption, they remain lawbreakers, and the full weight of their sin will crash down on their heads. The Lord's words to them will be final: 'I never knew you. Depart from Me, you lawbreakers.'" A tear streamed down his cheek, and his voice broke, "All they needed to do was call on Him. Like the prophet Nahum said, 'The Lord knows those who take refuge in Him.'"

Joel stared at the souls in torment on the other side of the Abyss. He tilted his head. "So, hell will be what follows the Great White Throne Judgment?"

Chapter 24

Phanuel swallowed and nodded. "The lake of fire...for all eternity." He shed another tear. "What you see over there is nothing compared to their final torment."

Joel felt a swell of pity. The plummeting souls now numbered in the tens of thousands. "And the only difference between here and there is belief in Jesus."

The breeze blew again.

Phanuel nodded. "Or before His Incarnation, calling on the Name of the God who was going to send Him...which only required that they *seek* Him." He tightened his lips and shook a fist in apparent frustration. "When people seek Him, He always reveals Himself to them. He made His Name known through every major empire in history: Egypt, Ninevah, Babylon, Medo-Persia, and Rome. He has even revealed Himself in dreams...many times across the millennia."

After some time, Joel finally broke his stare and looked around. "So, this is what we have to look forward to after we die?"

Phanuel wiped his eyes. "Not in your time, Joel. What you see here is what Jesus described when He told of the Rich Man and Lazarus."

Joel remembered. "This is the Bosom of Abraham."

A woman nearby spoke. "Who's Abraham?"

Phanuel looked at her. "Abraham hasn't been born yet, friend." He looked at Joel. "Jesus used that phrase to describe this place to His fellow Jews, descendants of Abraham, stewards of God's Name and Temple Presence on earth."

"I see." Joel was still a little confused.

Phanuel stepped closer to him. "Do you remember Jesus comparing Himself to Jonah?"

Joel nodded. "Yes. He said He'd be in the heart of the earth for three days and three nights."

"And His last words on the cross?"

Joel thought about it. "'Into Your hands I commit My Spirit'...and 'It is finished.'"

Phanuel held out a hand for emphasis. "So, He yielded His Spirit to the Father—"

Joel's eyes widened, "And His soul came here."

The woman gasped. "The Messiah is coming here?"

Phanuel nodded. "Yes. He'll spend those three days and nights with you...and the same Holy Spirit who will raise Him from the dead will take all of you up to Heaven at the same time." Phanuel looked around. "A few souls will even resurrect physically with Him as a sign, but only temporarily." He looked at Joel. "The Great Resurrection will come at the breaking of the Sixth Seal, after the great persecution." He directed his next comment to the souls surrounding them. "That's when you'll get your bodies back...*incorruptible* bodies."

Joel nodded. "I saw the beginning of that persecution." He looked around. "I feel His Presence here already."

The souls nodded and smiled.

Phanuel nodded with them. "Like David said, 'Where can I go to escape Your Spirit? Where can I flee from Your presence? If I go up to Heaven, You are there—'"

Joel continued, "'If I make my bed in Sheol, You are there.'" He thought of the words that followed. "'Even there Your hand will lead me; Your right hand will hold on to me.'" He took a deep breath and looked around. "This isn't so bad."

Chapter 24

A soul interjected. "Bad? It's wonderful here, and we will get to see our Lord."

"I agree." Joel looked at Phanuel. "I just don't mind so much being left here."

Phanuel shook his head. "Oh, you aren't staying here, Joel, and by the time you die, this place will be empty."

Joel felt a new surge of hope. "So, I'm going back?"

"Oh, yes." He held the scepter out and squeezed his hand. The staff disintegrated with a burst of dust. The white orb fell into his open left palm.

Joel blinked. "I'm surprised you'd destroy your scepter."

Phanuel furrowed his brow. "This thing? This wasn't my scepter." He held out his right fist, and an identical scepter appeared in his grasp. "*My* scepter is completely different."

Joel stared.

Phanuel's expression broke into a broad grin.

Joel enjoyed the moment. He stared at the orb in Phanuel's hand. "You know, I think I finally figured out why Enoch made more than one device." He looked up into Phanuel's eyes. "He didn't."

Phanuel nodded. "You're right. Now we can close the loop forever."

Joel pointed. "So, you're going to destroy it now...once and for all?"

"Yes, right after I use it for one last portal." He clutched it in his left hand, lifted it high, and flung it to the ground. It exploded with a puff of white dust and left a blue portal a few feet across.

Joel stared into the portal. After everything he had been through, he was finally going home. He heaved a sigh. "Then...I'm finished?"

219

Chronos: Revolution

Phanuel shook his head. "I'm afraid not, my friend. You still have much work to do."

Staring into the portal, Joel slowly apprehended the full meaning of that. He lowered his head. "That's why you told my father he wouldn't see me again."

Phanuel nodded slowly.

Joel couldn't have been more disappointed. He had expected to die that day. Now, he wasn't sure he wanted to go on living. "I'm tired, Phanuel. I just want to stay here."

"I understand, Joel. Your rest will come one day...but this is not that day."

Thousands of souls looked on with sad eyes.

Joel kept staring into the portal. It was a gateway from Paradise back into the War of the Ages, and he hated it. "Phanuel?"

Phanuel stood next to him. "Yes, Joel?"

"Will I see you again?"

"I guarantee it."

"Will Anna be alright?"

Phanuel took uncomfortably long to answer. "You'll need to trust God."

Joel's heart sank a little deeper. Phanuel put his hand on Joel's shoulder. "But there is something else you need to know."

Chapter 25

Year of Creation 1656

Joachim fell through the portal on top of the screaming Uruk. They thumped onto a grassy field with a loud oomph.

Joachim was grateful to have landed on top. He rolled off Uruk, groaned, and pulled himself to his feet. He looked down on Uruk, and his heart swelled with pity.

Uruk still clasped the gold-encased orb at his side. A moment later, he groaned and slowly got up. He stared at Joachim. "Where did you bring us?"

Joachim stared. "Where you can hurt no one else, Uruk." The earth rumbled beneath them. "You had all of us fooled, Uruk, but you never really believed, did you? How frightening it must have been for you...to go through all of that with no faith in the Savior."

Uruk looked around. He furrowed his brow and glared at Joachim. "Where, Joachim? Where did you bring us?"

Wind swept across the field and pressed the long grass down in fluttering waves. The rumbling grew louder, and the ground trembled under their feet. The temperature began to plummet.

Uruk jerked his head around. "Why is it getting cold?"

Chronos: Revolution

"The canopy is condensing, Uruk. Part of it is freezing into crystals that are being magnetically drawn to the poles before falling. The earth's atmospheric pressure is dropping by half, and with it, the temperature."

Joachim stared. "No...you didn't."

"It's not too late, Uruk...not yet. You can still call on His Name, even now."

A series of trumpeting cries drew their attention to one side. A herd of wooly mammoths lifted their trunks, cried out, and shuffled in confusion. One of them charged away. The others followed in a stampede.

Uruk stared at Joachim. "How could you? You fool!"

Joachim gazed at him with eyes of compassion. "Call on Him now, Uruk. He's waiting. Call on Yeshua."

The earth's trembling grew into a violent, back-and-forth lurch. The temperature dove below freezing. The wind became a bitter gust. It began to snow.

Uruk looked frantic. He extended a palm, and a blue spark appeared.

Joachim waved a hand and swept the spark away. "I won't let you portal, Uruk."

The snowflakes became larger. Soon they weren't flakes at all; they were clumps. A foot of it had already accumulated. A roaring sound came from the east.

Uruk stared toward the approaching roar. His eyes became saucers. "No! No!" He stared at Joachim. "We must escape, Joachim. Let's escape together."

Joachim folded his arms. "Call on Yeshua, Uruk."

Chapter 25

"Please! Please, Joachim." He shook his head and wept. "We can escape together."

The roar grew louder. The snow was almost waist high. Joachim sighed, folded his arms, and looked to the east. The entire horizon lifted high as a massive wall of water and debris surged toward them. Uruk screamed, turned away, and trudged through the chest-high snow, pushing it to the side as quickly as he could.

The roar became deafening.

Uruk turned back and looked up, his eyes wide with terror. He clutched the orb at his side with one hand and raised his other in a vain attempt to shield himself.

Joachim closed his eyes.

The wall of freezing water crashed down.

Chapter 26

Around the year of Creation 1000

Kemuel stood on the grassy hilltop and savored the rich air and sweet fragrances. He looked down on the headstone. "I did it, Adinah. You would have been proud of me."

A gentle breeze swept across the field. It blew a petal off a flower someone had rested against her headstone.

Kemuel tilted his head. He was pleased that someone else would leave a flower for her. He stepped to a nearby tree, sat, leaned against its sturdy trunk, and gazed where his wife's body lay peacefully in the earth. "I let her go, Adinah." He drew his legs up, rested his forearms on his knees, and looked around. "And I finally got to come join you." He plucked some grass and twisted it in his fingers. "One day I'll come see you for real."

A gentle breeze rustled the leaves in the tree above him. He looked up, took a deep breath, and sighed. He was ready. He reached into his tunic pocket, pulled out the leather binder, and opened it.

Dear Son,

I figured out today that a good friend has been deceiving me for decades. I saw you in the distance

Chapter 26

and heard you cry out, "How could you?" In that one moment, everything made sense.

I don't want you to regret saying that, Son. You're a man of great conviction, so I know those words must have felt completely justified. I respect you for that.

What's more, I promise you I'll do everything within my power to reach you again and tell you the truth. A man derives much of his own legacy from his father, and the enemy is robbing you of that. I intend to give it back, and I pray I'll succeed.

Son, whatever happens, know that I love you, and I'm tremendously proud of you. When we fought incursions, I felt so proud seeing you command your warriors—and seeing how much they respected you.

You have fought hard in this war, and you have seen more than one man's share of death. Don't look back on that with regret, Son. Instead, remember that you have been through a remarkable, man-shaping adventure, and you have led other men through, as well. You have fought courageously in the bitter combat of war. You have saved countless lives. You have been tested, and you have passed with flying colors. You are a strong, brave, courageous man. What's more, you are one of the most tenderhearted men I know. Don't lose that.

One more thing: By the time you read this, you will have not only lost your wife, but you will have been forced to let your daughter go, as well. I want you to know that I kept an eye on her from a distance. You would have been so proud of her, Son. She was courageous to the very end, and, like you, she saved many, many lives.

Chronos: Revolution

Now, don't be miserable forever, alright? Grieve their loss and move on. They would want no less. You've spent most of your life in our simulations of a pre-Flood atmosphere, so you have many years ahead. You're only 354, Kemuel, still a strapping man by our standards.

Look around you. There are plenty of widows from our war who need a husband and orphans who need a father. When you're ready, open your heart to the possibility. Do it with my blessing.

Your Proud Father,
Joachim, son of Mahalalel

Kemuel closed the binder and pressed it against his heart. He leaned his head against the trunk, closed his eyes, and listened to the breeze.

A sweet soprano voice echoed over the hilltop. He opened his eyes just enough to see.

A young woman walked slowly up the hill carrying two bunches of flowers and filling the air with her song. Her hair blew to one side, and the hem of her robe fluttered in the breeze.

Kemuel recognized her right away. He had carried her off the station.

If she saw him, she showed no sign of it. She strode slowly into the cemetery and finished her song. Kemuel was sorry to hear her stop.

She knelt in front of Kenan's headstone, laid a bunch of flowers against it, pushed her hair over her shoulder, and said something in a

Chapter 26

low voice. A few moments later, she stood, walked over to Adinah's headstone, and knelt in front of it.

Kemuel opened his eyes all the way.

She laid the second bunch of flowers against the stone.

Kemuel had to swallow hard. He marveled that the widow of one of his own fallen soldiers would open her heart so much as to remember *his* late wife.

"Commander Kemuel?" Her young son surprised him from the side.

Kemuel reached out and scratched the back of the boy's head. "Yes, Jared?"

"Would you like to have dinner with us?"

Chapter 27

Modern Day

Will landed on a rural, two-lane highway. He flexed his knees as he struck the pavement, then straightened himself. He had just done one of the most painful things in his life. He had left his son in someone else's hands, knowing he would never see him again. His heart was heavy with grief.

Tires screeched.

He looked up.

A van nosed down hard with a rapid series of rubber-on-pavement yelps and stopped inches away.

He slammed his hands onto the van's hood and looked up at the driver.

It was Jamie.

In the passenger seat, Kat dove forward and placed her hands on the windshield's interior. Her voice was muffled, but Will recognized the words her lips formed. *Where's Joel?*

Will swallowed hard, tightened his lips, and shook his head.

Kat settled back into her seat and stared at Will with pain in her eyes.

Chapter 27

An hour later, Jamie wound the van along a lonely, mountainous dirt road.

They had driven in near silence. From the van's middle seat, Will looked over Kat's shoulder. He could tell her heart was as heavy as his. No parent should ever have to suffer the loss of any of their children. It was understood that parents were supposed to go first.

Caught up in the epic war, however, he and Kat had lost all four of theirs. Will had no idea how they would ever truly move on, how they would ever be able to open their hearts again—maybe even to each other.

They crested a tree-laden hill and rode through a gate into an open space. The road smoothed into a paved drive that led to a cluster of warm-looking buildings with smoking chimneys. Several large, single-family dwellings surrounded an almost hotel-like structure and another inviting lodge that looked like it could be a central, community hub.

Kat was looking back and forth. "This place is big." She turned to Jamie. "Just how many people live here?"

Jamie steered them along the drive. "Quite a few. Grandma and Grandpa took more and more children in over the years. Eventually they had to build this place."

"That would be hard for two people."

Jamie smiled. "Oh, they didn't run this by themselves. We still have a group of wonderful brothers and sisters in the Lord who have chosen to join us and...well...be parents."

Will glanced at the floor. He wasn't ready for other people's children, at least not yet.

Chronos: Revolution

Jamie pointed to one of the single-family homes. "Chris and I live there." She pointed to the next one. "And that one's yours."

Will stared at the house. "You're giving us a home?"

She shook her head. "Not exactly."

"I thought you inherited this from your grandfather."

"I did." Jamie pulled up to the main lodge and threw the van into park. "Come with me." She stepped out and waited at the door.

Will climbed out, opened Kat's door, and gave her a hand into the building. Her limp was subtle, but she needed more time to fully recover.

Inside, a teenage girl greeted them. "Welcome home, Dr. Michaels."

Jamie nodded. "Hello, Jeannie. Is everything ready for our guests?"

Jeannie nodded.

Jamie led Will and Kat into a warm, carpeted room with a burning fireplace and two soft, high-backed leather seats facing a large, wall-mounted screen. Between the chairs, an end table supported a pitcher of water, two glasses, a box of tissues, and a remote control.

Jamie gestured to the chairs. "Please, have a seat."

Will helped Kat into her chair, then took his own.

Jamie poured them glasses of water.

Will chugged his. Having just left the battle on the station, he was parched.

Jamie pointed to the wall. "We'll be in the next room waiting for you." She picked up the remote and handed it to Will. "My grandfather left you a message."

Chapter 27

Will furrowed his brow. "Professor Aufseher?"

"Just hit play." Jamie closed the door behind her.

Will looked at Kat. She shrugged. Will pointed the remote and pressed the play button.

The screen came to life. Aufseher's face appeared immediately. Will scanned his outfit. It was a one-piece technician's uniform.

Will widened his eyes and pointed. "*He* was that guy on the ground shuttle...the shuttle that took us to the *Chronos* spacecraft."

Kat glanced at Will, furrowed her brow, and looked back at the screen.

Aufseher cleared his throat. He looked past the camera and nodded. "Thank you, Jamie."

Kat gasped, placed her hands over her mouth, and jumped to her feet. "How did I never see..."

"See what?"

She pointed. "It's..." She shook her head.

Aufseher spoke. "Hi Mom. Hi Dad."

Will's heart ripped out of his chest. He jerked his head toward the screen.

"Time is short, so I have to make this quick. I so, so wanted to get a message to you."

Kat limped to the screen and touched it, looking at Joel's white hair.

"For Jamie...for you...I'm recording this message only a few days ago. For me, however, this is the day of your launch. I just smuggled Kemuel on board, and it hit me that this would be my last chance to use the orb...in my lifetime, anyway." He looked down for a moment. "Mom, you will have just flown to Montana from DC. Dad, you will

Chronos: Revolution

have just...*dropped in* from the battle at the station, and a few days ago, you both attended my funeral without knowing it."

Kat caressed the screen with her hand and whispered. "Joel." Tears streamed down her cheeks.

"I wanted you to know what happened to me. Jamie can show you my journal and fill you in on a lot of the details, but the short of it is that I went back to 1942 Germany to get the orb that Uruk stole. God gave me a new name to go with my new calling. It was quite an adventure," his expression sobered, "and not all of it was good." He looked to the side for a moment. "Mostly, I want you to know"—he looked up with a faint smile—"that I was *happy*. I found Grace...her real name was Anna...and we spent many wonderful years together." He almost laughed. "And since we were able to invest money with a lot of foresight...we did pretty well for ourselves."

He shook his head and smiled. "Oh, these years have been happy." He looked past the camera. "You can ask Jamie. She saw a lot of them." He looked into the camera. "Don't be too hard on her, by the way. Sure, she kept secrets for me...but keep in mind how devastating the consequences would have been if she hadn't. I wouldn't have even been born. Besides, she didn't know you were her great-grandparents until after the *Chronos* mission."

He looked over to the side, then faced the camera again. "I can't hold this portal forever. There's one more thing. I always felt so guilty for letting those imps kill my brother and sisters."

Kat almost shouted. "That wasn't your fault, Joel."

Will squeezed a fist. "Why didn't I talk to him about that?"

"I know...I was only eight...but I always blamed myself, and it tore me apart every time I saw you both hurting because of it." He

Chapter 27

raised both hands in a quick gesture. "I'm sorry again...I don't mean to open old wounds." He stared intently into the camera. "But I want you both to look around you in the months to come. This compound belongs to both of you, to Jamie, and to Chris. I hope you can find it in your hearts to bless these children as you have blessed me."

He glanced to the side. "I have to go. I love you both, so much. Now...go see Jamie in the next room. I left something for you." He gave them a warm smile, and the image froze.

Kat reached out to the screen and caressed the image of Joel's face. She spoke without looking back. "He was right there all along, and we didn't know."

Will was still trying to process it all. He had just left his son on the station. Now he was learning of his son's entire life—after the fact.

Kat looked over her shoulder. "I know what he's saying is the right thing to do...opening our hearts to all these children...but I don't know how to do it. How can you keep loving when you've hurt so much?"

Will walked up to her. "Maybe we just need some time." He caressed her shoulder and gently turned her to face him. "I can promise you this...hurting or not...I still love you as much as I did that moonlit night by Lamech's fire." He bent down, gently kissed her, and gazed into her eyes.

Her eyes glistened with tears. "And I love you."

Will looked around. "I can't think of a better place to grieve... and heal."

Kat wiped her eyes and nodded. "Our son had good taste." Her gaze seemed to fade into the distance. "I wish we could honor his memory better. It's just *wrong* that everything we've done is buried in

Chronos: Revolution

classified reports. I want the world to know what we learned...how much he sacrificed...but who would believe us without evidence?"

Will reached into an inside jacket pocket, pulled out a thick, gold pen, and drew his lips into a mischievous smile.

"Is that the pen Dr. Sekulow gave you?"

Will nodded, grasped the pen at both ends, and pulled. "I had to take a swim in the Potomac earlier, but so long as this seal was watertight..." The lid popped off and revealed a USB connector. Will held it out so Kat could see.

Kat's eyes widened. "That'll shake the world."

Will resealed and pocketed the pen. "The Truth always does." He wrapped his arms around her, and they rested in each other's embrace for a long moment.

After a few moments, Will gestured to the door. "So...are you ready to go see Jamie? I don't know about you, but I'm pretty hungry."

Kat huffed a brief laugh, wiped her eyes, and nodded.

Will wrapped his arm around her waist and helped her to the door.

She pulled away just far enough to take his hand into hers. "I can walk. We can do this together."

Now that they were going, Will dreaded what they would see next. He needed time. He wasn't sure what he needed it for, but he knew he needed it. He hoped Kat might have more strength of heart to see the children who lived there. He opened the door to the hall for her.

She stepped through, walked down the hall, stopped in front of the open set of double doors where Jamie said she'd be, and looked in.

Chapter 27

There had been many times when Will had wanted to be Kat's rescuer, her knight in shining armor. Now, he hoped to draw some strength from her. He watched for her reaction, hoping against hope that she could give *him* some courage without having more pain heaped on her.

What he saw horrified him.

Kat covered her mouth with both hands. Her fingers trembled, her breath shook, and she fell to her knees. Her mouth contorted, and her eyes moistened with more tears.

Will ran forward to pull her away. He couldn't let her be hurt like this again.

From inside the room, three children shouted. "Mommy! Daddy!"

Will froze. He couldn't believe his ears.

Joshua, Christina, and Joy bolted out of the room into their mother's arms.

Kat squeezed them tight, lavished them with kisses, and dampened their cheeks with her tears.

Will's whole body shook. He was overwhelmed. His son had gone back and rescued their children. He had given them a second chance.

Will dropped down next to Kat, threw his arms around his reunited family, and squeezed them tight. Still shaking, he looked up and smiled as he wept. He had so much to thank God for.

Epilogue

Karl Aufseher watched the van speed away. "Father, please help him." He smiled. "Of course, I know you will. You already have."

He watched his younger self run around the corner. "That's a fine, young man over there." He laughed, grimaced, and clutched his hand against his side.

His hand was instantly wet and warm. He looked down. His side was red with blood, and black fluid was oozing from the wound. He spotted a park bench just off the road. He looked around for his cane but couldn't find it. "Criminy."

A familiar, weary voice came from beside him. "Use mine, my friend."

He turned and found the elderly version of Phanuel, who held out his cane.

Karl glanced at it and looked into Phanuel's weary, blue eyes. "That's not a cane, sir." He pointed. "That's a scepter."

"Well, I'll be proud to let you use it."

Karl accepted it and pressed it against the ground. The pain in his side made him double over.

Phanuel reached his old arms around Karl and ambled beside him toward the park bench. Once there, he lowered Karl into the seat, then sat beside him.

Epilogue

Karl held his hand against his side, squeezed his face together, and heaved a heavy breath.

Phanuel looked at him. "You did it, Joel."

"Oh, now I'm Joel again." He laughed and grimaced. "Please don't make me laugh."

"Fair enough. Hang in there, Joel. You've done it...and you're right." He stared down the street. "That *is* a fine young man over there."

Joel laughed and grunted in pain.

"Oh...sorry."

Joel's breaths were becoming labored. "I'll hit you for it later."

"And I'll let you."

Joel heaved another laugh and a pained grunt. "Darn it...I said *don't* make me laugh."

Phanuel reached an arm around the aged Joel's shoulder and gently pulled his head against his chest. "Soon, my friend, soon. Your rest is coming. You have certainly earned it."

The pain in Joel's side grew sharp and piercing. He gritted his teeth, and his chest began to seize. It became harder and harder to draw air into his chest. He wheezed in and out.

Phanuel stroked his hair. "Soon, my friend."

The pain dulled to a throb. His head swam. He drew in a tight wheeze, grunted, and seized every muscle.

A rush of wind blew the pain away, and Joel relaxed. He lifted his head and glanced up.

Phanuel sat in full glory, his white robe fluttering in the breeze, his golden breastplate shimmering in the sun, his gold, orb-bearing

Chronos: Revolution

scepter leaning where the cane once was. He looked at Joel and smiled. "You did it, my friend."

Joel stood, placed his hands on his chest, and looked down. He turned his hands in and out. They looked young again. He spun to look at the park bench.

Phanuel stood with his hand gently supporting the head of Joel's body. He carefully lowered the head so the body could slump onto its side.

Joel blinked. "I guess I won't be needing that anymore."

"Don't worry, you'll get it back, and in mint condition."

Joel felt his chest again. "So, this is what those souls felt like."

"How is it?"

"Weird, but okay. I feel complete...but not, you know?"

"I can imagine. Like I said, this is temporary...only until the Resurrection."

Joel nodded. He kept nodding, and his expression melted. "I couldn't have done it without you, my friend." He stepped forward and collided with Phanuel in a firm hug.

Phanuel hugged him back with a tight fist against Joel's back. "And I couldn't have helped you without Him." He stepped back and pointed up.

Joel smiled. "Oh yes." He looked up. "Thank you, Father. Thank you so much." He suddenly had a hopeful thought. "Oh, my goodness. I get my wish now, don't I?"

"You do, indeed." Phanuel stepped beside him. "Are you ready?"

Joel nodded with wide, hopeful eyes.

Phanuel placed a hand against Joel's back, looked into the sky, stretched his wings up, swung them down with a whoosh, and

Epilogue

pulled Joel into the air. He flapped his wings as they rose, leaned forward, and gained an impressive rhythm as they sailed forward.

Joel was fascinated by the experience. "Is it just me, or is the wind different?"

"You don't have a body to feel it anymore. What you're feeling is spirit."

"Is that why you only have a hand against my back?"

"Souls are pretty easy to lift, especially ones as light as yours."

"Is that a compliment?"

Phanuel grinned.

They sailed south and followed the Potomac. Joel looked to his left as they passed the Capitol Mall. Then he looked down as they passed over Hains Point, and he gazed ahead at the white Ferris wheel above National Harbor where the *Timekeeper* had been, or rather *was to be*.

Phanuel looked over. "Anything else you'd like to see on the way?"

Joel looked back. "Is this normal procedure?"

"Not exactly, but your story is pretty exceptional. So, how about it?"

Joel shook his head. "I'm ready."

Phanuel smiled. He looked up, and they soared straight into the sky. He pulled his wings up and down hard. They shot through a layer of clouds like a rocket, then another, gaining speed the whole time. The sky above dimmed from blue to purple to black.

Joel glanced down at the beautiful shrinking blue-green earth with clouds feathered all around its surface. He was struck by how similar it looked to the orb.

Chronos: Revolution

He looked back up just in time to see them streak across the moon's surface. He grinned as it sped by next to them. Then he watched it sail away behind them.

He looked ahead.

A point of light shimmered in the distance. It grew quickly as they approached, a shining, white city suspended in space. Its light flashed and subsumed them completely.

Joel stared with wide eyes. "What is this?"

"The spirit realm, Joel. This is Heaven."

They sailed above grassy fields and rolling, forested hills. A herd of white stallions ran toward them. One of the horses crested a hill, reared up with a loud, echoing whinny, and whipped its front hooves in the air. It settled to the ground and frolicked on the hill, jumping and rearing.

Phanuel pointed to the steed. "He recognizes you. You and he will be partners on earth in the Millennial Kingdom."

Joel grinned. "Wow." He waved as they sailed past. The stallion shook its head and whinnied back.

Two tall, white spires rose in the distance. Between them, two huge gates slowly swung open. As they flew between the spires, two dazzling bursts of glittering fireworks jetted from their top, and two sets of angels trumpeted an antiphonal fanfare. All along the gold, glassy road that stretched ahead, people turned, looked up, clapped, and cheered.

Phanuel sailed straight along the road between gleaming white buildings. An unspeakably beautiful set of chords sounded from the distance: *Holy, holy, holy...is the Lord God Almighty...who was... who is...and who is to come.* The chorus repeated over and over,

240

Epilogue

tickling Joel's ears. He had never heard anything so mesmerizing and exquisite.

In the distance, the road sloped up toward an emerald-green rainbow that arced high above a tall, gleaming, silver-white temple. On each side of the edifice, two huge, glorious beings faced each other and stretched their wings over their heads to meet in the middle, forming a vast canopy. Surrounding the structure on each side, four amazing creatures stood, held aloft by striking sets of spinning wheels. Joel realized at once those creatures were the source of the mesmerizing song of praise.

Joel stared at the angelic beings, then at the wheels. They seemed to spin and stretch across length, height, width, and dimensions beyond.

Around the four creatures, a long set of thrones surrounded the temple. Seated on the thrones, white-robed angelic beings cast their crowns before God while the four creatures sang their chorus of praise.

As they approached the temple, the gold, glassy road beneath spread into a vast sea of iridescent orange, like fire burning and flickering within glass. It stretched to each side in front of the massive temple. The fiery crystal sea led to a set of broad, shallow steps that climbed to a burning altar at the temple's entrance. At the bottom of the stairs, a large group of people watched them approach.

Phanuel lowered his legs, flapped his wings in graceful, sweeping motions, and settled slowly to the shimmering surface just in front of the crowd.

Joel planted his feet on the floor. He looked up and smiled.

Chronos: Revolution

Their arms around each other's shoulders, Joachim and Kemuel grinned broadly. Joachim stepped forward and gave Joel's hand a firm shake. "Welcome, Joel. It's a pleasure to see you again." Kemuel grinned, shook Joel's hand, and lifted him up in a bear hug.

As he settled again to the ground, Joel spotted his father's best friend. He grinned. "Khaliil!" He reached out and gave the man's hand a firm shake.

Joel spotted the next man, Kat's father, and gave him a hug. "Grandpa!"

Another man approached. He grasped a long, white garment in both hands. He held it out and invited Joel to insert an arm into one of the sleeves.

Joel turned, slipped his arm in, and completed the turn as he inserted his other arm.

The man tied a gold sash around Joel's waist, then reached out to shake his hand. "A white robe for the redeemed. You have no idea what a pleasure this is, Joel."

Joel finally recognized him from pictures. "You're Joshua Stark... my grandfather." He gave his grandfather a firm hug and drew back. "Man, it's great to see you. Dad got your letter. He called on Jesus, too."

Joshua Stark nodded with watery eyes. "Thank you, Joel. Thank you. Jesus told me when I got here, but it's still great to hear it from you. We'll make plenty of time to talk, but first—" He gestured behind himself.

Joel looked past him.

Joseph and Elsa Michaels smiled broadly while the rest of the crowd began to stream up the broad, shallow stairs. Joseph hurried

Epilogue

forward and hugged Joel, "My dear friend." He drew back, "It's good to see you." He gestured with his head behind himself.

Joel looked past Joseph. The crowd of a couple hundred had formed a long line up the shallow stairs. Joel practically whispered to Joseph, "Who are all these people?"

As if on cue, the people in the line each extended one hand. The gesture was more than enough to spark Joel's memory. He covered his mouth with one hand, moved beyond words. He gathered himself, extended his own hand, and slowly ascended the stairs, touching each hand on the way, looking into the faces of all the people he and Anna had smuggled out of Germany. The French drivers were there, too, and near the top of the stairs, a man weeping out of control. Joel looked into his eyes and was pleasantly surprised to recognize the SS captain he had last seen tied up on a cattle car near the crossing into France. He smiled and shook the captain's hand, "You called on Jesus."

The man nodded, still weeping. "I don't deserve to be here, but the others were kind enough to let me join them."

Joel grasped his hand with both of his own. "None of us deserves to be here. I'm so glad you came." Joel continued from person to person to the top of the stairs, knowing full well who would be waiting at the top. When he got there, he grinned from ear to ear.

Her white robe flowing down, her dark hair flowing over her shoulders, Anna bathed him in her own warm smile.

Joel stepped forward, held her arms with both hands, stared into her beautiful eyes, and pulled her gently into a warm embrace. "My little Grace from God. Oh, Anna, I've missed you so much. I have so much to share with you."

Chronos: Revolution

She drew back and wiped a joyful tear. "We'll make time...but first," she gestured into the temple, "He's waiting for you."

Joel's heart leapt. He nodded, turned, gazed into the silver-white temple, and walked in. Inside, seven torches on a golden lampstand illuminated the interior with jet-hot flame.

Joel walked past them, filled with awe. Beyond them, a steady stream of fragrant, prayerful smoke rose from a golden altar of incense. Amidst the smoke, thousands of voices uttered praises, gave thanks, and lifted tearful petitions. Joel inhaled deeply. The most fragrant prayers by far were tearful and joyful expressions of love. "You, Jesus," they said over and over, "I long for more and more of You."

Joel walked around the altar and savored the rich aroma.

Farther still, a rich, dazzling, sapphire throne rose high above the floor.

Awash in glory, Joel fell to his knees, took a deep breath in awe-struck wonder, and slowly looked up.

The Father sat on the sapphire throne in all His dazzling love and greatness, as bright as the sun.

Joel squinted and turned to the side. Even here, he couldn't fully take it in. Here in the Father's Presence, he could understand why Jesus had to be born...not created...outside of time as the Glorious Bridegroom. The Godhead bore Him so He could enter time and space to look on His beloved creations; so they could look upon Him; so He could *touch* them; so He could *rescue* them; so He could *marry* them. The thought filled Joel with anticipation for all that was still to come.

Epilogue

The lampstand surged brighter, and Joel felt the Holy Spirit's gentle tug. He looked down and to his left.

There, another throne rose above the floor to the Father's right.

Joel's gaze dropped immediately. Now that he was finally here, he found himself overwhelmed with anticipation.

The temple filled with white smoke, and Joel felt himself whisked away, suspended in time. For him, it was a familiar sensation. Soon there was nothing there but the surrounding smoke, the white throne before him, and the One seated on it.

Still kneeling, Joel's gaze remained fixed on the floor. He tried to pull his eyes up, but they kept falling. He caught a glimpse of two bright, sturdy legs approaching and understood immediately why Isaiah and John had struggled to do justice to the image. His legs were like burnished bronze, firm and immovable in their strength.

Joel pulled his eyes up a bit more.

His dazzling white robe was deep red at the bottom, as if it had been dipped in blood. It flowed behind as the Wearer approached.

Joel had longed for this moment all his life. He had even seen his Lord standing on the Mount of Olives, but this was different. So different.

Jesus stopped right in front of him.

Joel stared at His golden sandals and spotted the deep holes in His feet. He could hear the vicious hammer strikes that pierced his Savior's flesh. He lowered his face to the ground and kissed Jesus's feet.

He pulled himself back up to his knees and slowly drew his gaze up but froze once again. Overcome, he couldn't lift his head anymore, much less pull himself to his feet.

Chronos: Revolution

Jesus reached down, wrapped His thumb and forefinger around Joel's chin, and gently drew Joel's gaze up to meet His own.

Joel's eyes met his Creator's, and even more than that day in Jerusalem, he was undone by the overwhelming love in His eyes. There was such an intensity to that love, like bottomless pools of water, and like lightning at the same time.

Joel stared into Jesus's eyes and just breathed in and out. Even though he had long asked for more, he could have stayed right there forever.

Jesus held out His hand.

Joel reached up, took Jesus's hand, and immediately felt His wound. He took Jesus's hand in both of his own, turned it palm-up, placed his fingers in the hole left by a Roman nail, and stared in grateful, awestruck wonder.

Jesus gently grasped Joel's hands and drew him to his feet. His voice was strong and warm, and His smile pierced Joel's heart with love. "Well done, Joel. Well done...good and faithful servant...treasured friend...and beloved son."

Too overwhelmed to speak, Joel stared into His eyes and treasured every word.

Then Jesus added something He probably didn't say often. "When I looked down on you from the Mount of Olives, I was so proud."

Joel's heart melted and surged at the same time. All the grief from his life welled up at once, mixed with all the joy of that one moment. He began to weep, and he began to laugh.

Jesus smiled, curled an index finger, and wiped the first tear from Joel's cheek. His own eyes watered, and His voice trembled,

Epilogue

"Whenever you remember and weep, Joel, I'll be right there to wipe the tear. I'll be right there with a shoulder for you to cry on. I created time, so you can bet I'll always make more for you."

Joel's tears became sobs, mixed with boisterous laughter. He gazed on His Lord through watery eyes and smiled as all his life's emotions poured out.

Jesus's smile melted into an intense expression of compassion and desire. He squeezed Joel's shoulder with one hand, placed His other hand against Joel's face, and wept with him. He planted a firm kiss on Joel's cheek, then rested His forehead against Joel's and stared through His own tear-filled eyes. He drew back just far enough to hold Joel's face with both hands, "Welcome home, my beloved, precious son." He kissed Joel again, dampening His beard with their combined tears before resting His forehead against Joel's once again and staring into his eyes, pouring love into Joel's soul. "Welcome home."

The sweet mix of love, empathy, and desire calmed Joel's sobs into quiet tears of joy. For the first time in his existence, he began to apprehend just how passionately Jesus loved him, how much Jesus had longed for this moment, how He, too, had waited in near agony, wanting Joel even more than Joel wanted Him. He marveled that he, with all his sins and failures, could ever be the object of such intense desire.

Jesus swept that thought away, "I desire you, my dear, beloved son, because I see you for what I made you to be—for all you are *going* to be. And trust Me—you're wonderful. I wouldn't make you any other way."

Joel laughed again through his tears. Every combined moment of worship during his life on earth suddenly seemed so paltry. Jesus deserved so much more.

And yet, Joel felt not even a hint of regret or condemnation from his beloved, heroic Savior. Instead, Joel bathed in what felt like liquid love, it was so tangible. With every fiber of his being, Joel gazed into Jesus's eyes and returned that love, but it was like the moon trying to outshine the sun. The best he could do was reflect it back.

He knew there were still many, many wonderful things to come—receiving an incorruptible, immortal body in the First Resurrection, marrying Jesus as part of the spotless Bride, reigning with Him in His Millennial Kingdom on earth, and living for the rest of eternity in the New Jerusalem—but none of that seemed to matter at that moment. There, face-to-face with His Beloved, Joel felt more satisfaction than he ever knew was possible. He couldn't imagine any way his situation could get better.

But it did.

At long last, Joel got his lifelong wish.

His eyes glistening with tears, His face beaming with a smile of sweet satisfaction, the Everlasting Father slipped one hand onto the back of Joel's head, drew his face onto His shoulder, slipped His other arm around Joel's back, and squeezed tight. Joel felt every beat of Jesus's heart against his chest, the swell of each breath, and the warmth of each tear-stained kiss on his cheek as his Savior held him in a long, joyful, healing embrace.

The End

CPSIA information can be obtained
at www.ICGtesting.com
Printed in the USA
LVHW112054300920
667550LV00001B/51